Unholy Passion

Amara Holt

Published by Amara Holt, 2024.

Copyright © 2024 by Amara Holt

All rights reserved.

No part of this book may be reproduced, distributed, or transmitted in any form or by any means, including photocopying, recording, or other electronic or mechanical methods, without the prior written permission of the author, except in the case of brief quotations in book reviews.

This is a work of fiction. Names, characters, places, and incidents are the product of the author's imagination or are used fictitiously. Any resemblance to actual events, organizations, locales, or persons, living or dead is coincidental and is not intended by the authors.

CHAPTER ONE

Skull

As soon as the helicopter lands, I'm the first to jump out. I automatically reach for my *Glock* in its holster at my waist and scan the environment. The field we are in is open and filled with greenery; there's only a shed near the riverbank, and on the other side, I see a dirt path. Two containers narrow a possible escape route, and I stare at it, somewhat confused. Clearly, a stupid idea made by some idiot; I roll my eyes, the author of this deserves a bullet. In front of the large doors, I see four armed guards, smiling beneath my mask.

"He's inside," I hear the voice of the contractor, and I turn. I can't even remember his name, he's that insignificant. He steps down from the helicopter, looking a bit nauseous. "Please, sir, you may go ahead."

I walk forward with determined steps; the guards, noticing my presence, form a barrier. One of them raises his hand.

"No weapons in here."

"How about you get out of my way before I get annoyed?"

"No weapons in here!"

He repeats, in a threatening tone. I narrow my eyes, and out of the corner of my eye, I see the others ready to move. Before I can draw my weapon and start the game, the shed door opens. The guards quickly step back, eyeing me suspiciously, but I don't care. I look inside and see Albert Ritchson, the United States Diplomat. My gaze fixes on him as I approach. Upon seeing me, I can tell he's nervous, even though his expression tries to remain impassive.

"Mr. Skull," he greets me with an outstretched hand. I look at it and don't move an inch. "Well, take a seat! I hope the trip..."

"Get straight to the point, *Diplomat*. Your time is valuable, just like mine. What's the job?"

He quickly nods, searches for a black folder on the table, and hands it to me.

"It's quite complicated," he replies as I observe some photos of several men on the first page. More precisely, allies of the enemy government. "It's a delicate operation that requires discretion. We need you to capture the target and take her to the second meeting point. We learned she will be used as a bargaining chip for negotiations." He lets out a sigh, then I stare at him. "We're talking, Mr. Skull, about the release of captured members of these terrorist groups, the withdrawal of our troops from areas and regions that are usually taken over by these criminals. She is the key to initiating an imminent war. And that's why we need someone like you, Skull. Someone capable of leading, knowing how to act, and ensuring that she doesn't escape, or worse, get kidnapped by the enemies."

I glance at the photos for a moment, assessing each face with a calculating expression. I flip the page and come across the target. Confused, I just stare at that photo: a teenage girl. I search for her name in the file and as soon as I find it, I notice the age beside it. 18 years old. I'm drawn back to the photo and fix my gaze on it. Her skin is fair, her hair long and blonde, her eyes are different. One is blue and the other green, oddly complementing her beauty. I remember where I am and look back at the diplomat.

At no point was I informed who she was and why she was so important.

"And what about payment?" I ask, suppressing my real question.

The Diplomat smiles subtly, as if anticipating this question.

"I was informed that your rates are high," he says, and again goes to the table, grabs a silver briefcase, and opens it in my direction. "1 million dollars for your service. Here's half, and the other half will be at the second meeting point. And the best part, you won't have to share your money with anyone else. That has already been agreed upon."

"Others?" I repeat, and when I receive a nod, I shake my head. "I don't work with anyone else, just me."

I notice his apprehensive look and analyze him slowly.

"I'm not doubting your capability, sir. However, you should consider that a squad will be of great help in case of unforeseen events. These are men who obey without question, ready to take a bullet for you."

"Mr. Diplomat," I step closer and stop right in front of him. He holds his breath, and even though the place is poorly lit, I see his tension. "Do you think I'm afraid of getting shot? I don't need a pack of dogs behind me; I work better alone."

He nods slowly and takes a step back.

"As you wish," he says and then clears his throat. "In the file, you'll find her location and where to leave her. As I said, half the amount will be there. Just drop the girl off and go. Remember, the fate of an entire nation may depend on the success of this mission."

"Understood. You can consider the job done."

With that, I turn my back on them and leave with the briefcase. The helicopter is still waiting for me; I rush to it and settle into my seat.

As the helicopter resumes flight, I lazily scan the target information. I leaf through the file and realize that her importance goes beyond what the diplomat revealed. If she falls into the wrong hands, the consequences could be catastrophic. My eyes fixate once again on her image, trying to decipher any hint in her expression.

The Catholic orphanage was her only home, and the absence of information about her parents seems intentional. Someone made a point of hiding her past, making her a mysterious and vulnerable figure at the same time. A key piece in a power game where the players are willing to do anything.

My deep breath is not only to calm my nerves but also to prepare for the challenges ahead. The fogged window reflects my serious gaze beneath the skull mask. Eveline is the link between peace and war, and the responsibility weighs on my shoulders like lead.

After a few hours of flight, I spot my car parked in the same spot I was picked up. I hurry down and head to the driver's seat. As soon as I settle in, I place the briefcase on the passenger seat and retrieve the phone I keep hidden under the seat. I dial the numbers and bring the receiver to my ear, waiting a few seconds.

"I need a favor," I inform as soon as I'm answered. "Now."

"*What do you need?*"

"Weapons, a phone, and a plane."

At the end of my speech, I hear a brief laugh.

"*I need at least 3 hours for all of that, Skull.*"

"That's the time it'll take me to get there."

I end the call and quickly start the engine. The roar of the motor echoes along the road as I head toward Pablo's isolated cabin, a reliable acquaintance who becomes a valuable ally in times of need. My fingers grip the steering wheel of the large jeep tightly; my gaze is fixed on the road, but I'm alert to everything around me.

After a few hours of driving, I finally spot the solitary wooden cabin among the trees, a flickering light indicating that Pablo is home. I park the jeep, grab the folder, and step out with the briefcase in hand, stopping in front of the door before I can announce my presence.

Pablo appears at the door, his imposing figure illuminated by the dim light inside the cabin. His dark eyes study me for a moment before a subtle smile appears on his face. I remain serious, which makes him smile wider.

"Always so friendly, my friend. It's good to see you well; it's been a long time, hasn't it?" With my silence, he steps aside to let me pass; my hand goes to the *Glock* as I enter the cabin. "I managed to get what you asked for; the plane was a bit complicated, but I have my contacts."

I nod subtly and place the briefcase on the table. Inside the cabin, the smell of burning wood smoke fills the air, mixed with the scent of guns and fuel.

"It's yours!" I announce and watch him. "For this favor and the one from Syria."

Pablo smiles and grabs a cigarette, his gaze fixed on the money.

"What's the current mission? How much do you have there?"

I watch him take the bills.

"Half a million." I reply, and Pablo stares at me. "Where's what I asked for?"

After lighting the cigarette, Pablo leads me to a room where the weapons are displayed on a table. I see an open bag, then he gestures. I walk over to the wall and start to help myself. I put into the bag: weapons, 9mm magazines, and more. Once the bag is full, I pick it up and turn to Pablo.

"The plane is in the hangar," he murmurs and turns his back to me. "I'll take you there."

I follow him in silence; we walk to my jeep, and even though I don't like it, I let him drive. I hide the file in another compartment of the bag.

Finally, Pablo leads us to a nearby clearing, where a plane is on the runway. It's a U.S. Air Force plane; I see the emblem I know so well on the fuselage. I scoff and glare at Pablo.

"If you scratch my car," I begin, my voice muffled by the mask. "I'll kill you."

"*You're welcome,* Skull. You know if you need my help, just say the word."

With everything ready and in hand, I nod and head toward the plane. I go to the cockpit and sit in the pilot's seat. I put on the headphones and begin the takeoff procedures. I press the buttons and adjust the GPS on the controls. I gently accelerate to the recommended takeoff speed, then lift the nose of the aircraft. With the altitude stable, I click on autopilot and lean back lazily.

There alone, I remove my mask and rub my hand over my face. I run my fingers through my short hair and look to the side. I search for the file again and this time focus on the enemies; the trip from Washington D.C. to Yukon in Canada will take about 14-19 hours of flight. I study every detail of the plan and everything provided to me. There is no room for errors. Eveline is in the hands of fate, and fate, for now, is guided by me.

CHAPTER TWO

Eveline

The cold, gentle breeze caresses my skin as I rest in the peaceful field just a few meters behind the orphanage. The sky, tinged with a deep blue, gives me a good sense of peace, with soft clouds moving slowly, like fleeting thoughts. Lying on the soft grass allows me to feel the earth beneath my body, a direct connection to the nature that surrounds the place I grew up.

Silence is my truest companion, broken only by the soft chirping of birds and the distant buzzing of bees. I close my eyes to absorb the serenity of the moment, letting myself be carried away by the subtle aromas of the flowers blooming around me. Red roses, white lilies, and daisies dance gently in the sunlight, creating a spectacle of colors and shapes that hypnotizes my senses.

As I contemplate the sky, my mind wanders to thoughts of what my future would hold from now on. In a few days, I would turn 18, and like all the girls reaching that age, I needed to make a decision.

Stay here and work to have food and a place to sleep, or venture out into the world. That scared me quite a bit, but a part of me knew that new horizons could be a good thing.

"Ah, there you are!"

Hearing that familiar voice, I turn my face toward the sound and smile at my friend Abby.

"Hey, I just came to rest a bit," I murmur, turning my gaze back to the sky. "It's so nice to be like this; lie down here with me."

Abby lies down right next to me and sighs.

"I just came from Principal Aarons' office," she informs, glancing at me curiously. My friend keeps her hands clasped in front of her uniform. "I thought I was going to get in trouble because I took Ethan's box of cigarettes and his lighter."

"You what?" I ask. Then, under my shocked gaze, I see her lift her leg and pull out the mentioned items from her long socks. "Why did you do that? You're crazy."

She laughs, unfazed, and carelessly grabs a cigarette.

"Want some?" she asks. I shake my head, still watching her, and as if it were the most normal thing in the world, she lights it and brings it to her lips. "Hmm..." she mumbles with the cigarette between her lips, and when she tries to speak, she coughs on the smoke. "This is really bad."

"Then why did you take them? You don't even smoke, Abby."

I let out a brief laugh without holding back.

"Ethan always uses them," she comments, examining the cigarette. "I thought it might be good, but it's crap." I watch her exhale the smoke and fall silent, though it doesn't last long. "I never thought about leaving here. Have you?"

"Actually, yes," I reply. "I was thinking about it a few minutes ago because you know, I'm turning 18."

"It sucks, doesn't it?" she says, and I nod, smiling.

If anyone heard Abby speaking or behaving so indecorously, she would definitely be grounded. So, when we were together, she allowed herself to act and use those expressions. I hope she continues, but as I watch her closely, I notice she's hiding something from me.

"What did the principal want?"

With a sudden motion, Abby sits up, and I follow her lead. Our blonde hair, like mine, is loose without the usual braid. We could even be mistaken for sisters since we look alike: fair skin, naturally rosy cheeks, long blonde hair—the only differences were our ages and our eyes. Abby was blessed with bright blue ones, while I have one green iris and one blue, almost gray.

"It seems someone came looking for me."

Hearing that makes my heart race, and selfishly, I hope for a laugh and a "*Just kidding, I'm not getting out of this crap hole*." However, she just stares at her hands.

"Is the someone you're talking about a relative?"

"Actually, a pretty fancy lawyer," she shrugs, searching for my face with her eyes. "He showed me a document and asked that tomorrow I go with him and one of the sisters to a lab in town. It seems I need to prove that I'm the person he's looking for." Then, disbelieving, she shakes her head. "It's almost a joke. Me proving I'm who they're looking for, when I'm not looking for anyone. It's confusing, Evie."

Not knowing what to say, I clasp my hands in front of my gray skirt and pull a thread from the fabric.

"At least someone is looking for you," I finally say, letting out a brief sigh. "Look on the bright side, Abby; you won't have to make that dreaded decision," I laugh to lighten the mood, but my friend just stares at me. "If it's confirmed that you are who they're looking for, then you should go. You don't have to stay here and become one of those bitter old hags."

This time, she smiles at me.

That was the affectionate nickname Abby had given to the superior sisters. Principal Aarons was the Mother of the Bitter Ones, a rude old lady with a huge double chin and a wart on her chin the size of a button. Whenever she walked through the dining hall corridors, it seemed like she was looking for someone to punish just because she was in the mood. In my childhood, I always feared when that horrendous look was directed at me.

"And do you already know what you're going to do?"

With the question, I snap out of my daydream.

"I don't know," I murmur, looking beyond the brick walls and rusty bars. "I think I don't have the courage; here I still have a roof and food."

"Then I'm going to stay here with you," she said in that determined tone she always used. "If you want to become a bitter old hag, then let's go for it. You'll be a good teacher, and I can teach good manners. That old lady from Durham needs to retire, so I'll take her place."

I can't hold back my laughter as I shake my head.

"Principal Aarons would freak out about that!" I assert, then give her a small smile. "You're still so young, Abby."

"I'm three years younger than you."

"So you're still young," I retort. "You'll meet other people; you might even study with them in a different class than ours."

"And I'll kiss a lot of boys?"

"Pretty as you are, I'm sure you will."

"Wow, when you say that, you sound like a bitter old hag," Abby pokes at me, but then laughs. "I'm going to want to have sex with them too."

"With all of them?"

"No, one at a time. Wanting them all at once is a sin, and I don't want to go to hell." After saying this, she rubs the cigarette on the sole of her shoe and then throws it away. "What's it like to have sex?"

I lie back down on the grass with that on my mind.

Some time ago, Principal Aarons had called Ethan to fix the water pump that supplied the orphanage. And being the curious person Abby was, she had called me to go to the handyman's room; she wanted to know what a man's room looked like. After all, he was the only man in the orphanage. We were even surprised by how tidy the room was, with a different smell, like a stronger essence. However, what caught our attention was the slightly open drawer next to the bed.

"It must be strange," I finally say, "but something necessary."

"You talk like it's some kind of obligation," Abby complains, poking me. "Don't be a bitter old hag."

"Stop," I ask, pushing her hand away. "If you think about it, what a man and woman do is pretty strange. I mean, how can it be good? Considering the difference between their bodies."

Beside me, Abby grumbles.

"Wow, this place is crap. Do you know how I feel?"

"Like a bitter old hag?"

"No. I feel trapped in a century I don't belong to," she said, looking at me. "It's ridiculous that we can't go out for a walk now and then, or maybe have a computer that actually works."

"But the one in the library works," I counter, and Abby looks at me tiredly. "It takes a while to boot up, but it still works."

"That computer has been here since we arrived, and you can be sure it was here when this place was created."

I sit back up; Abby is restless, and it's so noticeable.

"Want to complain to the principal?"

"No." She shakes her head, and as if she's had a spark of inspiration, she smiles. "Come with me?"

With a jump, she stands up and extends her hand to me. That look was her signature sign that she was going to do something mischievous.

"Why don't you just forget about it for now?"

"Because you're having doubts and you've dragged me into them. Let's go!"

As soon as I stand up, Abby pulls me, and we start to run. We dodge as best we can from the girls and the sisters complaining about us running. We cross the stone path, and when I finally spot the corridor to the principal's office, I stop, pulling her back.

"Do you want to go into the principal's office?"

"No, I want to mess with her computer."

With a shove, she moves away and walks until she stops in front of the wooden door. I look back and, as expected, there's no one around. I turn my gaze back to Abby as she knocks three times on the door. I quickly approach to pull her away, but she's quicker and opens the door.

"Abby!"

I run after her, completely scared of getting caught, and while she heads to the computer, I stand guard at the door. For a moment, I scan the books around the room and feel the urge to grab one, but I shake my head. If the principal discovers this invasion, it'll definitely mean punishment.

"Evie, come here!"

I look at her, confused, and shake my head. Who's going to watch the door?

"No, get out of there before the principal comes back!"

I say nervously, and then I peek through the crack in the door: the corridor remains empty. I turn back to Abby again and see her writing something on a piece of paper. Her expression is serious; for a moment, I think about asking what's going on, but when I look back at the corridor, I feel my blood run cold as I spot Ethan approaching.

I close the door and gesture for Abby. She quickly leaves her spot, hiding the paper between her breasts. As soon as she stands next to me, the door opens, and Ethan stares at us.

"What are you doing here?"

"We were looking for the principal," Abby lies, and I silently thank her. Because if I dared to try to answer, I would give us away unintentionally. "The door was open, so we thought it was strange. Something might have happened to our principal."

Ethan smiles, clearly not believing us. He knew Abby got into trouble a lot; she was known for being grounded for bad behavior. For a moment, I try to imagine what he would do if he discovered we had entered his room. Remembering that detail brings me back to the slightly open drawer, filled with magazines of naked women. As Abby continues to defend herself against the accusations of snooping around, I allow myself to analyze him carefully.

His light brown hair, almost blonde, was messy. His green eyes didn't show anger but amusement instead. His tanned skin appeared well cared for, giving the impression of being soft to the touch. His naturally pink, full lips are now curled into a mocking smile. Ethan seems to enjoy this argument. I subtly swallow and return to sizing him up. The beard, which had been scruffy a few weeks ago, was now neatly trimmed. I lower my gaze to his shoulders and arms, noting that they are strong.

Ethan was a handsome man.

I glance quickly at his face and startle as I realize he's staring at me.

"Let's go, Abby!" I say quickly, impulsively. "The principal must be in the library."

Noticing my desperate look, she nods.

"Or in the prayer room; Principal Aarons is a fervent woman."

"How can you be so cheeky, Abigail?" Ethan asks with a smile. "You're really the terror of this place."

"How rude to say that to a young child like me! Come on, Evie."

"Young child," Ethan mocks, stepping aside from the door. "Don't cause any trouble, Abigail!" he commands, and when he looks at me, he nods his head.

I pass by him and suddenly feel so awkward. Abby is still talking when I look back and see Ethan staring at me with his arms crossed. I quickly turn back around and take a deep breath.

"Why did he only tell me not to cause trouble? You were with me."

"Because you always cause trouble, Abby. I only tag along to try to instill some sense in your head," I laugh to lighten the mood, but inside, I still feel shaken. "Did that clear your doubts?"

"No, let's drop it," she said, then looks at me in surprise. "It's almost time for roll call, isn't it?" she asks, and I nod. Roll call was always done near the end of the afternoon. "Let's go; hopefully, we can shower before and go together to the dining hall. It seems there's soup again today."

"Better than nothing."

Abby links our arms, and we walk toward the dormitory.

My friendship with Abby was born a long time ago, around the time I was seven and she had just arrived at the orphanage at six. She had lived in another orphanage that had to be closed, so as a consequence, she came here. We never ran out of things to talk about; she always cheered me up when I was sad. With a huge heart and a personality that captivated everyone, she was always in a good mood and full of plans to get us into trouble.

I smile at that last thought.

A life without her would be a torment, but I would be happy for her.

AFTER THE SHOWER, WE ran to the dining hall and joined the line of girls. Abby and I, along with three others, were the only older ones in the entire orphanage; most girls, upon reaching adulthood, chose not to stay. After roll call, we sat down to eat, and even though I tried to start a conversation with Abby, it was clear she was distracted.

And I understood her.

The day had been full of surprises for her and, in a way, for me too. When we finally finished our dinner, and before I could say anything, she got up and left. I followed her quick steps with my gaze, wondering what she was up to. Still wanting to solve her doubts? A sigh escaped my lips, and with the other girls, I picked up my plate and Abby's. Today was my day in the kitchen, but the good thing was I would have company.

Hours passed, and with my task done, I dried my hands and looked at the wall clock. There were fifteen minutes left until curfew, and by that time, I hadn't seen that airhead again. Trying not to worry, I left the kitchen and headed to the dormitory. Some girls were already getting ready for bed; I greeted a few out of politeness and left when I couldn't find my friend.

Even though I wanted to run, I kept walking. Only Abigail had the knack for making me worry, and later, when I scolded her, she would complain as if she hadn't done anything wrong. I descended the stairs, intending to go to the library; she must be there. Just before I could turn the corner, I heard the principal's voice and the supervisor's. I froze in place and turned around; if they caught me there, I was sure I'd get a scolding or worse. Since there wasn't time to run back to the stairs, I entered the first room I saw with the door ajar and hid behind it.

"Are you hiding?"

Startled, I notice Ethan smiling at me. Only now do I see him crouched with a tool in hand; I bring my fingers to my lips in a plea for him not to say anything. His eyes, previously amused, become confused, and as he stands up, the door swings open. I huddle closer, holding my breath.

"Are you finished, Mr. Williams?"

"Just this one, Mrs. Director," he replies, stepping closer to the door, purposely hiding me from the visitors. "Do you need me to do anything else?"

I hear a cough, but she speaks again soon after.

"I expect you to fix that part of the wall tomorrow morning. I don't want it to fall on anyone."

"Sure, ma'am. I'll take care of it tomorrow morning."

My heart feels like it's going to leap out of my mouth; I had never been this close to a man before. The strong but pleasant scent slowly intoxicates me, filling me with a desire to let out a sigh. In truth, it was a feeling of restlessness.

But what could it be?

The moment he closed the door, I knew we were alone. So when Ethan stepped away, I could finally breathe deeply.

"Thank you."

"What are you doing here? Did you know that if she had seen you, I would be in trouble?"

I gulp.

Ethan watches me without looking away, seemingly trying to understand my intentions.

"I was just looking for Abby," I respond, while trying to calm my racing heart. "If I got caught in the hallways, I could end up grounded, and I didn't know you were here."

His analytical gaze sweeps over my face, lingering longer on my body. After my shower, I had worn a different uniform, consisting of a black skirt that reached my knees, matching stockings, a white button-up shirt with sleeves that extended slightly below my shoulders, and my shoes were black and well-fitted. If I hadn't had the task in the kitchen, I would already be in my nightgown and in my bed.

"Ethan," he finally says. "Don't call me sir; we don't need that formality, *Evie*."

Feeling awkward at how he said that, I divert my gaze to where he was before.

"I'll be going; I don't want to bother you anymore."

"You're not bothering me," he denies. "It's not something that requires my full attention," he murmurs, walking over to the toolbox. "Today has been hectic, just like yours. I'm curious; what were you doing in the principal's office?"

I watch him gather the materials, then cross his arms in front of his body.

"Abby wanted to talk to the principal," I lie, and automatically feel my face flush. Ethan stares at me; it was so obvious he didn't believe me. "Personal stuff."

My eyes travel down his face against my will, and it's so inevitable that I let out a sigh. Ethan is wearing the same outfit as earlier, but now he has left the two buttons of his shirt open.

"I heard you're turning eighteen," he comments, and I look at him, surprised. "Excited?"

"A little." I smile nervously. "Actually, very much."

Ethan laughs and steps closer.

"Do you know what you want to do? Are you going to stay or go?" he asks, his expression pure curiosity. "If you stay, it will be nice to have a friend close to my age."

I gulp.

"And how old are you?"

"31." As he answers, he studies me for a few seconds. "Too old?"

"No, but it's not close to my age," I smile, receiving a smile in return. "Well, I really have to go. It's time to gather, and Abby must be looking for me."

Ethan leans against the door, fully closing it. I glance at him, a bit startled, and try to keep my breathing calm. After all, one more step and he would invade my personal space.

"I think we can be good friends," he murmurs softly, and with his other hand, he touches my cheek. "What do you think?"

I shy away from the contact, which feels so intimate, and with a trembling hand, I fumble for the doorknob. I try to open it, but Ethan's hand stops me.

"Please, let me go."

He stares at me for a few long seconds, and when I try to open the door again, I succeed. Without looking back and like a coward, I dash out. In the corridor, as I run toward the dormitory, I feel my heart racing. I have no idea how I should behave, and I also don't want him so close.

As soon as I reach the dormitory hallway, I spot the door still open. So I run a bit more and enter; leaning against the wood, I close my eyes for a few seconds. If I had taken any longer, I would have been stuck outside. I open my eyes and find Abby sitting on my bed, wearing a half-smile as she waves at me.

"Where were you?" she asks as I stop next to the bed. "I was looking for you."

"I was looking for you, Abby!" I retort, searching for my nightgown on the pillow. "Why did you disappear? Don't tell me you were on the principal's computer again?"

"Wow, it's good to see you trust me," she comments, watching me change clothes. "And no, I wasn't on the principal's computer," she whispers. "I was in the file room."

"What?"

I ask, startled, even more so when I see Abby pull a folder from under my pillow. I quickly glance around and feel relieved when I see the girls lying down.

"This is your file, Evie! At that moment, on the principal's computer, it was open and looked like it was being filled out. I noted down its number and went to look for your folder after dinner. I have one just like it."

Because of the large glass window, the remaining moonlight brightens the dimness of the room a bit. I open the old folder, which smells of mildew, and I'm surprised when I read *Eveline Novikov*.

"Novikov? Is that my name?"

"I think so! Look on the other page; there's a photo."

I turn the yellowed page and pause for a second. The photograph isn't very old, but it's a bit damaged, and even torn in half with the face of a man scratched out, I can still see him. He seems to be smiling, hugging someone, but it's not certain. He wore a very nice suit with some pins. I look at the back and see something written that I can't understand.

"I wonder what it says?"

The handwriting is different and somewhat faded due to time.

"I don't know," she shrugs, then sits down next to me. "But don't you see? It's something about your family! Look, I was scared to go because I didn't want you to stay in this place, but what if you have a father or a mother?"

"If I really had them," I say after swallowing hard. "Why am I here and not with them?"

Abby looks at me, and it's so clear that she doesn't have an answer for that.

"Let's sleep! Tomorrow, when we're calmer, we can figure this out." I nod; my eyes don't leave the photograph. "I love you so much, my friend. Tomorrow we'll discover this together."

I receive a kiss on the cheek, and I watch her go to the bed beside mine.

Before I lie down, I take the folder and place it under the mattress, but I keep the photograph with me. Already snug and wrapped in the thin blanket, I reach for the photograph and gaze at it for a while. Who was that man with the scratched-out face? My father? And what was written on the back? I let out a completely frustrated sigh, wanting to have the answers early tomorrow, and decide to sleep.

CHAPTER THREE

Eveline

After several hours of trying to sleep, I sit up and grab my hidden file. Because of so many questions, I can't clear my mind and get a good night's sleep. Every time I close my eyes, the information dances in my mind. After all, I have so many questions. I open the folder again and begin to read the paper titled *admission*. Right in the first paragraph, I discover that I was left at the door of the orphanage a few months after I was born, and that is a surprise to me. I had been told once that I was abandoned with the umbilical cord near some trash.

As if I had been born and left to fend for myself.

I bring the photograph of the eyes closer, trying to see the face of the man better, but it's in vain. A bit unsettled, I read on, hopeful that there would be more about me.

However, there is nothing else interesting. Just some medical records, which I believe all the girls have. Finally, I put the folder back in its hiding place, and with the photograph under my pillow, I close my eyes.

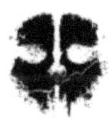

When I open my eyes again, it's daytime and some of the girls are awake in their beds. Subtly, I move my hand under the pillow and look for the photo. With the daylight, I can see some details that I couldn't last night and in the early morning. The man wore a black shirt with sleeves under a torn jacket, but I can't decipher the place where he was.

"Tell me you at least slept?"

I look at Abby and her messy blonde hair. She has her eyes closed, but upon noticing my silence, she stares at me.

"I did," I reply, then let out a sigh. "I need to find out who this man is, but where do I start?"

I sit down, being imitated.

"Could asking the director be a bad idea?"

"I think so," I say, unsure. "She will want to know where I found this photo, and I don't want you to get in trouble."

Abby sighs and gets out of bed, coming toward me.

"Ethan must know what that means on the back. You should ask him," she suggests, taking the photo from my hand. When she sees me opening my mouth to retort, she continues, "If I ask, he might not even answer."

"And if I do, will he?"

"He will," she confirms, standing tall. "Because you're polite and sweeter than I am."

I take the photo again and keep staring at it.

"Do you think he's my father?"

"We'll find out, Evie. Now, shall we take a shower? Before one of the bitter ones shows up."

I hesitate for a few seconds, but soon nod, and before going, I hide the photo with the folder. As I follow Abby, I'm already decided on what I'll do. I was going to seek answers and wouldn't rest until I discovered everything. I take a quick shower, and when I return to the room, I take the photo and hide it in the inner pocket of my gray skirt.

We leave for breakfast, and when we finally eat, we head outside.

In the large courtyard, I see some girls scattered around, and the two sisters sitting on a wooden bench while carefully watching everyone. Further away, on one of the benches, is Ethan. I stay with Abby, pretending to talk, and when he gets up to leave, Abby and I stealthily follow him. We pass by the sisters and politely greet them. With one hand, I hold my friend's arm, while the other keeps the photo in my pocket.

Ethan carries a briefcase and politely waves to some girls. My eyes don't leave him, afraid of losing sight of him. As soon as he enters another corridor leading to a quieter courtyard, we quicken our pace.

I see the wall that Director Aarons mentioned last night.

"Ethan!" I call, and at that moment he turns around, and I see the surprise on his face, followed by a smile. "Good morning!"

"Good morning, Evie," he replies and then focuses on Abby. "Abigail, how are you?"

I look at Abby, who has a furrowed brow. Her gaze shifts between me and Ethan.

"Fine," she responds suspiciously. "We need your help."

"My help?" he asks, somewhat confused, looking at me. "What can I do for you?"

Abby nudges me, and then, a bit nervously, I glance back. Confirming that we are alone, I slip my hand into my pocket and pull out the image.

"I wanted to know if you know what this means on the back?"

I hand it to Ethan, and under my watchful gaze, he examines the front image but soon flips it over.

His gaze meets mine.

"Where did you get this?"

"It's her father," Abby replies, and Ethan can't hide his surprise. "But we don't know what that means."

Ethan is silent for a few seconds, but then looks at me.

"I'm not sure," he murmurs, looking back at the image, "but are you sure this man is your father?"

I swallow hard, and hesitantly shake my head.

"I don't know, but it was in my file."

"Was there anything else in it?" he asks, and I frown. He seemed very curious. "I just want to know if there's anything more that could help figure this out."

"It had Eveline Novikov written in her file," Abby says. "So that's her name. Can you find out what that means? The computers in the library don't let us access the internet, and we can't go back into the director's office."

"So that's what you were doing yesterday?"

Startled, I stare at Abby, who widens her eyes, shaking her head at me.

"Could you find that out for me, please?" I ask, looking directly into the green eyes in front of me. "I barely slept last night with this on my mind; it's so awful to be left in the dark."

The masculine eyes analyze me, then he smiles and nods.

"Alright, I'll look into it for you. But you'll have to go get it in my room; I can't be seen in the girls' dormitory."

I swallow hard and turn to Abby, who quickly nods at me.

"Alright," I confirm, even though my good manners think it's wrong. "At curfew, I'll stop by your room?"

"Yes, I'll find out whatever is needed. Don't worry."

"Thank you, Ethan." I smile happily.

"It's Ethan, thank you for helping us."

Then, without waiting for him to speak, Abby pulls me away from there. I'm practically dragged by her, and when we reach the first courtyard, she stops in front of me.

"Why did he call you Evie?" she asks, hands on her hips. "I'm the only one who calls you that. Who does he think he is stealing the nickname?"

"He said we didn't need formalities," I say, and I see Abby make a disgusted face. "That we could be friends."

"He's old," she replies as if it's obvious. "Don't let him call you that; it's my nickname for you. And what's this? He said you didn't need formalities and that you could be friends? When did he say that?"

"Yesterday," I murmur softly. "I went to look for you, and to avoid being caught by the director who was in the hallway, I entered a room and he was there." I glance around to see if anyone is nearby. "Then he said, and..."

"And... what?"

Abby looks at me eagerly. I consider mentioning how close he got to me, but I decide not to say anything.

"And that's it," I look away but soon return to watching her. "Nothing more."

The expression on Abby's face was a mystery.

"The fact that he's helping doesn't make him your friend. Don't let him do anything to you; don't be silly. Be like Director Aarons. Not bitter like she is, but serious, firm when she says something. Everyone is afraid of her, so you should be like that too."

"Aren't you being too worried?"

"No!" she replies and pulls me to start walking again. "It's just that you're so sweet; you accept everything quietly."

"I'm polite, Abby. It's different."

"Then don't be!" she exclaims and enters the hallway leading to the library. "Make me proud, okay? After all these years with me, something has to rub off on you."

"One Abby is already too much; imagine two."

I joke, and I receive a grimace in response.

Further ahead, we find Director Aarons talking to the sister in charge of the filing room. My gaze searches for Abby's, but she doesn't seem fazed. We approach to enter the library next door, but we are soon stopped.

"Miss Eveline?" she approaches, her gaze accusatory. "Can we talk?"

"Yes, Madam Director."

I try to stay calm, even though my heart feels like it's about to stop at any moment. The fear of being discovered pounds in my chest, but one thing I'm sure of: I'll accept any scolding. Abby beside me raises her eyebrows quickly and then enters the library. I turn my attention back to the director and walk alongside her. The time it takes to get to her office feels like an eternity to me. As soon as we enter, I watch her sit in the large chair and point to the seat in front.

"Are you nervous?"

I swallow hard and shake my head quickly.

"No, ma'am."

"I called you here, Miss Eveline, for a reason you are already aware of." For a moment, I'm at a loss for words, so she continues. "You will finally turn eighteen. What do you plan to do? I need to know so that everything can be organized; I have other girls to talk to."

I clasp my hands in a nervous gesture, thinking it over as I watch her type on the computer while I remain silent. What can I respond?

"Well, I don't know yet, ma'am. I still have doubts."

"You have doubts about staying here where you have security or starving on the street?"

Her harsh words hit me like punches to the stomach; I know she's right, but I could have a chance out there.

"Actually," I say, trying to maintain a serious tone, echoing what Abby advised me just minutes ago, "I'm unsure if I should stay here to become just another person who ended up with a job they didn't want, or if I should try my luck in the world."

I see the exact moment the director's double chin inflates, and I swallow hard. My gaze focuses on the wart, and with great effort, I have to hold back the expression of disgust. From where I am, I can see some hairs on the wart alongside a few yellowish bumps around it.

"You disdain what we do for you?" she questions, her gaze serious. "I'm surprised by that, Miss Eveline. I didn't know this petulant side of you."

"I'm sorry, Madam Director."

I apologize, extremely embarrassed; it was the wrong moment to be courageous.

"Get out of my office! Come back here tomorrow and give me an answer, and we'll put an end to this. Go!"

I nod and ask for permission to leave.

Outside, I shake my head in denial. I feel so stupid.

I go in search of my friend, and when I find her still in the library, she asks me what I talked about with the director. I briefly tell her what happened, and without any surprise, she starts laughing at my embarrassment. I try to act offended by her lack of understanding, but I can't hold it for long, and I join her laughter.

We're shushed by all the girls who are focused, and that makes us quiet.

At lunchtime, I see from the kitchen window Ethan passing by with a bag of cement on his shoulders. I remember he promised to find information about the photo, and that reignites the anxiety I had almost forgotten.

Almost at the end of the afternoon, to our surprise, the lawyer appeared, and with that, Abby and another sister went to the nearest town. The orphanage was located in an isolated area; the last time I had to leave there, I was still small, and I remember thinking the journey from there to the city center was long. I said goodbye to my friend and wished her good luck; her expression was scared and anxious.

A few hours remain before I meet Ethan, and my anxiety is killing me right now. Officially, it would be my second time alone with a man, but this time I wouldn't get nervous; I would stay serious and confident.

Curfew arrives, and as I make my way through the dimly lit hallways, I stand in front of Ethan's room door. He sleeps in another wing of the orphanage, but in the same building. In front, I can see the dark courtyard, as there's no lighting like in the first courtyard. Before I even knock on the door, I hear a conversation inside, and seconds later, it opens.

"Ah, you really came." I nod and wait for him to hand over the photograph and information. However, he opens the door wider and gestures for me to enter. "If they catch you out here, it will complicate things for me; it's better to come in; it won't take long."

I look around and see only darkness. I take a deep breath and enter the room; it really wouldn't take long.

"Did you find anything?" I ask, my gaze scanning the room. The bed is made, and on a small table rests a bottle and two glasses. "Was it very difficult?"

"Don't you want to sit?" he asks, pointing to the bed. "I have some great wine; I only drink on special occasions."

"No, thank you," I decline and watch him go to the table; there he fills one glass and pours half the liquid into the other. "What did you find?"

"The writing is part of an ancient Cyrillic alphabet," he replies and takes a sip of his drink. "In other words, it's Belarusian writing."

"And what does it mean?"

Ethan laughs and approaches me with the half-full glass.

"*JA budu kachać ciabie ŭsio žyccio*" he replies, and I'm surprised by this. I didn't know he spoke other languages. "*I will love you for all my life.*" It's a phrase of love; I think they were both in love.

I nod and absorb everything I've heard. So, my parents weren't from that country?

"Do you know how I can get there?" I ask, twisting my fingers in a nervous gesture.

He looks at me, surprised, and continues holding the glass in front of me.

"You want to go to Belarus?"

"Maybe I can find more answers there."

Ethan shakes his head.

"You don't know what you're talking about, Evie. You shouldn't waste the opportunity to stay; I thought you were smarter."

Annoyed by his words, I cross my arms.

"Can you give me the photo?"

"Of course," he replies and smiles. After taking a single sip, he reaches into his pants pocket and hands me the photograph. I quickly take it and tuck it away. "Now, since I did you a favor, I hope you can help me with something."

"A favor?" I repeat, confused. "What?"

Without answering me right away, he goes to the room's door and locks it. My heart skips a beat, but I remain impassive.

"I've been watching you for some time," he reveals, catching me off guard. I had never noticed. "And I was happy when I saw you looking at me the same way."

"I don't..."

"Shh," he interrupts, touching his fingers to my lips. "You and Abigail are quite the pair, so I had a question... " Ethan pauses with a sly smile. "Have you two taken advantage of it?" As soon as he asks, I stare at him, confused. Noticing this, he smiles and pulls me closer, keeping our bodies together. I try to pull away, but he is stronger. "I want to know if you've rubbed against each other, you know how it is? The so-called female curiosity."

Alarmed, I try to push him away, but he easily holds my arms behind my back and starts kissing down my neck.

"Let me go! I'll scream!"

"Scream!" he encourages me with a smile. "Director Aarons will love to know what you and your little friend have been up to."

With a swift movement, he throws us onto the bed, positioning himself on top of me.

"No! Stop!"

"Answer me, Evie," he murmurs, the smell of alcohol and his actions making me feel nauseous. "Have you rubbed your little pussy against that troublemaker? You must be really tight."

I try to free my arms, but it's no use. I start screaming, and that infuriates him; one hand covers my mouth with extreme force, and the other manages to pin my arms above my head. In the midst of my panic, I hear a loud noise, like something exploding. Ethan pauses, and with a frightened look, loosens his grip on me. I don't waste any time and scratch his face, causing him to fall to the side.

I use that moment to run to the door, and even with trembling hands, I manage to unlock it and rush outside. My lungs burn from the effort, and as I cross the stone path, I hear gunshots and female screams.

I stop, scared, and then see some hooded men coming down the end of the corridor. I hide behind a pillar and from where I am, I can see the girls and the sisters on the first floor running in the opposite direction of the armed men. Even though I want to cry and stay still, I take a deep breath and run towards the back of the orphanage. Just before I can turn the corner, I feel a hand grab me, and alarmed, I try to break free.

"Calm down, girl!" I stop automatically and see the sister in charge of the filing room. "Go hide with the others in the second basement! Don't come out until one of us goes down there!"

"Did you see Abby?!"

"Go!"

She pushes me in the direction, but I shake my head, and under her terrified gaze, I run towards the dormitories. If Abby has arrived, she must be around there! I run as fast as I can, and as soon as I reach the stairs, I hear the angry male voices. They were speaking a strange language that I couldn't decipher; I think about turning back and running, but I'm soon grabbed by one of them who was behind me. I lower my head in fear, bracing for the worst.

However, he drags me by my hair into another room, and there I see only blonde girls. I scan my gaze over all of them and feel somewhat relieved when I don't find Abby there. I'm violently thrown to the ground, and one of the sisters quickly embraces me. I cling to her, my sobs full of pure horror. What is happening? There was no money or valuable material goods in the convent. So why are they here?

I subtly glance at one of them and realize he seems to be giving orders. When he finishes speaking, he pulls out a phone and points it in our direction. I cling tighter to the sister as she prays softly.

"I'm looking for a young woman," the man speaks in our dialect, his accent strong along with his serious voice. "So, if you can help, we'll leave, and all of you will be fine." The room is partially dark, and my fear of what could happen to us there is enormous. "Each of you, in order, take a step forward and say your names."

I look to the front of the line and see the first girl step forward and speak. The one next to what seems to be the leader shines a flashlight on Amber and does the same with the second. When it's my turn, I'm trembling; the man looks me up and down and smiles.

"E-Eveline," I murmur.

The light is directed at my face, and to my surprise, I feel my arm gripped violently. As I'm dragged outside, I try to look back, and with a broken heart, I watch those who were once my family being killed.

CHAPTER FOUR

Eveline

I am dragged toward the exit, and along the way, I see some bloodied bodies on the ground, as well as many debris still on fire. I try to escape, but the hand on my arm exerts more force, making me cry out in pain. Outside, I feel the cold wind hit my face. Part of the wall is destroyed, and parked right in front, I see a huge car.

The person holding me starts to speak in an authoritative tone, and trembling, I watch the group of men walk toward the car. Once again, I try to break free, and impatiently, another man slaps me.

The door is opened, and I am thrown inside. The men enter with me, looking pleased. They greet each other and raise their weapons in a gesture of victory. I curl up as much as I can; some look at me intensely, and I feel extremely uncomfortable. I look away and hug myself. Minutes pass, and no one addresses me, but I know we are on a dirt road. Everything shakes a lot. I wipe away the tears that keep falling, and almost at the same moment, the car stops.

The group looks at each other, and then we hear more gunfire.

Four of the men with me open the back door and slowly step out. I watch everything without being able to look away, and I see the moment all four fall at once. The other three, who remain with me, position themselves with their guns pointed outside.

"Who's there?" the man asks furiously.

I watch him gesture and point outside.

Then the glass separating the front from the back shatters. I scream as I see the bodies fall, lifeless. I cover my lips in fear and hear footsteps outside. My gaze follows the noise, and then I see him.

He has a different gun in hand, points it in my direction, and in fear, I close my eyes.

"Let's go," he says, then I look at him, confused. "We have a long journey ahead."

His gaze shifts to one of the men on the ground; he does a quick search and finds nothing. When he realizes I haven't moved yet, he looks back at me. He wears a black mask with a skull design; I can only see his eyes, but even so, I notice he huffs out a faint puff of smoke due to the cold air. I don't move, and this time he stands up and comes over to me. My arm is grabbed again in the same spot, and I groan in pain. Already on the dirt floor, I nearly fall, but I am held up.

"Please! Don't hurt me!"

"If I were going to hurt you, you'd already be dead."

The tone he uses is determined; he doesn't seem to care that I'm scared or about what he just did. I feel the hair on the back of my neck stand up.

"Who are you? What do you want from me?" My voice trembles, barely able to articulate the words.

His blue eyes then lock onto mine. Even there, poorly lit, they shine with a chilling intensity, revealing a mix of determination and disdain.

He lets out a brief, sarcastic laugh.

"It doesn't matter who I am. What matters is that you're safe with me, for now."

His response only heightens my fear. What does he mean by "for now"? Why would I be safe with someone who hasn't even told me who he was? And who held me in the same way those murderers did?

"Please, I didn't do anything. I don't know why I'm here," I plead, tears beginning to flow down my face. "They invaded the orphanage, killed my friends, the sisters..."

He watches me for a moment, as if weighing my words. Then, without a word, he drags me to another car hidden among the trees. I look on expectantly; I have a plan. The orphanage can't be far, so I think I can run back there. The masked man opens the car door and follows my gaze, perhaps understanding what I would do. He sighs and decides to put me in the back seat.

"To avoid any headaches, okay?" he murmurs, and with a rope, he ties my arms behind my back. "Don't test my patience."

With that, he locks me in the car, and frightened, I watch him return to the bodies on the ground.

Skull

I GLANCE BACK QUICKLY and see her leaning against the window. I let out another sigh and move toward the large van. I observe the bloodied bodies and, without wasting time, I begin to search each one. In a pocket, I find a cellphone, but it asks for a digital lock. Cursing under my breath, I bend down to place the dead man's finger on the screen. I try twice, and on the third try, I succeed. The last app open was the camera, and I touch it. A video catches my attention.

I can see a row of blonde girls; they check each other's eyes, and when they reach Eveline, they recognize her. I search for more information, and when I don't find anything relevant, I take my tactical knife and force it into the device, splitting it in half. I remove the SIM card and break it in two, and when I notice a micro USB card, I take it. I toss the pieces inside the van and step back.

I need to get out of here, as quickly as possible.

Once in the driver's seat, I glance at the rearview mirror and notice Eveline silently crying. I don't pay much attention and take a shortcut. The plane is two hours away, in an abandoned hangar.

Hours pass, and I finally approach the runway. I park near the plane and get out. Even in my combat gear and mask, I feel the cold wind. I search for the weapons bag, throwing it over my shoulder, holding the AK47 in one hand and grabbing the girl's arm with the other. We walk briskly to the plane, and I glance subtly at Eveline; she looks surprised.

"Wait! Please!" I stop to hear her, even though I want to ignore her. "Why are you taking me? Please! I need to go back; I need to see if my friend is okay. Everything happened so fast, and..."

"You're not going back!" I cut her off rudely. "Your life in that orphanage is over"—I continue, and she cries more. Annoyed, I let out a sigh and pull her toward the plane. "I was hired to save you and take you to the meeting point." With my response, she tries to break free. I pull her, bringing her face to face with me. "So if you're smart, you'll obey me and stay quiet. Do you understand, Eveline?"

She furrows her brow, her gaze fixed directly on mine, and for a moment, I feel unsettled. Those differently colored eyes were even more beautiful in person. I involuntarily lower my gaze down her face, noticing her slender nose, rosy cheeks, but one side of her face is bruised. I clench my jaw, and when I realize I'm staring at her, I look away. She hugs herself, maybe from the cold or fear; I can't tell. I make her climb the stairs ahead of me, and then my gaze lands on her uncovered arm. There are marks where I held her tightly; I remember being rough with her the entire way.

I don't apologize because I have no reason to.

But this time, my hand goes to her back. I guide her to one of the seats, and when she sits down, I watch her closely.

"I'm not going to tie you up," I warn seriously, "but it's best if you don't touch anything." I place the weapons bag beside her and help her buckle her seatbelt. "When we take off, I'll let you know, and you can unbuckle and lie down if you want."

A few tears fall, and she quickly wipes her face. She nods and looks away. I grab the weapons bag, adjust the AK47 to the side, and head to the cockpit. I take the same seat as before and perform all the necessary procedures.

Eveline

AFTER A FEW MINUTES, I look at the small window behind me and observe the bright lights below. The sky is dark with scattered clouds as we fly between them. I feel a mix of emotions as I watch the blinking lights, each representing a life, a story, a destiny. It's as if we are in another world, distant and isolated from the hustle and chaos below.

I can no longer cry; I feel physically and mentally exhausted. However, I still feel fear. My thoughts keep going back to Abby; not knowing what happened to her is killing me.

I let out a sigh, then I hear the door where he is being opened. I adjust my position, my eyes never leaving his masked face. I wonder what is going through his mind at this moment. He is a man of mystery, exuding an air of danger with every move he makes. I lower my gaze to his hand and see a package and a bottle of water.

"You can unbuckle now," he says, extending what he has brought. "Eat, and if you want to sleep, I recommend it. We still have two hours of flight. We're heading straight to Chicago; you'll be able to use the bathroom there if you can't hold it..." He pauses as if thinking about it. I frown, not understanding him. "You can use this bottle."

"I am not going to relieve myself in a bottle!" I retort, but quickly shrink back. I don't want another slap. With trembling hands, I take the items. "What are we going to do in Chicago? Who sent you? I don't even know your name..."

He simply watches me in silence.

I unwrap the package and discover it's a sandwich. Before taking a generous bite, I smell it and glance at the masked man.

"It's not poisoned."

Ignoring him, I turn toward the window. If he wouldn't do the bare minimum to answer my questions, I wouldn't reciprocate. I start eating the turkey sandwich, holding back from devouring it all at once. The clouds begin to disappear, leaving a clear sky filled with bright stars.

I wake up with a jolt and, dazed, look at the small window and see dawn slowly fading. The sky is tinged with soft shades of pink and orange as the sun begins to rise on the horizon. The clouds seem to be brushed by a celestial hand, reflecting the soft colors and giving the impression of a constantly changing painting.

"*If you're already awake, put on your seatbelt,*" a voice sounds loud and clear over the speakers. "*I'm going to start the landing.*"

My gaze goes to where he is, and through the little glass door, I can see him. He still wears the mask; why does he wear it? I feel another jolt and remember the seatbelt. I put my arms through, as he did yesterday, and fasten the clips until I hear the click. I try to look through the small window again and spot a place with other planes, smaller than this one.

The plane descends, and I feel a shiver run through my body. What awaited me down there? After a few minutes, I see the masked man exit, holding a large black bag and a gun at his side. A loud noise fills the air, and when I look—much to my surprise—the hatch of the plane opens. The wind blows through my hair; I can see the sun flooding the interior of the plane and touching my skin.

"Let's go."

As he speaks, he walks past me without looking at me. Quickly, I unbuckle and follow him, keeping him in sight. Outside, he heads toward a car and tosses the bag into the back seat. There's another man who speaks briefly, hands over something, and then heads toward the plane. He doesn't even look at me; he just enters. I walk quickly to the masked man waiting for me near the car; his gaze follows my steps without wavering.

I settle into the front seat, and he does the same.

I watch him fasten his seatbelt and mimic him. Out of the corner of my eye, I see him start to drive. I wait a few minutes, and when we are on the road, I let out a sigh.

"Could you please stop somewhere?" I ask, and he looks at me. "I want to use a bathroom."

"Didn't you use the bottle?"

His tone is serious.

"I'm not an animal to use a bottle like that." He breathes deeply; I see his chest inflate. I wait for a response, but he remains silent. "I need to pee!"

He looks at me once more and makes a maneuver, pulling over to the shoulder. Cars pass by at high speed; I look at him, confused.

"Your bathroom," he points to the vegetation beside me. "You have two minutes."

"I'm not going to pee in that brush," I refuse, horrified. "I want a bathroom! Someone might see, or some animal could bite me."

"Don't test my patience," he warns in a tone of advice, pointing outside again. "Now go and come back in two minutes."

I cross my arms and lift my nose. I wouldn't give in to this humiliation, not even if it cost me another slap.

"I want a bathroom! And I'm hungry! I'm not going into that brush without knowing what's in there. I'm not an animal! So find a decent place, or I'll do it right here."

I watch his eyes narrow, his piercing gaze drilling into mine with a chilling intensity. He inhales deeply, as if searching for patience amid my irritation.

"If you were in a war, and your life was at risk, you can be sure you wouldn't have even that to relieve yourself," his voice is sharp, laced with a rough tone that makes me instinctively recoil.

I gulp, struggling to maintain my composure in the face of his blunt response. I look away, unable to meet his gaze as the words echo in my mind.

"I'm not in a war, so please find a decent bathroom," my voice comes out weaker than I'd like, a mix of frustration and resignation.

With a sudden motion, he goes back to driving, the vehicle shaking under his firm control. I cross my arms over my chest, keeping my gaze fixed on the horizon, trying to block out the tumultuous emotions swirling within me. It's a silent battle, but I know I can't afford to falter now.

After a few minutes, I'm restless in my seat, let out another sigh, and glance at the back seat. There's only the black bag. I adjust my position and continue with my arms crossed. From my window side, I can see a huge establishment appear, and even from inside the car, I can spot some people inside.

"Go to the damn bathroom and you have one minute to come back. If you take too long, I'll come after you, and you won't like that." He states, and I just nod. He seems nervous. "I'll order something for you to eat."

"Could it be the same sandwich as yesterday?"

I ask; I had really liked it, and at the orphanage, we rarely got to eat that.

"Sure. Go."

I agree and get out of the car. As I walk to the entrance, I can read the word Pub in huge letters. My gaze scans the area curiously; cars and motorcycles are parked side by side. When I reach the door, I push it open and step inside. A bit surprised, I see that most of the patrons are men, and they look me up and down. I gulp and approach one who is drying a glass.

"Good morning! Can I use the bathroom?"

"Of course." He smiles, revealing some yellowed teeth. "Just go straight ahead; the first door on the right."

I thank him and follow his directions.

As soon as I enter the bathroom, I head to a stall and lock the door. It's a relief not to have to use the brush for this. I wish I could take a shower and maybe change clothes; mine are completely dirty. But I don't want to test the masked man's limits; he seems quite nervous. I don't linger inside, and when I finish, I wash my hands. I take the opportunity to splash some water on my neck and face.

I dry my hands and step out.

For a moment, I pause and observe the men inside. Could I trust them and ask for help? Or would they not believe my word? Is it safe? When I think about thanking them and leaving, two of them approach me.

"Hi," one of them says, stopping beside me. He smiles, looking me up and down. "Need help, princess? You don't look so good."

"If you need, we can help you."

His smile reminds me of Ethan, it's the same one he had before he attacked me.

"You don't have to," I say simply and try to pull away, but my arm is grabbed. "Let me go!"

"Calm down, princess," he smiles, attempting to touch my face. I push him away forcefully and try to step back, but I'm grabbed once again.

"Let me go!" My voice comes out in a growl of indignation, struggling against the grip of his hands.

"It's better to obey her," a voice emerges from the corner of the counter. I immediately recognize the masked man by the outfit he's wearing, as he's not wearing the mask at that moment. Surprised, I observe his low, almost blonde brown hair and his blue eyes—a more intense color. His beard is short, like a shadow on his face. My gaze fixes on the prominent scar that crosses his face. "I suggest you back off, or I'll be forced to use force," his voice is firm, his posture threatening as he stares at the man holding me.

A shiver runs down my spine as I sense the tension in the air.

I feel my arm being released, and I take the opportunity to move closer to my savior. I stop beside him, and he hands me a white bag and a huge white cup with a straw. I observe his face for a few seconds, but quickly look away.

"And who's the *faggot*?" the man who was holding me inquires, his voice filled with disdain. "Or are you going to tell me she's your little whore? Dressed like that, do you think you intimidate anyone?"

I feel my face burn with embarrassment at the insult. After questioning, he crosses his arms, and then others who were sitting before approach us. Scared, I hide behind the masked man. He simply stands up and surveys everyone.

"Believe me, you don't want to know who I am or what I'm capable of," he replies calmly, his voice echoing with a cold seriousness. Then he looks at me sideways. "Let's go."

"You're only leaving here when I let you," the man speaks again. "And when I get a kiss from the *hot little nymph*."

They laugh, and I'm left confused. Are they talking about me? I look at the masked man with some confusion, noticing his expression of disapproval. It's so clear now without the mask. His eyes are focused on the man in front of us. I gently tap his arm, but he quickly pulls away and walks forward. Everything happens so fast that before I know it, the man who spoke receives a punch that makes him fall.

He moves with agility as he takes down two more, my eyes can barely keep up. When he finishes, he lands a kick to another's face. I swallow hard, watching him; he's not even tired.

"Let's go."

CHAPTER FIVE

Skull

I keep my focus on the road; by my calculations, we would reach the meeting point the next day. It wasn't the plan, but I don't want to stress myself out again today, so we would sleep in a motel tonight. I glance quickly to the side and see Eveline dozing off. Some strands fall over her sleeping face; she has a serene expression, different from yesterday. She seems calmer too, and even with my excessive rage in that *pub,* she didn't show any fear of me.

Sleeping, she doesn't look like the stressed-out bossy type she is. I scoff disbelievingly and continue driving. How could someone so small be so cheeky? And stand up to me like she did just hours ago? Even though I don't want to admit it, I have to acknowledge she's brave. Another girl would have stayed quiet and obeyed, but not her.

I look at her again and am surprised when I notice a small smile. She's still asleep. Once she's delivered, I plan to live in isolation. Maybe in a small farmhouse with chickens and two cows? For me, this life I lead has run its course. Years serving a country that turned its back on me at the first opportunity. All that's left for me is to try to seek justice with my own hands. Much blood has been spilled on my journey, so this will be my last mission.

If I'm to die, let it be far away from everything and everyone.

I keep driving, and when I spot the neon sign of the roadside motel, I change my route. I park in an available spot and retrieve a stack of money from the glove compartment. To avoid drawing attention, I take off the top part of my tactical long shirt, leaving on a black t-shirt. I glance at Eveline one last time and exit the car.

I go to the reception and ask for a room with two beds. I hand over the money and receive the key. As I approach the car, I see Eveline watching me.

"Today we're sleeping here. Tomorrow, if you cooperate, we'll reach the meeting point."

I see her eyebrows furrow, expecting a sassy response. However, she just shrugs and gets out of the car. She takes a few steps forward and approaches the porch. I quickly grab the weapon bag and follow her. I stop in front of the room we would share and open the door. She enters and touches all the furniture, goes to the bathroom, and comes back. Her gaze stops at the two beds.

"Who hired you?" she asks while sitting on one of the beds. I open my mouth to say that it's none of her business, but she's quicker. "I just want to understand why all of this is happening. I mean, I don't have parents, and I don't know anyone from my family, and out of nowhere, I'm kidnapped. It's not fair to me, so if you could tell me something, just so I'm not completely in the dark, I'd be grateful."

I analyze her in silence. The pleading look in her eyes makes me uncomfortable; I avert my gaze and go to the window. I pull back the curtain and observe outside; everything seems normal.

"Those men who kidnapped you were going to use you for bargaining." I say, and she looks surprised. "They were mercenaries, rebels, allied with the Iraqi government. It seems you're quite important. I was hired to rescue you; tomorrow we'll go to your last stop. We'll part ways there."

"But who hired you?"

"Someone from the United States government." Her expression becomes even more confused. "Now go take a shower and rest. Tomorrow morning we'll hit the road again; we'll arrive by late afternoon."

UNHOLY PASSION

I sit in a chair and hold my *Glock*. My gaze follows Eveline; she enters the bathroom and closes the door. I lean back in the chair and stretch my legs; spending hours driving used to be enjoyable, but today it just brings me fatigue. A few hours later, Eveline returns, still in the same clothes, reminding me that this was all she had.

"What's your name?"

I look at her; this time she's lying on the bed. Her blonde, damp hair is spread out on the white pillow. Strangely, the tip of her upturned nose is reddened. Had she been crying?

"Skull."

"Skull?" she repeats, frowning. "Are you a cop?"

"No."

"Are you a soldier?"

I let out a sigh and stare at her. Doesn't she ever tire of all these questions?

"I used to be, once. Aren't you tired?"

"I'm scared," she replies, my gaze locking onto hers. "Not knowing if I'll be okay... or who's behind all of this is terrifying. Skull, it may sound like a stupid question, but in the orphanage, I wasn't taught. Is Iraq in Belarus?"

I find her question strange and shake my head.

"They are different countries. Iraq is in the Middle East, in Western Asia. Belarus is in Eastern Europe."

She sighs and stares at the ceiling.

"Then I don't understand," she murmurs, pulling out a crumpled paper from her skirt pocket. "My parents are Belarusian. I found out before they invaded. So, I must be too."

"How did you find that out?"

"My friend Abby saw it on the director's computer," she answers and gets off the bed. "Well, in my file, there was this photo. We thought it could be my father. When I turn eighteen, I'll need to choose whether to stay in the orphanage and work there or leave. Abby thought that maybe I could look for them."

I take the image and fall silent.

The photograph is quite worn, and even with the man's face scratched out, I can clearly see who he is. It wasn't the Diplomat. I turn my gaze back to Eveline; she doesn't seem to be lying about the information she shared with me. My mind drifts back to my conversation with the Diplomat; he mentioned that they knew about Eveline, that everything had to be kept absolutely secret, and I was hired so no one would know. Everything was starting to make sense to me.

For a moment, I try to analyze the entire situation.

I turn the image over and frown. A message of love, with a surname underneath it.

"Novikov?"

"What?"

"*I will love you for all my life.*" I read aloud. "H. Novikov."

I hand the image back, and she furrows her brow.

"Yeah, I saw that name in my file, but I didn't know it was here too."

"You can't read?" I ask, curious. After all, if she's from this country, she should have some understanding. But I quickly realize I've been rude. She lifts her upturned nose and turns her back to me. "So the answer is no."

"I can read! But I can't read this. Why are you so rude?"

I let out a sigh and turn my gaze back to the window.

"Go to sleep; it'll pass."

"Your rudeness won't go away like that."

She grumbles from the bed, and my lips pull into a brief smile. Then I stop. Since when do I smile? Uncomfortable, I turn back to the entrance of the room. I urgently need to finish that job and get some proper rest.

Novikov.

The surname didn't seem strange to me, but I couldn't recall its origin. I check my *Glock* and wait for dawn; I'm not sleepy despite everything. It was never a good idea to let my guard down; terrible things happen when we're not alert.

When dawn finally breaks, I'm ready to continue the journey. However, Eveline is still asleep. I think about waking her, but in the end, I let her sleep until 7 a.m. In the meantime, I check my weapon and tuck it into the waistband behind my pants under the black t-shirt. A few minutes later, I call Eveline, and she sits up quickly. Her breathing is rapid, and I can see she's still sleepy.

"We have a long way to go."

I wait for her to head to the bathroom, and when she returns, I indicate the outside.

I hope she'll say something at some point, but she remains silent. Out of the corner of my eye, I notice her hands clenching; she's nervous. I imagine she's hungry, but nothing is said. I remain silent, but when I see a sign for a restaurant 5 km away, I decide we'll eat. As soon as I take the road to the restaurant and park in a spot, I inevitably search for Eveline's face.

She smiles subtly, and I wait for her to look at me and say something.

"Are you hungry?" I ask when she doesn't speak.

"Yes, but if it's going to hold you back and delay you, I can wait until we get there."

Her look is sad; I feel sincerity in her words, but I don't like how it sounds out loud.

"I won't let you go hungry," I say, and she smiles at me. My stomach twists, but not in a bad way—rather, it feels strange. That had never happened before. "Just don't draw attention to yourself."

"Have you looked in the mirror, Skull?"

Automatically, I feel a bitter taste in my mouth. It was obvious my appearance wasn't the best, and that shouldn't affect me the way it does. Her expression changes, and when she opens her mouth, I simply exit the car. I hope she stays by my side, and together we enter the restaurant. The door signals with a bell as we enter, and after looking around, I point to a table by the window.

I sit across from her, but my gaze is on the parked car.

"I'm sorry," she says; I don't look at her. "It's just that..."

"Look at what you're going to eat and don't take too long."

Her gaze shifts to the menu, and even though I don't want to, I watch her.

She's really beautiful. Her face is perfectly shaped, her blonde hair, her two-colored eyes, her sharp nose, her rosy cheeks... even her lips are inviting. But that outfit definitely doesn't help. The waitress arrives and quickly takes our orders. Eveline looks at me, and I continue to stare. I think she'll look away, embarrassed, but she holds her ground. Seconds pass, and her eyes drop to my scar; I don't find the repulsion I expected. Her gaze feels like embers on my skin, and when it descends to my lips, I see her blush.

The food arrives, and I bring the unsweetened coffee to my lips.

"I didn't call you ugly," she suddenly says. "It's just that you're handsome, and asking not to draw attention was a bit strange. Your presence alone already draws attention, Skull."

"You'd better eat well; you're talking nonsense."

Eveline smiles at me.

"I'm starving, but I'm not talking nonsense."

With a fork and knife, she cuts a piece of pancake and examines it closely. Then she brings it to her mouth, chews, and closes her eyes. I drink more coffee without taking my eyes off her. The events of last night soon return, and deep down, concern arises. What will the diplomat do with her? Because in my way of living, when there's something that could jeopardize the plan, it's eliminated to achieve success.

"What else was in your file?"

She looks at me, surprised, and shrugs.

"My first and last name, that I was taken there as a baby. Medical histories, nothing more."

"So, when you were taken, you already had that name?"

Even with a confused expression, she nods.

"I think so."

"That man in the photo," I continue. "You have no idea who he is?" I ask and receive a negative shake of her head. "Didn't you have a TV in the orphanage?"

"Well, sometimes we watched some movies," she replies innocently. "There were some computers, but they only worked for typing; the internet was really bad. In fact, they barely turned on. We had other things to pass the time. I learned to cook, clean, work in the garden, and sew."

"Yesterday, you talked about leaving the orphanage or staying," I mention, and she nods. "Why is that?"

"It was a rule. Once we turned eighteen, we had to choose between staying or leaving. Director Aarons asked what my answer would be, but I didn't get the chance to speak."

"And what would it be?"

She sighs and leans back in her chair.

"I would choose to leave. I wouldn't want to become bitter."

Eveline smiles, but soon her expression changes to sadness.

"You'll have your answers soon; I'm not a good person for that."

"I think you're a good person," she says, and I scoff. "I'm serious. You didn't have to stop at that place for us to sleep, or even here, but you cared about me. And I appreciate it."

Annoyed, I shift in my seat and look away. I don't feel comfortable.

"Have you finished eating?"

"You have this way of acting like you don't care, but you have a good heart, Skull. By the way, your name is really strange. Is it really Skull?"

I smile quickly, and Eveline mimics me.

"Everyone knows me like that, and I prefer it."

"But what happened to your real name?"

I shake my head. I haven't used my name for about five years; I had to kill my old self so that Skull could live and have the chance to make those who took my purpose in life suffer. I let out a sigh when I realize she's still looking at me.

"Let's hit the road. Do you want anything else?"

Eveline stops smiling and shakes her head.

I leave some notes on the table and gesture toward the exit.

CHAPTER SIX

Eveline

I pay close attention to the road we're following; my heart feels like it's going to leap out of my mouth. Since we left the restaurant, I've kept silent, lost in thought. Skull, next to me, drives focused on the road. My gaze now scans the sides of the highway, where the weeds and plants appear as blurs. The fact that Skull hasn't said anything about where we're going to stay or who will be there makes me very anxious.

It's strange, but I trust Skull. His presence makes me feel calmer, despite my earlier fear. His intense blue eyes convey security, but also secrets that I believe are too heavy to bear. I let out a sigh and lean my head back.

"Are you hungry?"

His voice surprises me.

I look at him and shake my head; I'm not hungry, I'm scared. I grip the hem of my dirty skirt and begin twisting the end. As the car enters another highway, I see several leafless trees; it's still winter, and that's my favorite season. Whenever it snowed, Abby and I would sneak out to the back and lie down, enjoying it. Remembering my friend gives me a tightness in my chest; I have no idea what happened to her.

"Do you need to go to the bathroom?"

"No," I shake my head. "Thank you." I appreciate it, and taking advantage of his more talkative mood, I watch him. "Where are we going?"

Skull sighs and glances at me quickly.

"We're in Chicago, but our destination is Evanston."

I thank him and turn my attention back to the window. I cross my arms and lean my head against the glass, feeling so lost and restless. I close my eyes to try to distract myself, but it's worse; intrusive thoughts come and go. I fall asleep, and when I wake up, my gaze shifts to the window. It's late afternoon, and my stomach growls. I look around, a bit dazed, and realize we're in a remote area. There's nothing but forest around us, and that makes me anxious. My frightened gaze goes to Skull; he has a furrowed brow.

"Are we there yet?"

"Almost."

From the glove compartment, he retrieves his mask and puts it on. He then takes out a gun and holds it. The car stops in front of a huge cabin, and I analyze the place. The door is closed, but the small screen door is slightly ajar. Skull gets out of the car, and I follow him. Next to the house, I notice some chopped tree trunks scattered on the ground. Before we can enter, I see a huge man walk up and stop in front of the door. He opens it, and his cold gaze falls on me. I move closer to Skull, who, still holding the gun, watches the man in front of us.

"You took your time. What happened?"

"Where is he?" Skull questions, not even bothering to answer. The man in front of us inhales deeply, and soon behind him, two more men appear. One of them is holding a large black bag.

"He's going to be a little late," he replies after a few seconds. "Here's your cash. Take it and get the hell out of here."

Then he throws the bag at Skull's feet, who continues to stare at him.

"And you, princess," he points at me. "You can go inside the house."

I swallow hard and notice another man staring at me from the window. I shake my head and practically hide behind Skull.

"I'm not going in!" I refuse and turn to Skull. He holsters the gun on his thigh and bends down to grab the bag. "You're going to stay, right?"

He sighs and, with the bag over his shoulder, looks at me.

"I was hired to drop you off here."

Incredulously, I watch him walk past me; I run after him and stop in front of him.

"Do you know them?" I ask, and he shakes his head. "Then how can you leave me here with them?"

"Eveline..."

"No! Please! I don't trust them; don't leave me here alone with them! Please!"

He sighs and walks past me. My heart skips a beat, but I see him toss the bag in the back seat and turn back to me. Without saying anything to me, he walks toward the front of the house. I run after him and stay very close.

"The deal is just for her to stay," the unidentified man says. He seems angry.

"The deal was to keep her safe here," Skull retorts, and I subtly see his hand hover over the gun. "And for now, I'll wait until the contractor arrives. Now get your ugly mug out of my face."

The two men behind him try to move forward but are stopped by their colleague. I shrink back in fear, while Skull remains unmoved.

"You can come in."

I enter with Skull, and in the room, I face the other member. The four men spread out in the space; some look at me, and I see malice in their eyes; others glare at Skull with deadly intent. On the coffee table, there are some weapons and glasses with drinks.

"Who are you guys?" I hear Skull ask.

"We were hired to come with you to get the *princess*, but it seems the plans have changed."

Skull sits down, and I follow. I wouldn't be foolish enough to distance myself from him.

"I imagine. What time does the Diplomat arrive?"

Diplomat? I look at Skull, confused, but I can't say anything.

"Maybe tomorrow, or over the weekend. We're not sure."

I shiver with fear at the tone used. My gaze searches for the man by the window, and he smiles at me unabashedly.

"Since when have you been here?"

"About a day or so," he replies, sitting in an armchair. "You can go." He smiles. His skin is tanned, and his hair is shorter than Skull's. They all wear similar clothes: black pants, black t-shirts, and boots. "She'll be safe with us. You don't need to keep this burden."

I feel offended and wait for Skull to deny it, but he remains silent. I look at him in surprise; he seems to be analyzing everyone there, and then my doubt arises: am I a burden to him?

I hold back the urge to cry and try to stay calm. He wouldn't leave me there, not with those unfriendly men. I sit quietly. We all remain in silence when a cellphone rings. The man who handed the money bag to Skull answers and informs that I'm there, but that Skull is too. Then, after he agrees to something, he hands the phone to Skull. He sighs and answers.

He remains silent for a few minutes but soon confirms and stands up. I follow him, and when he heads toward the exit without looking at me, I go after him. Someone tries to hold me back, but I push him and run to Skull.

"Where are we going?"

He stops, sighs, and looks at me.

"You're staying, Eveline."

"But I'm going to stay with them?" I question, and before he can answer, I continue. "Take me with you! I promise I'll stay quiet, I'll pee in the brush, I don't care. Just don't leave me here."

"Eveline..."

"Skull, please! Take me, I..."

"You're not my problem!" he explodes, and I stop, startled. "You're not my responsibility! You're nothing to me! Why do you think I'd risk anything for you? I was hired to save you and bring you here. After that, it's every man for himself. Do you understand?"

A few tears escape my eyes. I quickly look away and nod. I don't have the courage to face him; he's right, but it's so hard to hear.

"I-I'm sorry."

I hear footsteps beside me, and when I turn, my arm is gripped tightly. I don't look at Skull, but I know he's standing in the same place. As we're in the room, I continue to cry as I look at each of them. Their smiles are disgusting, and out of pure fear, I try to run outside. However, I'm caught and feel a slap sting on my face. I become a bit dizzy but try to escape again.

I receive another slap.

Skull

I WATCH HER BEING DRAGGED inside, and I force myself to get into the car. As soon as I take the driver's seat, I start the engine, make a U-turn, and accelerate. Then I stop a few meters away. I feel extremely furious and restless, as if I've done something wrong. It's a feeling I've never felt before. After all, I've killed before and tortured enemies, but I've never felt this way. Involuntarily, I glance at the passenger seat where Eveline was, and I close my eyes. Did I save her only to leave her at the mercy of four unknown men?

I back up while watching the rearview mirror, and when I stop in front of the cabin, I get out of the car with my gun drawn. The door is open, and the room is empty. Just as I'm about to call her, I hear a muffled scream coming from upstairs. I rush up there, and when I stop in front of a room door, I kick it open. I don't stop to analyze; I shoot three of them, making them fall onto the bed. I point my gun at the one left standing; he has his pants undone and is unarmed. I look at Eveline and feel the guilt wash over me. Her face is bruised, and her shirt is torn. She hugs herself, hiding her breasts while her pained, tear-filled eyes stare at me.

I look away, and without holding back, I shoot the bastard in the foot and thigh who is still standing.

"Son of a bitch!" he screams from the floor. I approach him and press the hot barrel of the gun against the bullet hole. His scream is one of pure agony.

"Let's talk downstairs."

I warn and grip his hair as I drag him outside. When we reach the stairs, I push him down from the top; he falls and groans in pain.

"Y-You're going to die..."

I holster the *Glock* on my thigh, and still filled with rage, I throw the bastard onto the glass table. It shatters. I pace back and forth, feeling like a caged beast. I notice his hand fumbling for a nearby weapon, and in fury, I grab him by the hair and throw him in the opposite direction.

"What were you planning to do with her?" I ask and, with a clenched fist, punch him in the nose. "Was it part of the plan to take advantage of her?"

"Yes!" He laughs, and I freeze with my hand in the air. "The Diplomat... paid us to make her disappear, but first... allowed us to have our fun with her." I look at him, incredulous, analyzing him. He laughs, then grimaces in pain. "What did you think would happen to her? Were you that naïve?"

I land another punch, blood staining my hand.

"Where is that bastard of a Diplomat?"

"What are you planning?" He laughs derisively. "To kill him?"

"Exactly! Him and anyone else involved. Now answer me! After this, where were you going?" I question, and he looks at me furiously as I grip my *Glock* again. "Do you want a little incentive?"

"You can kill me! Do you think I'm afraid of dying?"

At the end of his question, I watch him closely.

"I don't think so, but I wonder... What would the Diplomat do? Do you think it would be a problem for you?" I want to know, and maybe I've gotten close. His expression shifts from furious to tense. "What did he promise? A lot of money? Do you think if you fail, he'll come after you or someone important to you? A woman? A daughter?" I ask, and he becomes serious. "Do you think it would be difficult for him to hire a hitman to eliminate loose ends?"

"I want you and him to go fuck yourselves!"

I stand up and grab my *Glock*.

"It seems like you're not going to say anything."

"As if you were..." I shoot him in the forehead, causing him to topple backward.

I put my gun away again and head to the bedroom.

Eveline is lying on the bed, covering her ears with her hands, still in her torn shirt. I let out a sigh of frustration as I walk between the fallen bodies on the floor. I sit on the edge of the bed, trying to touch her, but she abruptly pushes me away, screaming.

"Go away! You left me!" Her voice is filled with anguish and anger.

I swallow hard at her cutting words and get up, heading to a wardrobe to grab some clothes. When I turn to hand them to her, I see her gaze fixed on me.

"Put this on, and let's go." I hand her the fabric, but she doesn't move. "If you want to take a shower, see if there's another bathroom. The house is big. Gather some clothes to take. We'll leave in ten minutes."

I stand in the middle of the room, waiting for her reaction. My words sound empty in the face of her intense emotions. What more could I say?

"I don't want to be a burden to you. I understand I'm not your problem."

I take a deep breath, but soon I exhale. I remove my mask and sit close to her again. Her tear-filled eyes make me feel ashamed of what I did minutes ago.

"You're not a burden. I was wrong to leave you once, but that won't happen again. I promise I won't leave your side until everything is resolved. I know it's asking a lot, and I know I don't deserve it, but trust me."

I extend the fabric to her again, and after a few seconds of staring at me, she holds it against her chest. I get up and survey the room, noticing some photographs on a wall. Curious, I approach them and see a couple embracing. I look at the bed and realize it's a double bed. Without saying anything, I leave the room and go to another; it's empty.

I open a door and find several children's clothes.

I leave there and go in search of more answers. When I reach the kitchen, I step out the back door. In the backyard, I see an open grave and two closed ones. They really were going to kill Eveline, and probably the owners of that cabin are in the other graves. And what would happen to me? Would I be killed too? Would I be hunted?

I hear a cellphone ringing in the background, and I turn toward the living room. The phone thrown on the floor catches my attention, and I answer it on the fourth ring.

"*Is she dead?*" The Diplomat's voice is anxious and low.

"You've caused a big problem, Diplomat," I respond, keeping my voice steady. In the background, the call goes silent, but I can hear his tense breathing. "Tell me, why do you want her dead? Is she a problem for you? Or for our dear President?"

He remains silent for a few minutes, then clears his throat and speaks again.

"*This was a misunderstanding, Skull. I don't want her dead, and I didn't understand your insinuation. I only want what's best for her.*"

"Misunderstanding?" I repeat, my mind already connecting the dots. I walk to the window while continuing the conversation. "So let's see if I got this wrong. Eveline Novikov, a young orphan, who would soon leave the orphanage and possibly go after her parents. A president about to be re-elected, but a bastard daughter shows up... how does that affect his reputation?" I question rhetorically. I continue, "And her mother? I wonder what happened to her? I feel there are many secrets involved. Really, Diplomat, if the enemies had gotten her, it would be a massive catastrophe. The President would be in a tight spot."

"*You don't know who you're dealing with, Skull. I can forget all this nonsense you just told me if you hand her over to me. Otherwise, you will be seen as a traitor, and your head will be worth a bounty; I'm sure your enemies will love to help capture you.*"

I let out a hollow laugh.

"Don't worry, Diplomat. I'm making it a point to come after you; you'll understand that no one plays games or threatens me. And as long as she's under my protection, no one will be able to lay a finger on her."

I hang up the phone firmly, my expression serious as I return to the room. My suspicions about who Eveline's father is are confirmed, but I need more answers. Before I can call for Eveline, I see her come out of the other room. She's wearing tight black jeans, boots, and a pink sweater. Her hair is damp, and just by looking at her face, I can tell she has been crying in the shower.

I feel worse than ever. After all, I could have prevented that situation.

"I'm sorry if I took too long."

"Did you pack the bag like I asked?" I inquire, and she nods. "Great! Let's go; we still have a long way ahead."

"Skull," she calls me shyly. "I made one for you too."

Surprised, I divert my gaze and walk into the bedroom, seeing two backpacks on the dresser. I check them to confirm they contain her clothes and men's clothing. Not knowing what to say, I simply grab both and leave the room. I gesture for her to follow, and she passes by me with her head down. I see she doesn't even look around; her stride is steady. I walk quickly to the driver's seat and settle in. I glance subtly at Eveline; she remains silent.

I accelerate away from there, knowing that soon our calm would give way to total chaos.

CHAPTER SEVEN

Eveline

On the way back, I stay silent the whole time. I can't relax; the images of what almost happened to me in that room haunt my mind. I hug myself tighter and rest my head against the window. My reflection shows the marks from the slaps I received. The minutes I spent in that room were desperate, and when Skull appeared, I felt a relief that didn't last long. His words hurt me deeply, not because he lied, but because he told the truth.

By my calculations, we had been traveling for five hours. We had already eaten at a restaurant and returned to the road. The sky is beautiful, full of stars and with few clouds. I want to sleep, but I'm afraid something will happen, even though Skull says he won't abandon me. I was scared.

I want to know the plan and about the so-called diplomat, but I've realized that Skull doesn't like being pressured like that. So I just accept it for now. The highway is calm, with few cars, and there aren't many houses around, but there are plenty of trees scattered about.

Skull takes another lane off the highway, minutes pass, and then I can see the huge identical houses. Curious, I observe everything, glance at Skull to find out where we are, but I change my mind when he looks at me.

"What's wrong?" he asks, and I shake my head quickly. "We're spending the night at a friend's house. I need to think about what to do now." I nod; indeed, I was a burden to him. "He'll put some killer on my trail anyway, Eveline." I look back at him. "You, whether delivered or not, the loose ends are eliminated."

I spend a few seconds looking at his face without the mask. His scar always catches my attention; I want to know how he got it, but I can't imagine the possibilities. My gaze travels down his sharp nose, his stubbled chin, and then his lips. I'm caught by his gaze, so I clear my throat.

"Skull..." I begin, then let out a sigh. "Did you say diplomat?"

"Yes, he's the one who hired me to rescue you."

I'm surprised by that. In the orphanage's library, there weren't many books, and I don't remember hearing about the diplomat.

"Is he important?"

"In the political scene, yes," he replies, but seeing that I look a bit confused, he continues. "He works in international relations." Skull scoffs and shakes his head with a half-smile. "Basically, in other words, he cleans up the messes of the President, which are not few. We'll talk when we arrive."

"Thank you."

As my gaze turns to the window, I notice that the street is now poorly lit, but many establishments are open. I adjust myself better in my seat and look outside in fright; there are few people on the sidewalk. We move a bit further away and see a two-story house. It's huge, and on the façade, there's a neon sign of a woman's silhouette. In front of it, there are some motorcycles and a car. Skull parks.

"You don't need to be scared of him," he says, looking at me. "I've known him for a long time; he served with me in my special operations group. He owes me a favor."

"He won't mind being with me?"

"Don't worry about that. Stay behind me and don't wander off."

I quickly agree, and when he gets out, I follow him. I grab the backpacks with the clothes I set aside, holding them as if my life depended on it. I move to Skull's side, who is holding two black bags.

UNHOLY PASSION

We stop in front of the door, and when the entrance camera moves in our direction, it doesn't take long for the door to be opened.

I shrink back when I see a huge man standing by the door; he gestures for us to go in, not seeming to care about us. As we exit the end of the corridor, I first hear a very different song and then see some almost naked women dancing on metal bars. There are men scattered around, smoke filling the air, watching the women dance with fascination. I search for Skull's gaze, but he isn't looking at the women. His attention is focused on someone else, and when I try to see who it is, I notice a tall, big, handsome blonde man approaching. I grab Skull's arm automatically.

"Oh my God! Miracles really happen! Skuller!"

Surprised, I watch the newcomer hug Skull, who doesn't move. But as soon as he pulls away, he gives a nod.

"And look at you, moving forward with your idea?"

I look around and feel a strange sensation when I see a redhead sitting on a man's lap. They kiss in a completely shameless way.

"Well, my friend. And this princess, who is she?"

I look at him quickly, anxious. Those men called me that same way.

"I'm not a princess!" I retort nervously. "Don't call me that!"

He raises his hands and gives a weak smile. He looks at Skull, who just sighs.

"We need a place to spend the night."

"Come with me!"

My gaze insists on leading me to the couple still kissing. How can they do that in front of so many people? We climb a staircase and take a hallway. At the end of it, I see several doors. Skull's friend points to one of them and opens it. I'm the first to enter the room, and then I see the huge bed in the middle. I walk over and sit down. As I feel the soft mattress, I give a small smile and throw myself down, stretching out. The bed in the orphanage wasn't this good, nor the one at the motel. If I had to compare, I could easily say I'm lying on clouds.

"I'm going downstairs because it's a celebration," the man says. "Bachelorette party. I'll order food, and as soon as possible, I'll come back up to talk."

"Thank you."

The door closes, and Skull places the bags next to the bed. In silence, he walks to the window covered with curtains and pulls it back a bit to look at the street's activity.

"What's your friend's name?"

"Miller."

I sit on the mattress and go barefoot. I stretch my toes, which practically scream in relief, while keeping my eyes on Skull. I watch him sit in an armchair against the wall and sigh. My gaze roams over the combat gear he's still wearing. I can't even remember if he took a shower at any point; I did. I took two showers.

"Can you tell me now?"

He looks at me for a few seconds but then nods.

"They found out you were going to be kidnapped by the enemies, so I was hired. As I said before, they would use you as leverage, which would definitely trigger a war. The agreement was to take you to the meeting point, but it seems he had other plans. To kill you."

I'm surprised and don't know what to say. Use me as leverage? But I wasn't anyone important, so why is this happening? I swallow hard and turn my gaze back to Skull. He keeps his eyes on me, perhaps looking for some reaction.

"Is he my father?"

"I'm not sure yet, but I think not. I need to confirm."

I nod.

"So, what am I going to do?" I ask, feeling anxious. "I have nothing. The only thing I had was the orphanage, and I don't even know what happened to them. Do you think I can go back there?"

"No. You're not going back there or doing anything," he replies. "I promised I'd take care of it, and I will."

"Why?"

He looks at me seriously. I want to believe his words, but I'm scared of being abandoned once again.

"When I've resolved this issue," he murmurs, looking at me. "You can go anywhere you want. If you want, you can go take a shower first."

Noticing him change the subject, I just accept. He doesn't have to do this for me, but a part of me feels grateful.

"You're not leaving this room, right?" I question as I stand up.

"No, you can go."

I agree once again and grab my backpack. I enter the bathroom and close the door. Inside, I look around with curiosity; it's very beautiful. I place my backpack on the porcelain counter and gaze at my reflection in the mirror. My life changed drastically two days ago. Two days where I no longer know who I am or if my friend is okay. That uncertainty is killing me.

I don't take long, and being curious as I am, I open some drawers. I find some sealed toothbrushes and other hygiene products. I take a pink toothbrush and toothpaste. I set them on the sink and start to undress. Then, I pull my hair up on top of my head and head towards the shower. I get wet and grab some liquid soap.

My shower lasts a few minutes, and when I finally finish, I come out of the bathroom wearing different jeans and another warm shirt. Skull has his back to me, fiddling with the black bag, and I see he has different weapons inside. He turns toward me, making me look away.

"Don't leave the room without me."

I nod and sit on the bed.

I sigh and watch him grab the other backpack and enter the bathroom. My gaze sweeps across the entire room, and even though we're far from the bachelorette party, the music filters in muted. I hear the shower turn on and soon find myself staring at the closed bathroom door.

"*Hello?*" Someone knocks on the bedroom door.

I swallow hard and see a shadow through the crack of the door.

"Yes?" I reply a bit nervously. I don't leave my spot.

"*Mr. Miller asked me to bring food.*"

I remember he did say that, so I walk to the door. I open it slowly, and to my surprise, I recognize the redhead from earlier. She smiles politely at me and extends a silver tray.

"Thank you."

"You're welcome!" She smiles and tries to look inside the room. "I'm Layla, and you?"

"Eveline."

"Eveline," she repeats, smiling even more. "Well, it was nice to meet you."

After speaking, she turns her back and leaves. I still hold the tray when I go back into the room and close the door. I place it on the dresser and lift the two stainless steel lids. There are two plates with food. I'll wait for Skull to eat, so I put the lids back on and wander around the room. There are many drawers here. Curious, I go to one next to the bed and pull out the first one. It has a white tube with a flame design and several square packages. I grab both just as the bathroom door opens.

Skull is shirtless, his hair damp, and his pants undone, showing part of his black underwear. His body is enormous; he's so strong that I can't look away. His chest bears several old scars, some lines and others more distinct. In his hand, he holds a shirt that I had set aside for him, and as if I just noticed it now, I observe his arms covered in tattoos. The images are so mesmerizing that I question how I only just noticed them. I realize he's fixating on my hands.

"I found this in the drawer." I inform him and return what I took. "Didn't you like the shirt?"

"Too tight," he replies, walking over to the food. Then I see his back, where there are also several large scars. "I'll see if Miller has something for me to borrow."

"You have so many scars."

He looks at me for a few seconds but then goes back to the food.

"Your food," he simply responds, pointing to the meal. "Eat in silence."

I move closer to him and take the plate and utensils. Since there isn't much space, I sit at the edge of the mattress. My gaze follows Skull as he goes to the other side of the room and bends down in front of a cabinet. He opens it and grabs two bottles of water. He throws one near me, and the other stays with him. We eat in silence, even though I want to talk. After the meal, I head to the bathroom and brush my teeth. Then, Skull does the same.

My body is showing signs of fatigue, but I stay alert.

"I'm going downstairs and..."

"Can I come too?" I ask. Skull is dressed in the shirt, and it really is tight. "Don't leave me here alone. I promise I won't say anything."

"I'm just going to see if Miller can talk." He retorts, so I swallow hard and nod, sitting back on the bed. Maybe he noticed my hesitation, as he finally sighs. "Alright. I think tomorrow will be better for talking."

I smile in gratitude and watch him lock the door. It was already late at night, and even in jeans, I can feel the cold caressing my skin. My feet are freezing. I stay on the same side of the bed, but I burrow under the sheets. I wait for Skull to come, but he settles into the armchair. He mutters something, quickly removes his shirt, and tosses it to the floor.

"Isn't it better to come to bed?"

He looks at me and crosses his arms.

"You can sleep soundly; I'll stay here."

I snuggle into the sheets and watch him.

"I never saw you lie down on a bed," I comment, making it clear that I won't give in.

Then I have an idea. Under his curious gaze, I go to the dresser and grab two sheets from the first drawer. I return to the bed and build a barrier with them. It doesn't turn out as I imagined, but it's enough to mark our spaces.

"This is your side of the bed, and this is mine," I declare, determined.

"You don't need to," he replies, with a resigned expression.

This time, I huff in frustration and cross my arms.

"Oh my God, you are so stubborn! What do you think I'm going to do with you? Attack you while you sleep? Or are you scared to sleep in the same bed as me?" I smile at that possibility, teasing him. After all, a man that size scared of me?

Skull scoffs and laughs disbelievingly; I join him.

"Just go to sleep, Eveline," he orders and closes his eyes.

I roll my eyes and lie down, stretching out. I deliberately stretch my body, and I see him staring at me.

"Well, I'm going to sleep then. Happy because it won't be me who has back pain tomorrow."

I close my eyes, and after a few minutes, I feel the side of the mattress sink. I smile and surrender to exhaustion.

CHAPTER EIGHT

Skull

Before I even open my eyes, I sense a sweet perfume lingering in the air, so close it seems to envelop my senses. I hear a soft moan, and when I finally open my eyes, I realize Eveline is lying on my chest, her delicate presence filling the space around me. My first impulse is to push her away, to create distance between us, but before I can move a muscle, as if she reads my thoughts, she snuggles even closer to my body, seeking warmth and safety.

In that moment, I instinctively wrap my arms around her waist, my fingers brushing against the soft skin of her exposed midriff. A feeling of warmth and familiarity spreads within me, and I am unable to pull away from that comforting contact, even though my instincts warn me about the complications of this proximity.

Her breath is soft against my chest, a calm rhythm that contrasts with the turmoil of my own thoughts. I feel torn between the desire to push her away to avoid trouble and the desire to savor the moment of comfort and intimacy we share. I notice every detail of her so clearly, as if my gaze could capture every feature of her sleeping expression. Her hair cascades over the pillow, a blonde curtain framing her serene face. Her lips are slightly parted in a small smile, as if she is dreaming of something pleasant.

For a moment, I allow myself to relax in that sense of closeness, pushing away the worries and conflicts that haunt me. It feels like, in that instant, it's just me and her, two individuals lost in a world of uncertainties, finding refuge in one another.

Then reality imposes itself again, and the awareness of the dangers surrounding us returns with full force. With a resigned sigh, I gently stroke her hair, a final concession before making a decision. I can't allow myself to succumb to the temptation of comfort when danger lurks.

Carefully, I pull away from her, and I watch as she furrows her brow. Her hands fumble around the bed as if searching for something, and when she touches the pillow I slept on, she pulls it to her and hugs it. I don't know what to think, and I even stand there for a few seconds just watching her. But soon I remember to look for Miller. I head to the bathroom, take care of my hygiene, and then grab the tight shirt. Eveline is still sleeping peacefully, and I wonder how I didn't wake up when she hugged me in bed? If it had been an enemy, the worst could have happened. I wouldn't let my guard down again.

I step out into the hallway while putting on the damn shirt.

At the top of the stairs, I observe the aftermath of the party in the main hall. I can't help but smile upon seeing Miller sprawled on the stage. I approach and wrinkle my nose; there's vomit beside him.

"Wake up!" I slap his face, and he sits up, dazed. "You're a mess. With all due respect, of course."

"Who the hell was it!?" he asks, but as soon as he sees me, he smiles. "Skuller! My friend!" The stench of alcohol and vomit hits me hard. I turn my face away. "So it wasn't a dream!?"

I push him away when he gestures to hug me.

"Did you have a good time yesterday?"

I look around. Some girls are half-naked and sprawled on the sofas, and there's no sign of any customers. I turn back to Miller, who tries to stand but almost falls. I help him sit up.

"Triple blowjob," he says, grinning. "A redhead, a blonde, and a brunette. You need to... try it."

I let out a sigh and assess the situation. Miller is in no condition to talk today, but I don't want to linger. After all, it would only be a matter of time before we are tracked down to this place. With those thoughts in mind, I cross my arms.

"That hot blonde..." he begins, his voice slurred. I look at him seriously. "She was fucking hot... where did you find that del..."

"I suggest you respect her," I declare, yanking him by the collar of his shirt firmly. "Or I'll shove your head in the toilet and make you sober up real quick."

Miller seems surprised by my reaction, but he quickly backs down and grabs the bottle next to him. He downs it in one gulp, seeking momentary relief from his drunkenness.

"Sorry!" he pleads, his voice hoarse and regretful. "Now tell me, what the hell have you gotten yourself into this time?"

I take a deep breath, trying to stay calm. I quickly explain how my path crossed with Eveline, right there in that hall. Miller remains silent throughout, and when I finish and make my request, he nods his head.

"And that H. Novikov is her mother?"

"Everything points to yes," I reply, crossing my arms. "It's a last name I feel like I've heard before, but I can't remember where."

"It sounds familiar to me too," he asserts, rubbing his face. "Alright, I'll look into that person. And you, what do you plan to do?"

"Kill anyone who wants her dead," I say without hesitation.

"Why?"

"She can't go on living knowing that at any moment she could be taken."

"I'm not referring to that," he retorts, then I stare at him. "The last time we met, you said you wouldn't do these jobs anymore. And now you're putting yourself at risk for her? To others, you're dead, Skuller."

I remain silent for a few minutes, but soon I speak again.

"The last time, I tried to be a normal person. We know how that ended. I won't let it happen again, Miller."

He nods and looks away.

"If your suspicions are correct. Are you really going to kill the President of the United States?"

"I'm not going to gamble on it." I let out a sigh, then remember something. "I need clothes; can you get me some?"

"Why? That *top* enhances your sweet charm."

Just as I'm about to curse, we're surprised to see Eveline running down the stairs. She looks at me with tear-filled eyes and approaches. My gaze travels over her body, but I quickly return to her face. Her hair is a mess, and her cheeks and lips are rosy. Then I wonder, how is it possible for someone to wake up looking so beautiful?

"You scared me!" she exclaims, her voice heavy with emotion.

I exchange a tense glance with Miller, who raises his hands in a sign of surrender and leaves the room, leaving us alone.

"Eveline, I..."

"I thought you left me!" She interrupts me sharply, some tears escaping her eyes, but she quickly wipes them away with her hands. "Aren't you going to say anything?"

I feel a tightening in my chest at seeing her so vulnerable, her emotions on display.

"I'm sorry?" I ask, and she sniffles and regains her composure.

"I don't forgive you, no." I'm surprised by that response. I can't help but smile. "I'm not joking."

"I promised I wouldn't leave you, Eveline." I assert, and she meets my gaze awkwardly. "Not until you're safe."

I notice the blonde strands that fall across her face, suppressing the urge to tuck one behind her ear.

"Then you could have warned me you'd be down here."

"You used me as a mattress, Eveline," I warn, and she looks at me in surprise. "You didn't wake up when I got out of bed. Why would I interrupt your sleep when I saw you were extremely tired?"

"I-I didn't use you as a mattress." She denies, and it's clear she's lying to herself. "I had the barrier."

I smile openly, arms crossed.

"I woke up in the morning, and you were on top of me."

She furrows her brow in denial. Then for a moment, she pauses, crosses her arms, and smiles at me. A smile that disarms me, making my heart race.

"So you're confirming that you saw and let it happen?"

I swallow hard and remain silent. How can I explain that I was so exhausted I didn't even notice? Would she think I'm weak for succumbing and leaving us defenseless? I let out a sigh and stand up.

"I talked to Miller about H. Novikov," I murmur. Eveline stops smiling and becomes attentive. "We'll find out who she is."

To my surprise, she smiles at me gratefully. I feel a tingle, my chest warms, and involuntarily, I feel the need to smile back. But I hold back. I'm not one for smiles; I'm not weak in that way, so why am I behaving like this?

"Thank you so much, Skull. I don't even know how to repay you."

A part of me wanted to hear her say my name for real, but another part urged me to keep her at a distance. So, sure of what I should do, I shrugged.

"Anything so you can leave soon."

I turn my back to her, not having the courage to see her reaction. I head to the room. Inside, I feel completely disturbed, filled with conflicting emotions, and for a moment, I remember a time when I thought it was possible to give in to such feelings. Upon entering the room, I throw myself onto the bed and sigh. What am I doing?

Eveline

AS SOON AS I'M ALONE, I dry my face and swallow my tears. I don't understand him. Sometimes he seems to tolerate my company, while at other times, he doesn't. I clasp my hands in front of my body and think about what to do.

"Don't take his rudeness to heart," Miller says, approaching with a mug in hand. "Actually, you've already had more than I have."

"What do you mean?"

"We served together," he says, pointing the way. "Four years on missions in the Middle East: Iraq and Afghanistan. Two years in Latin America: Colombia and Nicaragua. And believe me, during that time, he never offered to be as polite and attentive as he is being with you."

"The first time we met," I murmur, drawing his attention. "He tied me up and threw me in his car."

"He stabbed me and shot me."

I look at him in surprise and wait for a smile, which soon appears. I let out a sigh of relief.

"For a moment..."

"The stab was here," he interrupts, lifting his shirt. His finger goes to the side of his abdomen, revealing an old scar. "And the bullet was in my thigh. I won!"

"And why did he do that?"

"Before we served together, I tried to kill him." He warns as we enter the kitchen. There are a few more girls around. "I used to be a mercenary like Skuller, but now I've settled down. I want to die old, preferably in the arms of a very hot woman."

I rest my hands on the counter, keeping my brow furrowed.

"That's so rude."

Miller ignores me and goes to the refrigerator.

"He has no manners," a woman washing dishes says. She turns to me and smiles. "Hi, what's your name?"

"Eveline, and yours?"

"Ellen. How was your night?"

"Good, thank you." As soon as Miller returns to me, I try to steer him into another conversation. After all, I want to know more about Skull, and I've already figured out that he won't tell me anything. "Miller, what's Skull's name?"

"He didn't tell you?" he questions. I shake my head. "Have you asked?"

"I have; he didn't answer."

"Then there's a reason, don't you think?"

"He's so closed off. He never seems to smile."

"He's suffered a lot, Eveline," he confesses seriously. "He's lost a lot, so be patient with him."

I let out a sigh, not understanding. I want to ask and understand what he meant, but he waves and walks away.

"You came with that handsome guy, right?" Ellen asks, and I nod as she smiles. "Do you two have something going on?"

"No, he's just helping me."

Ellen sits at the table and indicates the chair across from her. It doesn't take long for a few more girls to join us.

"You're so beautiful, Eveline." I smile at the compliment. "How old are you?"

I smile a little sadly.

"Today I turn eighteen."

"No way! Why the long face? Aren't you happy?"

I shrug and pour myself a glass of juice.

"I didn't expect to turn a year older away from my best friend," I respond, keeping my eyes on the juice. "I don't even know what happened to her."

"What do you mean?"

I lean back in my chair and explain what happened leading up to my arrival here. I'm not sure if I should talk or trust them, but holding that anguish in is eating me alive. At the end of my story, Ellen touches my hand.

"Do you know the name of that orphanage? We can look it up online."

"Really?"

She nods and reaches for one of the girls. I watch the phone being handed over, and with a trembling voice of nerves, I say the name of the orphanage. In anticipation, I wait for her to say something, but her expression is confused.

"Are you sure that's the name?" she asks, and I nod. "There's nothing here. It's like it never existed."

The phone is passed to me, and I'm left bewildered. Nothing appears, and I can't even see any images of it. I hand the phone back, feeling a bit dazed, my mind trying to make sense of what's happened. When I can't think of anything that makes sense, I remember that Skull didn't eat. I ask if I can take him breakfast, and they quickly agree.

I load a bit of everything onto the tray, thank them, and head out.

I ascend the stairs slowly, and when I reach the hallway by the room, I see Layla, the redhead from yesterday, leaving the room and adjusting her dress strap. I stop in my tracks, and as soon as she sees me, she smiles. As she passes by me, she keeps smiling and ignores me. Even confused, I continue walking, reaching the door and opening it. Skull is just in a towel, looks at me, but not for long.

"I-I brought your breakfast." My voice falters just imagining what they were doing in here.

"You didn't need to bother."

I place the tray on the dresser and glare at him, arms crossed. Isn't he going to say anything?

On the bed are new clothes.

"Did you just get out of the shower?"

Skull looks at me, not understanding, and subtly nods. Without caring about my presence, he gestures to take off the towel. I turn my back, avoiding looking at him; my heart feels like it's going to jump out of my chest from nervousness.

"Do you need anything?"

"No." I shake my head. "Are you dressed?" I ask, and I hear him agree. I slowly turn back and let my gaze roam over his broad chest. The scars are there, and they strangely suit him. "I saw Layla leaving here."

"Who?"

I cross my arms, and feeling a little calmer, I realize he isn't pretending. His gaze is confused as he puts on a black shirt and then looks for his gun.

"The redhead who just left here."

Skull sits on the bed and watches me.

"I came to bring the clothes I asked Miller for."

"Is that all?"

"What else would it be?"

My gaze roams the room; I don't know what I'm looking for. After all, he's the same as before. I look back at Skull, and he's still watching me. I shrug and walk to the other side of the bed. Barely laying down, there's a knock at the door. Skull goes to answer, and when he opens it, I hear Ellen asking for me. I sit up on the bed immediately.

"Miller let us celebrate your birthday, Eveline."

I move closer, completely surprised.

"But I didn't..."

"You were looking so sad," she interrupts, pulling my hand and making me leave the room. "It's not every day you turn eighteen."

I smile and turn to Skull.

"Is it okay if I go with them?"

Skull's gaze goes to each of the girls present. He stays silent for a few seconds, then sighs.

"As long as you don't leave here, it's fine with me. I'll go find Miller."

I agree and let myself be led by the girls. They all talk at once, and I'm left unsure of what to say. I hear them mention my hair and something about cutting it a bit, but I quickly shake my head, touching my strands. I like them long.

We walk down another corridor with several doors, and at the end, they push me inside. I see many mirrors scattered around, and some clothes hanging near the wall.

"Eveline, let's get you ready for tonight."

"Get me ready?" I repeat, confused. "What do you mean?"

Ellen smiles at me and leads me to a large mirror.

"Today, you stop being a teenager and become a woman." As she speaks, she pushes my hair back. "And what a beautiful woman you are!" I try to suppress a smile. "And your eyes are so lovely."

I smile, surprised, unable to hold back. She and my friend Abby were the only ones to give me that compliment. Remembering Abby makes me feel downcast, but deep in my heart, I hope she's okay. Ellen drags over a clothing rack and starts checking each item. The other girls do the same, so I sit in a chair, not knowing what to do.

"Can you trust us to make you look stunning today?" another girl asks, and even though I'm uncertain, I nod. "That's it!" She smiles and waves to another young woman. "Carmen! Get the things ready for hair removal! We have a lot to do."

Skull

WHILE MILLER IS AT the computer, I focus on reading the article from the old newspaper. No matter how much I search, I can't find anything specific about H. Novikov, but the surname sounds strangely familiar. I'm sure I've heard it somewhere before. I tuck the newspaper away in the file, determined to continue my search in other records.

Suddenly, Miller's voice pulls me from my thoughts.

"I found something," he says, and I quickly move over to him, eager for any lead we can find.

"What did you find?" I ask as he shows me the computer screen.

"Dzmitry Novikov was an engineer killed in the IPD explosion in 2001," Miller explains, pointing at the screen. "It appears to have been an accidental explosion, which rules out the possibility of murder."

I absorb the information, trying to connect the dots in my mind. The name Novikov resonates once again, but I still can't fully grasp its relevance. There's more to this story, and we need to uncover what it is.

"The Research and Development Facility?" I ask, already knowing the answer. Miller nods in confirmation. "And when it happened, it was overshadowed by other news."

Miller furrows his brow and stands up, seemingly lost in his own thoughts. Meanwhile, I return to reading the article, searching for any detail that might give us a clue.

"Remember when we escorted a team of five scientists from that facility to that godforsaken place in Afghanistan?" Miller interrupts my thoughts, and I strain to recall. "Three of them died for no apparent reason when we returned from the mission. Here."

He grabs the file and starts flipping through it, searching for the relevant document. My mind begins to spin as I try to connect the seemingly unrelated events. Is it possible that the scientists we escorted have any connection to Dzmitry Novikov?

"They were working on a military project, right?" I ask, seeking to confirm my suspicions.

"It was Level 5," Miller replies, his serious expression indicating the gravity of the situation.

I remain silent for a few minutes, absorbing the weight of what has just been revealed. Level 5 was the highest security clearance, reserved for projects of utmost importance to national security. This meant that the scientists we escorted in Afghanistan were involved in something incredibly sensitive and potentially dangerous.

As my mind spins with possibilities and implications, I realize we are facing something much bigger than we imagined. The connection between the seemingly disconnected events begins to reveal itself, and now I need to uncover the truth behind these governmental secrets.

"There's more here. He was married, worked four years at the IPD, and had three children: Aleksey, Andrey, and Halina Novikov."

As soon as he finishes, he stares at me.

"Halina? How old is she?"

I see him frown and go back to reading the article.

"At the time of her father's death, she was 25-26 years old," he replies, looking at me quickly. "If she's alive, she should be about 48-49 now."

"Do you think you can find out for me?"

Miller looks at me surprised but soon nods.

"I need a day or two," he responds, and I sigh. "If you want to know, it's because you plan to go see her. I'll ask a friend who owes me a favor for help. Don't worry; he's trustworthy."

"I don't want anyone to know about Eveline."

"Don't worry," he says, looking at me for a few seconds. "Are you going to leave her here?"

"No, she's coming with me," I warn, returning to read the newspaper article. "I promised, I can't break that."

With the sudden silence, I pull my eyes from the paper and stare at Miller. He looks at me confused, and when I think he's going to say something, he just sighs and turns his back to me. I expect something from him, but I get nothing. The office is huge, filled with many files.

"I'm surprised you keep all these files around here," I murmur, and he smiles at me. "You said something about settling down."

He shrugs.

"Settling down for suicide missions, Skuller. I don't have the same energy as I did years ago."

I start putting everything back in its place while Miller continues to talk, and then I hear Eveline's name; I turn to him.

"What about her?"

"Eighteen years old, who would've thought." I ignore him; he continues. "I hope you don't mind about the party."

"Why would I mind?"

This time I watch him, and when I notice his smile, I roll my eyes. I know what he must be thinking, and I hold back from explaining again my reasons for helping her. Once everything is okay, I'm leaving without a second thought. Then it would be goodbye Eveline, and goodbye to her stubbornness that suited her. I stop what I'm doing and let a brief smile escape. However, I quickly stop and check if Miller saw. He has his back to me, so I breathe a sigh of relief.

My thoughts drift back to Eveline, her smile, and how she made me a mattress earlier. If I just close my eyes, I can recall her scent.

I swallow hard.

I shouldn't be thinking these things. Not about her.

CHAPTER NINE

Skull

When night falls, I head straight for the room. I haven't seen Eveline all day, and I had to hold myself back several times from going after her. In the background, I can hear ambient music echoing through the empty corridors of the club. As soon as I enter, I see the bathroom door open, I approach and confirm it's empty. Nothing seems out of place; I check under the bed, and the bag with the gun and money is there.

I decide to take a shower and then head down to find Eveline.

I do everything quickly, putting on a pair of jeans, boots, and a dark green shirt. I don't take long, and I descend with a specific destination in mind. The waitresses are already at their posts, the security guards too, but I can't find Eveline anywhere. The music has changed to something with a stronger beat, and the lights are flashing. I take a deep breath. This isn't an environment for me.

"Get hyped, my friend!" Miller shouts as he comes toward me. He has two drinks in hand. "Enjoy being here; you can be with whoever you want!" He points around.

I accept the drink and look at what he shows me. I'm about to retort when I see Eveline appear from a more distant corridor. I freeze at the sight of her looking so stunning that I can hear my heart racing, as well as my breathing becoming uneven. I swallow hard and take her in from head to toe.

The damn white dress, with a deep neckline, reveals a sculpted body that I'm sure everyone else here can see too. The shape of her medium breasts captures my attention for a few seconds, but I quickly lower my gaze. She's barefoot, and somehow still looks beautiful. I press my lips together as she notices me and approaches with a smile.

The way her hair, once straight and now styled, moves with her walk is hypnotizing.

"Hi, Skull!" she continues to smile. "I was with the girls; we talked a lot." She comments, but upon seeing me silent, she adds, "You disappeared all afternoon."

"He was with me," Miller replies, and I glare at him. His eyes insist on focusing on her breasts, but when he realizes I'm glaring at him, he looks away. "I hope the girls didn't scare you."

"No," she denies, and with a delicate movement, she tosses her hair back. "Thank you for letting me celebrate here. It was kind of you."

"Of course, it's not every day you turn eighteen!" he shouts over the music and extends the drink to her. "On the house!"

Why is she smiling at Miller? I watch their interaction, feeling completely forgotten. Then, before accepting the drink, she glances at me. Not having shown any reaction, she takes a large sip. She makes a brief grimace but almost immediately smiles again.

I clench my jaw.

She is truly beautiful.

"It's bad, but I liked it!" she says, drinking a bit more and then looking at me. "You didn't say anything about my dress. Ellen, who picked it out, said I looked pretty. Did you like it?"

"No."

As soon as I finish speaking, I want to punch myself. Eveline looks at me, surprised, and I can tell she feels awkward. I take a sip of my drink and look away, controlling myself not to apologize. The drink feels like it's ripping down my throat, and from my peripheral vision, I see her pulling away. With Miller beside me, I let out a sigh and sit down in one of the cushioned chairs.

"Did you really need to be so rude to the princess?"

"Eveline!" I nearly growl, feeling the fury rise within me. "If you call her that again, I..."

"Calm down, lion!" He smiles casually. I let out another sigh and take a sip of the beer. "You're so hot-headed. You seem to have gotten worse over the years."

"Don't push it, okay?"

I shake my head as I search for Eveline with my eyes, finding her on the dance floor with a pole dance in the middle. Two of the dancers are chatting with her, and then I see one of them staring at me seriously. I return the glare; I won't let her intimidate me.

In the end, she looks away and goes back to talking to Eveline.

I lean back into the cushions and keep my eyes on Eveline. Did I like the dress? *Fuck!* That question is unbelievable. I'm still mesmerized by her beauty, and the bitter taste in my mouth makes it clear that I'm completely jealous. A genuine jealousy because she looks so temptingly sexy in front of everyone. I take another sip of my drink and glance at Miller; he keeps his attention on one of the dancers.

I return my gaze to Eveline; she's dancing with the same girls as before and drinks from one of their cups. Her movements are awkward at first, but she soon finds her rhythm. As she turns her back to me, my gaze drops to her shapely rear. I swallow hard and adjust in my seat. Slowly, to the beat of the music, the female hands caress their breasts in a sensual way. My body tingles immediately, and I feel my cock begin to harden inside my pants.

It's been a long time since I've had a woman in my bed. And in that moment, I hate myself for wanting Eveline.

From the entrance, I see the door open, and a few guys walk in. They look around with stupid grins; I watch them scatter, except for one. The only bastard stays still, staring at something on the dance floor, then I realize it's Eveline.

If he dares to approach her, I'll make sure to rip his arms off.

"What killer look is that?"

Miller shouts beside me. I ignore him because my attention is focused on someone else. Amid the pulsating sound of music filling my ears, I clench my fists as I see the guy approaching her. I can't control the wave of jealousy consuming me. I watch each step of the stranger with fierce intensity, my eyes fixed on the scene before me. I know I shouldn't care, but I can't help the possessiveness that overwhelms me.

I try to look away, but it's in vain. My masochistic side insists on watching that scene. He smiles and talks close to her. Eveline returns the smile and responds. His hands grip her slim waist, pulling her closer, so I decide to act. I down the rest of the drink and slam the bottle on the table.

I push through the dancing bodies like a hurricane, and when I'm close enough to the couple, I plant my hand on the guy's shoulder. He looks at me startled and a bit confused.

"Get out of here!" I growl, using my angriest and coldest tone. "Now!"

He obeys, almost running.

"He was going to dance with me!"

Eveline looks at me, upset; it's obvious. However, I find myself analyzing her beautiful face, with rosy cheeks and red lips. My first impulse is to kiss those lips that look so delicious, but I hold back.

What's happening to me?

"You're not dancing with any man," I say, and she crosses her arms. "So, settle for dancing alone."

When I think she will agree, I'm surprised by her refusal.

"I'll dance with whoever I want! It's my birthday, not yours!"

I swallow a curse and turn my back to her.

I don't recognize myself. Why the hell am I so furious at the possibility of another man touching her? I sit back down next to Miller and watch her. She's still crossing her arms, and I don't divert my gaze. It doesn't take long for a dancer to touch her on the arm.

"Let her dance with whoever she wants," I hear Miller retort. "You're not her father, for fuck's sake!"

I cross my arms, feeling in a terrible mood. My gaze returns to Eveline, and this time she's dancing while drinking a red drink. The music changes, and I see her jump to the beat. I sigh, as it looks like the night will be long.

Hours pass, and I'm still on my second drink; I can't remember how many times Eveline has drunk. Miller has left and hasn't come back yet. Alone, sitting at that table, my only reason for being there is her: Eveline. I take another sip of my drink and try to look anywhere but at Eveline. Then I notice a redhead passing through the crowd and walking in my direction.

"Want some company?" she asks, totally sultry. She sits down next to me and touches my thigh, sliding up to the waistband of my pants. "You're the only one not having fun."

I watch her hand rise and stop at my chest.

"If you don't mind," I say, looking her in the eyes. "I'd prefer to be alone."

I won't deny that she's beautiful, with straight hair down to her shoulders, heavy makeup that still doesn't hide her beauty. But I don't feel attracted to her. The red-painted lips are thin, yet I can only think about how they aren't Eveline's full ones.

She smiles and leans in closer. She kisses my neck, and automatically I search for Eveline, and there she is. Her gaze is fixed on me, or maybe on the redhead whose name I don't know. I feel her kisses moving up to my jaw, and to my surprise, I see Eveline turn her back on me and disappear among the people. I guess it's for the best; I don't want to create expectations where nothing will ever happen.

When I think of diverting my gaze, I notice the same guy from before making his way toward her. I don't waste any more time and follow his steps.

Eveline

I FEEL MY EYES BURNING, and I don't understand why I'm so affected by the scene I just witnessed. Skull isn't mine, so he can kiss as many women as he wants, but why right in front of me? Is he trying to prove something? I'm a bit dizzy, but I know I want to get to the room. The hallway is dimly lit, and some couples pass by without even noticing me. Earlier, the girls explained what they did and why there were so many rooms.

They also told me that they weren't obligated to do anything, but that they had it there as a home.

I lean my hand against the wall as everything starts to spin, stopping for a few minutes. I don't understand why I feel this way; I've only had a few glasses of whatever Ellen handed me.

"Hi," I turn quickly and nearly fall, but I'm caught. I look up and see it's the guy who asked me to dance earlier. "You look like you're drunk."

He smiles, and I return the gesture.

"I'm not drunk," I deny, but I'm almost certain that I am. "I think it's just exhaustion. I danced a lot."

"I saw, and by the way, you were delightful dancing," he smiles and touches my chin. "What's your name, gorgeous? Mine's Liam."

His eyes fix on me in a way that makes me feel invaded. I try to push him away, but he pins me against the wall and holds me.

"E-Eveline," I reply, and he lowers his gaze down my body. "I need to go."

"Is that guy your brother?" he asks, and I shake my head. "Is he your boyfriend?"

"No, I've never had a boyfriend."

Liam looks surprised but smiles.

"Really? You've never been with a guy before? But you must have kissed someone, looking that beautiful."

My hands rest on his chest, and my intention is to push him away, but I can't summon the strength.

"No, I've never kissed either. I want to go to my room, Liam."

"Can I come with you?" he inquires, and I shake my head, surprised. "Come on, just a little."

"No, I just want you to let me go." I plead, and he pulls me tighter against him. "Let me go!"

I receive a head shake in response, and when he pulls me closer, lowering his lips to my neck, I feel him pull away. Then I lock eyes with Skull; he's holding Liam by the collar of his shirt, his gaze furious, and I feel a bit scared.

"I should rip your fingers off and make you swallow them!" he says, not even stuttering. His voice is a mixture of aggression with a slight hint of threat. "Do you want to lose your fingers, you little shit?"

"N-No, sir!"

"Then get out of my sight!" Skull shoves him, making him fall. "If you come back to this club, you'll regret it bitterly."

From the wall, I watch him run away. As soon as Skull turns to me, I'm ready to retort, but I lose my balance and almost fall. Strong arms catch me, and with a quick motion, I'm lifted into his arms.

"I-I can walk!" I warn, but he ignores me, heading down another hallway. "Skull... I think I'm going to vomit."

"Don't vomit on me!"

I nod and cover my mouth with my hand, waiting until I'm in the room. Once there, Skull takes me to the bathroom and enters with me. I look at myself in the mirror and notice him behind me, arms crossed with a judging look.

"You don't have to stay here! You can go after Layla."

"Who is...? Oh!" he stutters, standing still. "Weren't you going to vomit?"

"No!" I deny, but as soon as I make a sudden movement, I feel my stomach churn.

I vomit into the toilet, and it's one of the worst sensations. Not even when I got sick at the orphanage did it feel this way. Remembering that place makes me cry in the middle of this situation. My hair is held back gently, and then I feel a hand smoothing my back. I vomit a bit more, and when I'm done, I feel weak. Without me asking, Skull helps me stand, flushes the toilet, and seats me on it.

I'm still crying; I'm completely confused.

I watch him open the drawers under the sink and pull out a small bottle with blue liquid. He pours a bit into a cup and hands it to me.

"It's not for drinking," he warns, and I nod. "Swish it around and spit it out."

I obey, then spit it into the sink. The bad taste of vomit is gone, and I feel a bit relieved. I try to stand, and he helps me. I look at the shower and then at Skull. He understands I want to take a shower, so he leaves the bathroom but leaves the door slightly open. I take off the dress I loved wearing but that Skull didn't like, and I step under the shower.

My shower isn't long; I don't wet my hair, just my body, and when I finally step out, my eyes feel heavy. I'm wrapped in a towel when Skull sticks his arm through the bathroom door and hands me the backpack. I open it and grab a pair of panties and a black long-sleeve shirt that goes down to the middle of my thighs. Shorter than the dress I wore. I open the bathroom door and see Skull making the bed for me to sleep.

"Why are you like this, Skull?" I want to know. He stops what he's doing, seeming not to understand what I want to say. "Why do you make me feel like I'm a burden to you? Yet you show care, like now?"

"I don't know what you're talking about, Eveline." He retorts, and I can't hold back my tears. I'm so sensitive. "You're not a burden. If you were, I wouldn't have you here."

"I was scared when you left me at that cabin," I say, recalling those terrible minutes that felt like hours to me. "Those men..." I cry. "They said that once they were done with me, they would throw me in a pit and bury me alive."

Skull stands there, looking at me. Then, to my surprise, he sits down beside me and gently strokes my cheek.

"I'm sorry for that," he says, swallowing hard. Is it guilt I see in his eyes? "You don't have to be afraid anymore. I made a promise, remember? I don't break promises."

I analyze what he said; he seems sincere about it.

"So promise you won't be rude to me anymore?" I ask, feeling sleepy. I see him take a deep breath and then sigh. "Just don't make me feel like a nuisance to you. I know you'd rather be somewhere else, far away, but..."

"Alright, I'll try to be less rude to you. It's just that you confuse me, Eveline."

"What do you mean?" I ask, almost closing my eyes. My body feels heavy. Skull doesn't respond, and when he thinks of moving away, I grab his hand. "Will you lie down here with me?"

"You want to make me your mattress again?" he jokes, a quick smile crossing his lips.

"I do," I say sincerely, and maybe he didn't expect that. He looks at me surprised. "I dreamed something nice this morning, but I don't remember. I felt safe in your arms."

I keep holding his hand, and in his eyes, I see the internal struggle; he seems to want to deny it. However, in the end, he just nods, and I give him space to lie down. As soon as he does, I lay on his chest. His body is warm, and mine feels a bit cold from the shower. I slide one leg over him.

He takes a deep breath but says nothing.

"Skull?"

He remains silent for a few minutes but soon responds.

"Yes?"

"What's your name?"

"It's Skull."

I smile; I'm still going to find out what his real name is. But for now, I'll settle for that.

"Why didn't you like my dress?" I ask, and he stays silent for a few minutes. I lift my head to see if he's asleep, but he's awake. "Huh?"

"You looked very beautiful in it, Eveline. Now go to sleep."

"You love not answering my questions," I grumble, and I snuggle closer to him.

I can hear his heart beating fast, and I smile slightly. I inhale his scent and let my hand trace the outline of some scars on his chest.

I snuggle closer to Skull, as if it were possible, and feel his arm wrap around my waist.

I let myself fall into a deep sleep, knowing I'm safe in his arms.

CHAPTER TEN

Eveline

Still drowsy, I open my eyes and notice the room is empty. I sit up on the mattress and look around. The backpacks are near the dresser, but Skull isn't there. My head hurts, which makes me lie back down. I can remember everything that happened last night, especially vomiting in the bathroom with Skull beside me. I bring my hand to my temple and rub it slowly.

Is this pain ever going to go away?

I've just turned eighteen, and I have no idea what to do. With the sheet, I make a kind of bandage and cover my face. I hear the door open, but I don't move.

"Headache?"

The question surprises me. After all, how would he know? I pull the sheet from my face and find him standing next to the bed. He's wearing dark-washed jeans, boots, and a black shirt. His muscular arms are exposed, allowing me to see the tattoos up close. I notice he's holding a glass of water in one hand and a pill in the other.

He quickly extends it to me.

"A little," I reply, sitting up. I take what's offered. "Thank you. I've never had a headache like this."

"It only gets worse when you drink."

As I take the medication, my eyes don't leave him. Why do I have the impression he's judging me? He drank yesterday too, and I only had a few colorful drinks.

"Thanks."

"Drink all the water," he commands with his arms crossed. "You need to stay hydrated."

I look away but obey. Finally, I hand him the glass, and he takes it to the dresser.

"Did you wake up early?" I ask, and he nods. "What are we going to do now?"

"At the beginning of the night, we're leaving," he informs, walking over to the window. "I got the address of Halina Novikov; we're going there."

"Halina?" I ask, surprised, suddenly my heart starts to race. "My mother?"

He looks at me for a few seconds, then sits on the edge of the bed.

"We're going to find out who she is," he says, and I nod. "I need you to stay safe before I can go after them."

"But you said you wouldn't abandon me. You made a promise!"

"Until you're safe, Eveline. I'm not going to leave you to fend for yourself out there." He retorts, and I swallow hard. "I asked you to trust me, so trust me."

I take a breath, but then I shake my head.

"And what if it's not safe?"

"If it's not, you'll stay with me until everything is over," he replies, and I can hardly suppress a sigh of relief. He furrows his brow, and when I think he's going to say something, he just looks away. "Take a shower and come down. I'll wait for you downstairs."

I nod and watch him leave the room. My head is still pounding, but much less now, so I go take a shower. I can't believe Skull found out about H. Novikov. I feel a flutter in my stomach and a fear of what might happen. What would I ask? What would she say? Would she think I was pretty? There were so many questions that for a moment I felt dizzy.

I head to the bathroom and take a long shower.

When I finally finish, I put on a pair of jeans and a sleeveless top. I only have two more outfits; I need to wash the ones I've already worn. Once I'm ready, I leave the room and head downstairs. As I approach the kitchen, I hear familiar voices. As soon as I enter, I see Layla sitting next to Skull. She talks animatedly while he keeps his eyes distant from her.

"Good morning, Eveline!" Ellen says, making everyone turn to look at me, including Skull. "Come, sit here; you need to eat well. Did you have fun yesterday?"

"Yes," I nod and sit in the chair next to Skull, "but I woke up with a headache."

"Ah, that's normal!" she smiles and offers me a cup of coffee. "With time you'll learn to handle it. I heard you're leaving today." She comments, and I nod. "I really wanted you to stay here."

I don't know what to say, so I take a sip of the coffee. Skull finishes his, stands up, and leaves, but before he exits, he turns and catches me looking at him.

"I'll be in Miller's office," he announces, I give him a smile. "At 5:00 PM, we're leaving."

I lean back in my chair and watch him walk with an air of ownership. The memories of yesterday remain vivid in my mind: the promise made, the apology for leaving me the first time, and how he found me beautiful in the dress from yesterday. Why did he lie last night?

"He was really worried about you this morning."

Ellen sits down in front of me.

"Yesterday, he said he didn't like my dress," I recall, and she nods, "but in the room, after helping me lie down, he said he thought I looked beautiful in it."

"I think he was jealous," one of the dancers speaks up; I don't remember her name. "And when that businessman's son showed interest in you, you could tell he was furious."

"Jealous of me?" I repeat, my smile growing just thinking about it.

"I don't think so," Layla interjects, crossing her arms. "Skull seems to prefer more mature women, women who have something to offer him. More sensual women who know how to kiss and drive him wild in bed, those kinds of things, but don't take it personally."

Her short laugh makes me stop smiling.

And I don't know why, but that hurts me. I really don't have anything to offer him; I'm not sensual, I don't know how to drive anyone wild in bed, much less kiss.

"Have you washed the bathrooms yet, Layla?" Ellen asks in a raised tone. "If you haven't done it yet, why not go do that instead of sitting here being bitter?"

From my peripheral vision, I see Layla stand up with indignation and leave without speaking to anyone. I take another sip of my coffee, feeling so embarrassed.

"Don't mind Layla," I hear someone say. "She's like this with all of us."

"No, it's fine. Either way, she didn't lie. I really don't know these things."

I feel a gentle touch on my hair, which makes me look at Ellen.

"Oh, my sweet angel, you don't know the power you have in your hands," she murmurs, leaving me confused. "You have a unique sensuality; you just need to learn to use it to your advantage. That's something we're born with, you know? And kissing is just practice."

"But those are things I'll never use," I reply, and she smiles, shaking her head. "I never imagined myself kissing someone or having sex. My friend Abby wanted that; she was always better at these things. I find it strange; how can *that* enter us?"

Now everyone is smiling, and I feel awkward.

"Are you talking about a dick?" one of them asks, and I look at her confused. "A penis is also called a dick."

"It's weird, Ellen. Back at the orphanage, my friend Abby and I found a magazine with naked women. It belonged to Ethan, and it was all so..."

"Who's Ethan?"

"He's the handyman there," I murmur, and she looks at me attentively. "I thought he was nice, but he's really not."

"I understand," she sighs and touches my hand. "Let's do this! You finish eating, and then you'll go to the dressing room; there we'll talk about sex and any doubts you have. If you want to, of course, and if you feel comfortable."

I smile, but at the same time, I feel like crying. Ellen is so nice; her gaze conveys warmth and genuine attention, concern. The way she speaks to me is always so caring.

"Thank you, I'd like that."

"Then finish eating and head over there. I have some paperwork to sort out, but I'll wait for you."

"Thank you," I say, watching her get up. "Can I wash some of my clothes? I have very few, and I don't know when I'll be able to wash them again."

"Of course! And we'll find some new ones for you."

Feeling grateful, I watch her walk away while others stay with me.

"She's like a mother, isn't she?" I glance to the side and smile at the brunette who's looking at me. "Ellen is one of the best people I've met in my life. Well, I'm off; I have more work to do today."

I wave and decide to finish eating.

After that, I wash what I've dirtied, and then I go to the room in search of my clothes. There, I see Skull's clothes folded; my first instinct is to grab his shirt and smell it. I close my eyes as I catch his distinctive scent, pleasantly fragrant despite the sweat. Before I get caught doing this, I gather everything and leave the room. With another girl, I head to the laundry, surprised by the new machines. Back at the orphanage, we had different ones. I load the washer and wait. I sit in a nearby chair and think about everything.

I still didn't know who my father was, and since Skull hinted that I'm something important, then my father must be too. Are we going to Belarus? I don't have any documents, just that photo. If my mother doubted me, how would I prove I was her daughter? Would I do the same as Abby did? With those thoughts in mind, my anxiety increased. If nothing goes right, then what would I do? Skull said I could stay with him, but I know I'd just be a burden.

Maybe I could go back and stay here. But would I have the courage to sleep with a different man every night? I let out a frustrated sigh and cross my arms. I really don't know what to do. Just feel.

In the end, when I finish drying the clothes, I fold everything and head back to the room. I put my clothes away and place his on the bed. Anxious for Ellen's advice, I head to the dressing room. In the hallway, I'm greeted by some girls, and I return the greetings. I stop in front of the door and knock; I hear permission to enter, then I do so.

"You look anxious," she says with a smile as I sit near her. "I know you're leaving today, but if anything happens, know that you have a home here."

I hold back the urge to cry; I'm not a crybaby. I swallow hard and try to smile.

"Thank you."

Ellen touches my face and then closes her laptop.

"Now let's get to work." She smiles at me. "Do you know anything about sex?"

"Only from the magazine I saw."

Then Ellen starts to explain things to me in an educational way. Occasionally, one of the girls interrupts to add a comment, which I attentively absorb. My biggest surprise comes when I see they have dildos of various sizes, shapes, and colors. Why do they have so many? Perhaps noticing my confused expression, Ellen says it's normal for them to use them alone or with clients. I'm even more surprised by the latter. They offer me one, but I politely decline. My face turns red just imagining Skull finding out.

At lunchtime, we eat in the kitchen, but neither Miller nor Skull showed up.

Afterward, we return to the dressing room, and I'm gifted two more dresses. They're so beautiful and new; they come with heels, but they hurt my feet. So, despite Ellen insisting, I don't take them. She gets called to take a phone call and leaves me with the other girls in the dressing room.

"Eveline, take these too!" Tracy hands me some silver packets. "These are condoms."

I'm startled. Who would I use those with?

"I don't..."

"You don't want to get pregnant before your time."

"No." I shake my head, holding them; they're just like the ones in the dresser drawer. "But I don't have anyone to use them with."

"What about that god with the bad boy look?" one of them asks, and my face turns to fire. "Don't you think something might happen?"

"Me and Skull?" I repeat, swallowing hard. "I don't know; I don't think he sees me like that."

"It doesn't hurt to take them," she insists, and I take them to hide among the dresses. "These are the large ones, and the thin ones that don't even feel like you're wearing one. Something tells me he's well-endowed."

"How so?" I ask, and the others nod in agreement. "Have you seen him?"

"It's years of experience," she replies with a smile. "When men have big hands or big feet, you can bet they have big dicks."

I look a bit incredulous. Is that really true?

"And that Skull has this wild vibe in bed," another comments to her friend. I glance at her, feeling a bit uncomfortable. "He exudes raw sex; I'd give it away for free to him."

I furrow my brow and stare at her in silence. How can she say this right in front of me? Without any shame?

"Whoa, Lindsay," Tracy murmurs, then laughs loudly. "Eveline didn't like those comments about her man."

Everyone laughs at their friend, but they stop quickly.

"About the kiss... do you want help?"

I turn to Tracy, who sits next to me. Her fingers touch my face, her gaze fixed on me.

"How would you help me?"

"I can show you on yourself," she says, brushing my blonde strands away from my face. "Three types of kisses."

She smiles, and I glance at the others, who are also smiling as they approach.

"You want to kiss me?" I ask to be sure I understood. She nods. "But we're women. Isn't that wrong?"

"No, of course not. It's normal. Sometimes we kiss and do more when we feel like it," she laughs softly. "If there's consent, anything goes. And we're in modern times, Eveline. Men together, women together, two men and a woman, two women and a man; it goes on. What do you say?"

I'm tense, unsure what to say. I've never kissed, and I never thought two women could kiss. Perhaps noticing my indecision, she smiles and points to two colleagues in front. They slowly approach and press their lips together gently. No one says anything, and they continue kissing like that.

"This is the peck," Tracy says, very close to my face, watching the scene. "Now the second." She points, and they kiss more closely. Their lips, in short sequences, caress slowly. I take a deep breath. "This kiss is nice, but I prefer the third." Then this time, the two open their lips wider. Their tongues touch while they begin to caress each other with their hands.

I watch the scene, unable to look away. What would Skull's kiss be like?

Just as I'm about to speak, the dressing room door opens. And in disbelief, I see him stop at the entrance. He's wearing a black cap turned backward and different clothes. I can't tell what his reaction is; he looks at the two who just ended their kiss, and then he looks at me. He remains silent, his gaze seeming furious, but what just happened?

"Let's go, Eveline."

His voice sounds serious. He stands by the open door, showing that he won't leave. I clutch the two dresses against my chest and say goodbye to the girls. As I pass by him, I hear the door slam shut. I look at him, not understanding; is he angry with me?

"Are you okay?" I ask cautiously.

Then he stops, rubs his hand over his beard, and looks at me.

"What were you doing in there?"

"Nothing," I shrug. However, he tilts his head to the side as if he doesn't believe me. "We were just talking. Ellen went to take a call and left me with the girls."

"So you decided to keep kissing?" he asks, and I shake my head. "That's what you were doing all afternoon?"

I hold back the urge to cry, feeling hurt by the way he speaks.

"You promised not to be rude to me."

Without waiting for a response, I walk past him as he remains silent. I head to the room, grab my backpack, and stuff my new clothes inside. From the window, I can see the late afternoon. It takes a few seconds, and he enters the room. I try to leave, but my arm gets grabbed.

"I didn't mean to be rude."

I look at him, but then quickly look away.

"Can you let me go?"

He does as I asked but says nothing. I hold the backpack and turn my back to him. Skull says I leave him confused, but what does he do to me? I descend the stairs, and near the entrance, I see Miller and Ellen talking quietly. I smile at them as they approach when they see me. Right behind me, I see Skull with the backpacks.

"It's a shame you're leaving already," Ellen murmurs directly to me, touching my face. "You'll always be welcome here."

"Thank you! I loved meeting you," I say and receive a tight hug. "I hope we can meet again someday."

"Of course!" She smiles, then looks at Skull. "And you take good care of her."

He nods and stops in front of Miller.

"When will I see you now?" Miller asks, pulling a yellowed envelope from his jacket. "Are you sure about what you're doing?" Miller seems tense, and Skull just nods. "I did what you asked."

"Thank you," he replies, glancing briefly at me. He takes the envelope, opens it, and I can see it contains a piece of paper and a credit card. Then, Skull hands over the two black bags. "Thanks for your help."

"Albuquerque, New Mexico?" Miller questions, and Skull agrees. I watch the two, surprised. Isn't my mother in Belarus? Still pondering, I see Miller take a cell phone and hand it to his friend. "You know you can call me, right? Don't disappear. I know you're always looking for that loudmouth Pablo."

Surprised, I watch Skull smile and give Miller a few pats on the shoulder.

After one last nod, Skull says goodbye and walks out. I hug Ellen once more; I will miss her. I smile at Miller, who returns it and watches us leave. I sit in the passenger seat and fasten my seatbelt. Skull enters silently and settles into the driver's seat. I glance back one last time at the two standing at the entrance and suppress the urge to cry. My gaze drifts to the window, where I can see the orange sky.

We've been on the highway for hours; I glance at the passing vegetation with boredom.

"I'm sorry if I was rude," he says again, and I let out a sigh. "Aren't you going to respond?"

I cross my arms, and this time I see him take a deep breath.

"They were just teaching me how to kiss," I reply, glancing at him quickly. "Actually, Tracy wanted to kiss me, but I didn't want to."

"Right," he mutters, his serious expression unchanged. He begins to drive with one hand but doesn't linger in my gaze. "Are you apologizing or not?"

"Is this your way of trying not to be rude?" I joke, but then I clear my throat, sitting up straighter. He seems uncomfortable. "So, we're headed to Albuquerque, New Mexico? Is it far?"

"About 13-14 hours of travel," he murmurs, glancing at me quickly. "She's using the name Candice Adkins. Works as a high school teacher at Southwest High School, has two daughters and a husband."

I look at him in surprise.

"Two daughters? How old are they?"

"One is sixteen and the other is twelve."

I turn to him.

Two sisters? Why was I the only one left behind? A wave of sadness washes over me, and my questions swirl in my mind, rising to the surface. Is it a good idea to go to her? Perhaps noticing my confused expression, he continues.

"If you don't want to meet her, you can wait in the car. Either way, I need to ask her a few questions."

"What kind?"

He looks at me hesitantly for a moment before taking a deep breath.

"Her father was an engineer, worked at a government facility. There was an explosion, and he died. But a few years ago, my team was tasked with escorting a team of five scientists to a remote location in Afghanistan. They were involved with the same research center as Novikov. Three of them died."

"Do you think it was intentional?" I ask, watching his expression as he focuses on the road.

"It's all very suspicious. At that time, they were working on a level 5 military project." He seeks my gaze before continuing. "Level 5 is reserved for extremely sensitive and potentially dangerous projects of national importance."

I nod and fall silent. So, did my grandfather work with them? But what does that have to do with me? I stare at my hands in front of me, wanting to say it all makes sense, but I'm completely confused.

"But I want to meet her, Skull," I say and give him a short smile. "I want to understand and meet my sisters. Do you think my father is the same as theirs?"

"I don't think so. Your father is the..." Before he can finish, I see smoke coming from the front of the car as it begins to slow down. "What the hell!"

"What happened?"

"Stay in the car."

I watch him get out and lift the hood. I look around, feeling a bit frightened; everything is dark, with vegetation surrounding us. Skull takes a few minutes in the front, but soon he returns to the driver's seat. He tries to start the engine, but the car doesn't respond.

"Is it broken?"

"Looks like the engine has a problem."

"What are we going to do?" I ask, scared. The road is deserted, and I don't know if it's fear, but I feel like someone is watching me from the vegetation. "We can't stay here."

He looks at me, and when I think he's going to say something, he stops and leans back. He closes his eyes and stays like that. I cross my arms against the cold, but my gaze is alert. In the distance, I hear a noise and look back. A car is approaching. Skull locks the door and reaches for the gun hidden in his jeans.

As the car pulls up beside us, I can see a couple in the front and two teenagers sleeping in the back. They lower the window and wave. Skull hesitates for a few seconds, but then he does the same.

"Need help?"

"N-no..."

"Yes!" I interrupt Skull, who stares at me. "The engine won't start."

"A few miles ahead, there's someone who can help," the man calls out, looking our way. "If you want, I can tow you there. It's dangerous to stay here on the road."

I look at Skull, who returns my gaze, and to my surprise, he looks at the couple and smiles.

"If it's not a problem, we'll accept."

The driver gets out of the car, and I watch as Skull follows him. The man hands him a rope and heads back to his vehicle. My eyes track Skull as he ties one end to the front of our car, and then the other driver, who is now in front of us, does the same. After a few minutes, we're driving down the highway, Skull at the wheel, his gaze focused on the road.

I hug myself and rest my head against the window.

CHAPTER ELEVEN

Skull

After a few hours on the road, we finally arrive in Wichita. The city is bustling, with several establishments still open at this hour. I glance at Eveline beside me and see that she's sleeping deeply, exhausted from the long trip. The car in front stops in a parking space, and then the man gets out and waves at me. I follow him and, with his help, manage to park beside them. He extends his hand, and I shake it.

"Thank you."

"No need for that! We wouldn't leave you stranded out here," he says, leaning his body toward Eveline. "Is she your woman?"

I look at Eveline, who's still asleep, and nod.

"Yeah, and thank you."

"I'm Owen," he smiles, pointing to the woman who's coming to his side while the teenagers remain asleep in the car. "This is my wife, Grace, and our kids, Chloe and Bryan."

I retract my hand, my gaze sweeping across the surroundings. I see a closed mechanic shop across the street. I return my focus to the two of them, who are still looking at me curiously.

"I'm James, and this is Layla," I say, using the first name that came to mind. For a moment, I hesitate; maybe I should have said another name. "Thanks again."

"Where are you headed?" Grace asks. "If you want a ride, we're heading to Oklahoma."

"We won't need it," I reply, trying to be as friendly as possible. "Thanks."

I hear the car door open and see Eveline stepping out, rubbing her eyes.

"Oh! She woke up! Hello, Layla, how are you?"

As I receive a confused look, I swallow hard. She walks over to stand beside me and then smiles politely at the couple in front of us.

"I'm good, thanks for helping us."

"No worries! We were just telling your boyfriend that if you want, you can come with us. We're going to take a break to eat and spend the night, but we'll be back on the road early tomorrow."

"Thanks."

They say their goodbyes and turn away from us.

"What's your problem?!" she asks as soon as we're alone. I'm surprised by her irritated tone. "I asked a question!"

"What's wrong?"

"Why did you say my name is Layla? Why that name, specifically?" she questions, and I sigh. "If you wanted her to come in my place, why didn't you bring her?"

"Eveline, you're being foolish."

"No, I'm not!" she retorts, poking my chest. "You know she was flirting with you, kissing you like that on my birthday, and now this?"

"And what does that have to do with you, Eveline?"

My question lands like a punch to her stomach. She freezes, and I see tears welling up in her eyes. I let out a sigh, and when she tries to step back, I grab her waist. Unable to contain myself, I push her against the car door. She looks at me startled, but doesn't flinch. I gently touch her face, using my thumb to caress her red lips.

"Don't confuse me, Eveline. I don't want you to get hopes up about us. I'm not the man for you. This will never work."

Tears roll down her cheeks, and I wipe them away tenderly.

"You can't ask me that, Skull," she murmurs, touching my scar. I close my eyes at her gentle touch. "You can't say you're not a man for me, that it won't work. Not after marking me as yours."

"I didn't do that."

"Then why didn't you let me dance with another man?" she shoots back, hitting the nail on the head. "You can't even stand the possibility of me being kissed by a woman. You're totally jealous, but you deny it at all costs."

I swallow hard, knowing I have no right to feel this way, but how can I control that feeling? A feeling I'm trying to suppress while acting indifferent. I can't have her. Even though my instincts scream at me and tear me apart inside.

"You're mistaken." She shakes her head and steps away from me. "Where are you going?"

"To find a man to kiss. I bet it won't be hard."

Possessed, just imagining it, I stride over to her and grip her arm, pulling her close to my body. My arm wraps around her waist, and without holding back, I capture her lips hungrily. Eveline holds my face by the beard and matches my kiss, maintaining a delicious rhythm that surprises even me. I cradle her face with one hand, feeling her soft skin under my touch. It stirs a desire in me to demand more from her, and that's exactly what I do. I pull her up to my height, pressing my tongue against hers.

I separate our lips for a moment, but she quickly returns to the kiss. I allow myself to smile between our swollen lips, but I kiss her again. Our tongues rub against each other sensually, and it reminds me of where we are. So I decide to stop before we attract attention. As I finish the kiss, I slowly pull away and see her delicate face flushed a deep red.

Eveline breathes heavily, her eyes misty, making her even more beautiful.

Her swollen, red lips are entirely inviting to me.

"No other man, woman, or whoever has the right to touch you, Eveline!" I roar, and she smiles shyly at me. "You like to tease, don't you?"

"I don't know what you're talking about," she shrugs, but doesn't step back. Her bicolored eyes are fixed on mine, more precisely on my lips. "I liked that kiss. Your beard scratches a little, but I liked it."

A quick smile escapes me. Her words sound innocent but stir something in me. She barely knows how much I want to have her right now, moaning and pleading for me. Especially in that dress she wore at her party.

I glance around and notice a group of men near a trash can. They shout in our direction, making crude jokes and comments that make me want to march over and knock their teeth out.

"I'll see if I can book a room," I say, and she nods. I notice her trying to disguise her feelings, but she always ends up staring at my face. "Are you okay?"

"Are we going to kiss again?" she asks, then looks me in the eyes. I fall silent; it would be so much easier if she didn't ask those questions. "Silly question, right? Forget it."

I hold her by the hand, keeping her close.

"It's a bit difficult for me, Eveline. I'm asking you to be patient, okay?"

She nods, looking sad, and I feel horrible for being the cause of her sadness.

I grab the two backpacks, lock the car, and we walk to the motel reception. Everything is quite simple but well organized. To my left, there's a 24-hour diner, where a happy couple eats by the window. On the other side, there's a man sitting in one of the chairs, his gaze traveling over Eveline, who is distractedly taking in the surroundings. I glare at him as we walk, until he notices me staring and quickly looks away.

At the reception, the attendant greets us. I request a room and wait for the key.

"Does the mechanic across the street work?"

"It only opens on Monday," she replies, handing me a paper. I sign at the bottom of the sheet. "Or Tuesday, I'm not sure."

I sigh and take the key.

Without thanking her, I gesture down the corridor to Eveline, who walks beside me. We climb a flight of stairs, and as soon as I spot the room number, I point to the door on the right. I open it and step inside, followed closely by Eveline. I watch as she makes her way to the bed and flops down on it. She stretches, undulating her body over the mattress. With her eyes closed and smiling, I can't help but be captivated by the sight. A smile spreads across my face, and a warm sensation fills my chest as my eyes stay glued to her.

She sits up and finds the TV remote on the dresser beside her. I close the door, lock it, and place the backpacks next to the bed. The channel is set to the news; I briefly glance at the screen and see the Diplomat. That piques my curiosity, and I watch attentively as the reporter speaks.

"This morning, Deputy Secretary of the Diplomat, Albert Ritchson, was found dead in his apartment. Stanley Smith, 33, had been working as a secretary at the White House for three years. Stanley disappeared three days ago, and this morning, neighbors reported a foul smell coming from his apartment. The police were called and confirmed the death. With no signs of forced entry, police rule out the possibility of a robbery and suspect suicide."

"Wow, he was so young," Eveline murmurs, looking at me. "What's wrong?"

"Stanley Smith was the person who connected me with the Diplomat," I confess, and she looks at me surprised. "He was the one who flew me by helicopter to Albert Ritchson, and now he's dead."

Worried, I grab the cell phone Miller gave me and dial the only number stored there.

"Do you miss him?"

"Stanley Smith was the one who took me to the Diplomat; he's dead. I don't know if it can be a coincidence, but be careful. They might be eliminating the clues."

"Are you both okay?"

"Yeah." I affirm, glancing at Eveline, who seems lost in thought. "I have to go." I warn and hang up. "Eveline..."

"It's my fault, isn't it?" She questions sadly. "People dying because of me... maybe..."

"No!" I interrupt her; she watches me. "It's not your fault! The ones responsible will pay for this, but not you."

She shakes her head, tears escaping her eyes.

"The girls from the orphanage and some girls there died because they were after me. My life isn't worth more than other people's."

"Eveline!"

"If it comes to a choice you need to make..."

"That'll never happen, Eveline." I sit beside her and take her hand. "I'll kill anyone who tries to harm you without a second thought."

My voice comes out more serious than I expect. And there, in that motel room, I was sure I'd never make that kind of choice, not with her. How could I? I gently touch her face and let out a sigh. Slowly, I lean our faces together and press our lips. I feel an electric current surge through my body, and the last time I felt this way was a long time ago. Then something compels me to stop. I stare into her eyes, but I can only remember when I allowed myself to dream of having a normal life. And then it all happened. It wouldn't be fair to drag Eveline down with me into the depths.

She would surely find her mother and have a chance at a normal life. I'd have my mission to finish those who would be a problem for her, and that would be it. I'd just be a memory in her life.

"I'm going to get food," I say, and she nods. "Don't open the door for anyone, and don't go out alone. As soon as I leave, you lock it and only open when I ask."

"Okay."

I gaze at her lips, holding myself back from kissing her again.

I leave the room and walk determinedly outside.

Just imagining Eveline building a family with someone else tears me apart inside. I exit the building and see the man I spotted earlier still sitting there. I head to the diner and order something for us to eat. The order takes a few minutes, and when I have it in hand, I pay and head back to the room.

As I reach the building, I don't see the man sitting there, and with a bad feeling, I walk faster to the room. I enter the hallway and see him standing in front of the door. He's holding the doorknob and trying to look through the peephole.

I approach silently, but he notices me and bolts. I curse and impulsively go after him, but then I remember Eveline.

"Eveline!" I call, and after a few seconds, I hear her trembling voice from the other side. "It's okay, I dealt with him."

The door opens, and to my surprise, she's dressed in a long-sleeved shirt. I can see her cotton white panties. Her trembling arms wrap around me.

"I-I was in the shower, and I heard a noise. I thought it was you, but no one said anything."

"It was a drunk," I warn, feeling her pull away to look at me. "Here, I brought food. He's not coming back."

She nods, takes the bag, thanks me, and sits on the bed. With the door locked, I decide to take a shower, and that's what I do. I place the other bag with the food on the dresser and head to the bathroom.

I strip completely, leaving my gun on the sink. As I stand under the shower, images of our kiss earlier flood my mind.

I feel my cock harden at just the thought of it and take a deep breath. The water is cold, but even that doesn't calm me. Unable to bear it, my hand descends to my cock, and I grip it. Slowly, I start moving up and down, always with thoughts of Eveline and our kiss. A groan escapes me, and I continue to masturbate. I feel like a teenager with raging hormones. I shiver at the nape of my neck, and I know I'm about to come. I quicken my pace, and as it happens, I groan thinking of Eveline.

I stand there for a moment, hearing the TV on, and for a split second, I fear Eveline might have heard me.

I finish my shower after a few minutes, stepping out with a towel around my waist and my gun in hand. In the room, Eveline is finishing her meal, but as soon as she sees me, I notice her shy gaze directed at me. Did she really hear? I pretend not to understand and place my gun on the bed, grabbing a clean pair of underwear and the same pants as before.

Dressed again, I sit down to eat.

Eveline finishes hers and gathers the trash, tossing it in the bin. Then she goes with her backpack to the bathroom. After a few minutes, she returns and lays on the bed. My gaze roams over her semi-nude body. Her thick thighs paired with her slim waist drive me crazy. Her eyes are fixed on the TV, which is showing some movie that I'm not interested in knowing.

Hoping to distract my gaze and thoughts, I finish eating. I head to the bathroom to take care of my hygiene.

As I return to the room, my gaze searches for Eveline.

"I liked the food you brought," she says while watching me. "What are we going to do if we don't have a car?"

"I'll figure something out," I affirm and lie down in the empty space. "Maybe we can accept that family's ride."

I see her grimace, and when her body turns toward me, I try not to look at her underwear peeking out. It's becoming increasingly difficult to hold back around her.

"I still don't understand," she murmurs. "Why did you say my name is Layla?"

"It was a name I thought of on the spot."

She sits up, looking offended. I allow myself to gaze at her; she's simply beautiful. Her large eyes scrutinize me with an accusatory look, her red lips—now that I know they're soft and delicious—are pressed together as if she's holding back from cursing me out.

"So you really think about her," she says, her eyes sparkling. "I don't understand you, Skull."

After making that accusation, she turns her back to me.

I shake my head and decide to accept what she says, but clearly, I can't hold it in. I approach her, allowing my hand to slide down in a caress over her soft arm. I kiss her neck, and with a smile, I notice the skin prickling. I lift the kisses to her earlobe and nibble on it. Eveline lets out a soft moan, which urges me to continue.

"You're being unfair," I whisper, pulling her body closer to mine. "The only one tormenting my mind lately is you."

"Tormenting?"

She repeats softly; I smile and brush her blonde hair aside.

"You don't leave my head, Eveline. And I've tried to put a limit between us," I confess, and she sighs as I lick the space of her neck, "but you tempt me in every way. Sometimes I think you want to know how far my limit goes."

"But I'm not doing anything," she retorts, and becoming bolder, I slide my hand down to her bare thigh.

"Skull... something is poking me."

I can't help but smile; I open my mouth to say that "the thing" is my erection when, by her own volition, she rubs against me. I suppress a moan and thrust my hips against her rear.

"Ouch! It's so hard, Skull."

In response, I hold her face, bringing it close to mine, and when our lips touch, I can't hold back my groan; I'm craving Eveline and I won't deny it. She turns towards me and we roll on the bed. I'm on top of her, our lips moving together in a synchronized, pleasurable dance. Her arms wrap around my neck, and with her legs open, I settle between them.

I grind my hips against her intimacy, protected by her panties, and I feel my neck being scratched. With my other hand, I slide down to her panties and touch her over the fabric. She breaks the kiss, bites her lower lip, and places her hand on mine. I rub her slowly, and Eveline rolls her eyes in pleasure.

"You in that dress made me hard as a rock," I comment, and she smiles to the side. However, it doesn't last long, and she opens her lips to moan. I push my fingers over her panties to her clitoris. "And just feeling you like this makes me feel like my cock is about to explode."

I notice her eyes drifting to the outline of my erection.

"Can I see it?"

I swallow hard at the request, and for a moment I ponder. If we cross that line, it would be hard to go back to how things were before. In the midst of my thoughts, Eveline pushes me, and I lie back on the bed. Her gaze scans my body as she sits on my legs. Her hands are clasped in front of her body, but I can see she's nervous from the way she twists her fingers.

"Are you sure?"

"Please," she begs, and after swallowing hard, she moves her hands to the button of my pants. "Can I?"

I nod, and I can see that I'm anxious to know her reaction when she sees me. She unbuttons and unzips my pants. Then, I see her eyes widen as I lower my pants along with my underwear. I hold my hard cock and, unable to contain myself, I start moving my hand up and down.

"Isn't this what you expected?"

She smiles and brings her fingers to her lips.

"She was right," she murmurs softly, but I hear and I'm confused. "Can I touch it?"

I agree, and as soon as she grabs it firmly, I groan. Her gaze is still surprised as she examines me, and I need a lot of self-control not to come at that moment.

"I'm at a disadvantage here, Eveline," I joke, and she looks at me. "Aren't you going to let me touch you?"

"I'm shy."

My low laugh catches her attention, and she smiles back. Her cheeks and lips are red, and when a strand falls in her face, I quickly tuck it behind her ear. I feel her hand moving up and down, pulling another groan from me. Eveline bites her lip without taking her eyes off my cock.

"In a just world, you would let me touch you."

I try again, and she smiles shyly but nods. Without delay, I move my fingers to her panties and find them wet. I observe her angelic face, and she gasps, opening her legs wider for me. As soon as my fingers slip under the fabric, I'm surprised.

"Waxed?"

"The girls who work for Miller did it," she replies, and I clench my jaw. Perhaps noticing this, she continues, "They just did that and explained a few things I had questions about."

"Like what?"

I'm really curious, but I can guess well. Besides the kissing lesson, for someone who's never held a cock before, she's bringing me to the edge.

"I just got confused," she says, holding my length with both hands. "How can something like that fit in someone? They explained things to me."

"What kind of things?"

"It's women's talk, you know?"

Smiling, she leans in to kiss me, this time on the cheek. With my finger, I rub her clit, and she moans, resting her head on my shoulder. I pull her in for a kiss, and when I think about deepening it, she pulls away, smiling, looking shy.

"Can I taste it?"

CHAPTER TWELVE

Eveline

As soon as I ask the question, I can see his surprise. My hand doesn't close around him, but I continue to caress him, eliciting groans that urge me to keep going. They were so raw and virile; my body is on fire and seems to ignite further every time he rubs his fingers against my intimacy. I glance at the backpack and remember the condoms. How can I let him know that I have them?

"Do you want to suck me?" he asks, and I nod eagerly.

"C-can I?" My voice wavers as I receive a more intense caress.

"He's all yours," he replies, but before I can begin, he makes me look at him. "If you let me do the same to you."

This time, I'm surprised.

Tracy had said that some men didn't like reciprocation. That often, they needed to finish pleasuring themselves. Why did I think it would be different with Skull?

"So? " he questions, and without thinking much, I nod. "Great! Now turn around and get on all fours for me. No panties."

I feel a tingle in my lower belly, and even trembling with desire, I obey. First, under his feline gaze, I remove my panties and let my hands cover my intimacy.

"Take off that top too," he commands.

After taking a deep breath, I do it. My first impulse is to cover myself, but this time I remain confident. His calloused hand grabs my breast and squeezes, repeating the motion on the other. Then he circles his finger. I remember he told me to get on all fours, and slowly I position myself on the mattress. I feel his thumb rubbing intensely against my opening; I almost fall onto the mattress, but I manage to steady my arms.

With his help, I find myself above him, and my mouth fills with saliva as I see him up close. His length is long and thick, a colorless liquid oozing from the robust tip, and I watch it curiously. Some veins protrude around it, which surprised me when I saw it for the first time. That cock is so... virile, and it perfectly matches Skull. So, knowing what I need to do, I grab it and suck the tip, feeling it soft between my lips along with a different taste. At the same time, I feel a lick that makes me moan louder. With some difficulty, I look back, seeing only his huge hands firmly holding me by the backside.

I return to placing the rosy head in my mouth and suck it. Always rubbing my tongue along its length. My body is soft and hot, it feels like I'm about to combust at any moment. I've never felt sensations like this before. The thought of sucking that part of someone's body had never crossed my mind before. However, providing that pleasure for Skull is something unique for me.

His tongue explores my intimacy, and then I feel it penetrating me. I sit up, and when I think about pulling away, Skull grabs me by the waist, keeping me in place. So, sitting on his tongue, I involuntarily start to move my hips back and forth. Rubbing and moaning in search of more pleasure. It's indescribable, so exhilarating that within minutes, my trembling body tightens.

I moan pitifully.

Before collapsing on him, Skull sucks and licks me. I hear him groan, and then my backside stings from the slap he gives me.

"Fuck! I could spend hours and hours sucking that delicious pussy."

His fingers touch me once again, and I moan, going back to all fours.

"Now it's my turn, Skull..." I warn and turn to face him. I position myself between his open legs and toss my hair to the side. He holds his cock, and I watch the up-and-down motions.

My intimacy remains sensitive; I touch slowly. Skull doesn't take his eyes off my hand.

"If you keep touching yourself and moaning softly like that, I'll be forced to fuck you until dawn."

I stop, surprised, and my gaze falls on his length. Even with Ellen explaining that I didn't need to be afraid, it was impossible. It would definitely hurt a lot. I lean in, and without breaking our gaze, I place him between my lips. I suck slowly and moan without holding back my desire. I remember some tips from the girls and let my tongue glide from the bottom to the top.

His fingers weave into my hair at the nape of my neck, and when I feel a tug, I release him to moan loudly.

"I'm going to cum on your lips," he states, seeming tense. Am I not doing it right? With that thought in mind, I decide to be bolder. I'll follow Tracy's advice. "Now it's your turn to stop!"

"But I want you to feel as good as I did," I murmur, and with both hands, I return to stroking him while my lips work on his glans. "You need to cum, so... just let it happen."

His hips, which had been still until then, start to move with my rhythm. I slide my hand down to his heavy testicles and give them some attention. Skull curses, and after a few minutes, I feel a thick liquid on my tongue. I pull back, paralyzed, and watch him cum. I'm fascinated by the sight; his cock seems to vibrate as he cums on my face and lips.

Skull collapses on the bed while I grab my top and clean myself.

A bit confused, I move closer to him and touch his cock. Skull quickly stares at me.

"Shouldn't he be limp?"

He laughs at me, his fingers brushing my face in a gentle caress. His gaze holds me captive; I feel at peace there and wish it were just the two of us. Maybe he and I in a little house far away from all danger, with a large garden and some animals. Waking up next to him every day until we grew old together. I smile at the thought, but soon reality crashes down on me. There wouldn't be a "we." Skull has already warned me about what will happen after he completes that mission.

I am just a mission.

I suppress the urge to cry by averting my gaze.

"What's wrong?"

"Nothing!" I say quickly, and he furrows his brow. "Did you not like it?"

"Are you kidding?! You did great," he praises, and I return him a smile. "Great enough for someone who's never done it."

"I'm a good student," I boast, but I'm being honest. "If I were staying at the orphanage, I would be a teacher, you know? Abby, with her style, wanted to teach good manners," I comment, and remembering my friend gives me a pang in my chest. "I don't know what happened to her, Skull."

He makes me lie on his chest as he strokes my hair.

"Was she at the orphanage during the invasion?"

"I don't know. She went to the city that afternoon for an exam. Her family found her and wanted to make sure it was really her." I snuggle closer to his chest. "She's the one who discovered my record and suggested we talk to Ethan."

"Who's Ethan?" he asks, and I fall silent. However, Skull makes me look at him. "Who is he?"

"The go-to guy over there," I reply, but he waits for more. I swallow hard. "We asked him for help to find out about the photo and the phrase. He told me to go to his room so he could tell me."

"I don't like where this is going," he says in a serious tone, so I fall silent. "Did he do anything to you?"

I shake my head a bit tense, but he keeps looking at me, and I sigh.

"He grabbed me and tried to do the same thing those men did in the cabin." I see his expression shift between anger and guilt. "He couldn't do anything! It was when the explosion happened, and I managed to scratch his face and run away. I don't know what happened to him."

"I hope he's dead. Because if I find him, he'll beg to die."

I lie back down on him.

What would it be like after he leaves? Would I be able to forget him? Would he forget me? How can I feel so safe in his arms? All that violence he rages should scare me, but it's the opposite. His words are a form of comfort. Am I going crazy? Or does he feel the same way?

"Don't worry about anything else, Eveline. You're safe with me, and about your friend... I'll ask Miller to find out where she is. He's good at finding people."

Surprised, I sit up abruptly and see the sincerity in his eyes. I hug him, even though I'm naked, and kiss him several times on the cheek.

"Thank you so much! Really! I knew you were a good person!"

I kiss him one last time and find it strange when I see something in his eyes. They look sad, but it passes quickly, and his serious demeanor returns.

"Let's sleep," he murmurs, glancing at his cock, which is still hard. "Tomorrow I need to sort out the car situation so we can continue our journey."

I think about retorting, but I remember that he might be tired. Tracy warned me that men tire easily, and if we're going to continue our journey early, it won't be me who hinders him.

"Can I sleep in your arms?"

He nods.

"Good night, Eveline."

The next day, we woke up early and went to have breakfast at the diner next door. My first reaction this morning was to rush to the bathroom until after a few minutes, I came out trying to look natural. I saw Skull smile, but he didn't say anything. I really was foolish. I sat near the window while he was on the other side of the street talking to a man in front of the mechanic. My stomach was rumbling, and the anxiety of knowing I would possibly meet my mother was killing me inside. The waitress placed our order on the table and left. I turned my attention to Skull and saw him handing a bundle of cash to the man.

In the background, I hear the bell ring, signaling that new people have arrived. The diner, although small, is quite cozy.

"Layla!" I look to the side; it's the couple from yesterday. "Do you remember me? Grace and Owen, we towed your car here."

"Yes, I remember." I smile and look for the teenagers, but not finding them. "Thank you so much for yesterday. Another couple would have left us stranded on the road."

"No need to thank us," Grace murmurs, glancing at the seat across from me. "And where's your boyfriend? James, right? Where is he?"

I look outside; Skull is approaching with a serious expression.

"He went to see if our car can be fixed."

"Our invitation still stands," Grace says, smiling. "If you both want to."

I smile and nod. I think they're going to leave, but they stand there looking at me. I adjust in the slightly uncomfortable seat, then mentally thank when Skull stops in front of them.

"We were reinforcing our invitation," Owen informs Skull, who remains serious.

"Thank you, but we've already talked to the mechanic." He looks at the two and continues, "Do you need anything else?"

Grace looks at me but quickly shakes her head. They both smile and step away. Skull sits across from me, his gaze following the couple until they leave the diner.

"They're quite helpful," I comment, and after a few seconds, Skull looks at me. "Did you get it?"

"The mechanic said the car will be ready in an hour. He asked for double to finish quickly, but we'll make it to Marfa by tonight," he pauses and watches me. "Then we'll see what to do."

I suppress the urge to say that we would stay together until everything was resolved, but I just agree. Just the thought of being away from him tightens my chest. I sigh and lean back in my seat; the food looks great, but I'm not very hungry. I steal a glance at Skull, and he's like me: lost in thought.

I start eating the pancakes, and he does the same.

Finally, when we finish, Skull heads to the mechanic's across the street, and I go back to the room. I lock the door as he instructed and lie down on the mattress. I turn on the TV and flip through channels, not knowing what to watch, when my mind drifts back to last night. I put the remote down on the bed, close my eyes, and slide my hand down to the middle of my legs. I'm wearing black jeans, a long-sleeve shirt, and boots, but deep down, I wish I were naked with Skull.

If he hadn't been tired last night, would we have had sex? I smile nervously and bring my fingers to my lips. What am I thinking? There's no way that cock could fit in me, but just imagining it makes me feel like I'm on fire. A shiver runs through my body, sending sparks of desire to my breasts and my intimacy.

I want to give myself to him, but does he want me the same way? Last night, he seemed very committed to pleasing me. I stretch out on the bed, wearing a silly smile. I don't recognize myself; the Eveline from before wouldn't have thought or done any of that yesterday. But now? My mind feels different; I feel different, and not in a bad way.

I sit up in bed, trying to shake off those thoughts for now when a news segment on TV catches my attention. A woman is crying as she's embraced by an older man.

"Teenagers kidnapped after leaving school," I read the headline.

I switch channels, feeling anxious. I can't imagine the fear she must be feeling. The next channel announces the start of the presidential elections in the United States. To my surprise, I recognize the diplomat, and behind him is a well-dressed man with blond hair and a big beard. I read the name Michael W. Carter, the current President. As he speaks, I frown when I notice a familiar face. I watch for a few minutes, then I remember the photograph.

I run to the backpack and search for the photo.

On TV, he looks older, but yes! It was him in my photo! I sit back down completely, surprised. Daughter of the president? Then everything makes sense. My mind is racing when I hear a knock at the door. I stay silent for a moment, then move. Is it the same person from yesterday?

"Layla?"

It's Grace's voice. Confused, I crack the door open just enough to keep the chain on.

"Hi," I murmur when I see her alone. "Is everything okay, Grace?"

"Can I come in?" she asks, but her gaze makes me a bit uncomfortable. "I wanted to talk to you."

"Oh, I'm about to take a shower. Skull is downstairs, and…"

"Who's Skull?" she asks with a sideways smile. I hesitate to say his name, and as I think of making an excuse, I'm startled by her hand on the door. "Let me in; it'll be a quick conversation."

"It's just that I really can't right now," I respond apologetically. "See you later."

"My daughter is feeling unwell," she says again, and I stop. "Maybe a kind word will help."

I ponder whether to go or not, but finally nod and tuck the photograph into my pants pocket. I wouldn't deny help to their daughter, especially since they helped us yesterday. I open the door and step past her without revealing the room, lock the door, and smile at Grace.

"Is she sick?" I ask as we start walking down the hallway.

"I think so. My husband went downstairs to see if he can get help."

I nod, and as we enter another hallway, I begin to feel uneasy in the silence. I risk a glance at her and notice her gaze on me.

"Where are you from?"

"North Carolina," she replies and, to my surprise, touches my face. "You're so beautiful, Layla. Your eyes are just enchanting."

"Thank you."

She points to the room, and we stop in front of the door. I wait for her to open it. Before entering, I see the bed neatly made. I step in cautiously, then I'm pushed inside. Grace closes the door, and across the room, I see two teenagers tied up and gagged. I recognize them instantly; they were the same ones I saw on TV. The bathroom door opens, and Owen appears, drying his hands.

Frightened, I rush to the door, but I'm quickly restrained by strong arms. Just as I think about screaming, he covers my mouth with his hand.

"Did anyone see you with her?"

"No!" Grace denies and goes to the dresser. "Her boyfriend wasn't there."

I try to move and scream, but it's in vain.

"You're going to keep these two company, but don't worry; you'll enjoy it a lot."

Then I see Grace approaching with a syringe filled with some liquid. Owen pulls my hair, exposing my neck, and when I feel the needle prick me, the door is kicked open violently. Skull appears, wielding a gun, and as soon as he sees me being held by Owen, he shoots him without a second thought. He then aims at Grace and shoots, making her fall to the ground.

My ear is ringing; terrified, I look to the side and see Owen with a bullet wound near his eye. I bring my hand to my ear, try to take a step, but stumble and fall onto the bed.

My vision is blurred, and my body won't obey me. Skull is furious; it's so palpable, but when he looks at me, his face turns to concern.

"Hey!" he murmurs, holding me gently. "It's okay! Look at me!"

I try to obey him, but I can't, and then everything goes dark.

CHAPTER THIRTEEN

Skull

Eveline doesn't respond to me; I press two fingers against her neck artery and breathe a sigh of relief when I realize she's alive. I glance to the side and see the two teenagers crying as they look at me. Carefully, I lay her back on the mattress and move towards them; I need to be quick or the police could arrive at any moment. I remove the gags from both of them and start untying them.

"Thank you!" The girl immediately hugs me, and I freeze, but a few seconds later, I push her away. "Are you a cop?"

"No," I deny, finishing untying her. "Pay attention!" I ask, and they nod. "Don't talk about me or her. Understood?"

"B-But you saved us!"

"It doesn't matter!" I speak more harshly, then take a deep breath. "I don't want the police on my tail."

"Okay!" the boy replies. "We won't say anything. Thank you!"

I nod and stand up.

The two are siblings; they were kidnapped a few days ago by that couple.

I saw their picture on the TV at the garage and remembered the couple. I noticed that the "children" hadn't appeared with them, and I found it strange that they were so interested in helping us, especially with the looks they were giving Eveline. The car was ready soon, and when I went to the room, I saw the couple putting two shovels into the car, along with a black tarp and ropes.

My mind connected the dots, and I was certain they were not good people.

"Go downstairs," I ordered, and they nodded. "Don't come back up here; the police are on their way."

"Thank you, sir!"

They run outside, and I quickly go to get Eveline. I lift her in my arms and walk out.

"Skull... what happened?" she asks quietly. "The teenagers...?"

"They're okay," I interrupt her, and when I reach the bedroom, I lay her down on the bed. "We need to go."

She sits up with difficulty and brings her hand to her head. I hold both backpacks with one hand and wrap the other protectively around Eveline's waist. The place is in chaos; some customers are in the reception with the teenagers. The girl is crying as she talks to someone on her cell phone, possibly her mother. The boy looks at me and nods subtly.

At the entrance, I see the mechanic maneuvering the car out front. I quickly approach him, open the passenger door, and wait for Eveline to sit.

"All set! Your car is like new..." I interrupt him by handing him another bundle of cash.

After placing the backpacks in the back of the car, I take my place in the driver's seat and accelerate away from the motel. As the place fades behind us, I turn to Eveline, my nerves still palpable.

"Why did you go after her?" My voice sounds heavy with irritation. Eveline looks at me with a confused expression.

"I wasn't to blame!" she replies, her voice echoing the tension in the air. "How was I supposed to know this would happen?"

I feel my heart tighten at the thought of what could have happened if I hadn't intervened in time. I swallow hard, my anger shifting into concern. Those two bastards could have taken Eveline away from me forever.

"Do you have any idea what they would have done to you if I hadn't followed you?" My voice comes out hoarse, laden with fear for what almost happened.

Eveline seems to grasp the seriousness of the situation and lets some tears slip; her expression turns more vulnerable.

"I'm sorry," she pleads, her voice almost a whisper. She averts her gaze to her trembling hands, emotion evident on her face. "I'm just a burden to you."

I feel torn seeing her like this, my heart aching with guilt. I reach for her hand and hold it firmly, bringing it to my lips in a gesture of comfort.

"I just got nervous! Don't apologize. Just next time, obey me," I murmur, trying to soften my voice so as not to scare her further. "Is that okay?"

She nods shyly, and I turn my gaze back to the road ahead. Silence reigns in the car, but the overwhelming sense of relief at having her by my side is undeniable.

"Skull?" she calls, and I glance at her quickly. "Is my dad the President of the United States? I saw him on TV with the diplomat. I compared him with the photo, and it really is him."

I confirm, of course, that she would find out through the TV.

"Yes, it seems so," I reply, and she pulls the image from her pocket. "There are more secrets involved. We'll figure them all out."

"Do you think my mom has those answers?"

"Let's hope so," I murmur, looking at her. "Are you feeling okay?"

"Yes," she nods. "They kidnapped those teenagers." She speaks sadly. "If we had accepted their ride, what do you think would have happened?"

"They would be dead because of me," I assert seriously. "No one is going to lay a finger on you, Eveline."

Her gaze returns to the photograph, and she stares at it for a few minutes. We still haven't kissed since yesterday, and I'm holding back with all my might. Feeling her kisses and the unique taste of Eveline brought me to the edge. My desire after she came on my tongue was to have her wide open and to bury myself deep inside that warm, sweet pussy.

Just imagining it makes my body cry out for it.

"...Skull?"

"Yes?" I respond, startled. Her eyes evaluate me as if waiting for an answer. "What?"

Then she sighs, seeming anxious.

"We're okay, right?" I frown at her question; she continues, "It's just that we did that yesterday, and you haven't said anything since."

"You ran away from me this morning," I reply, and she blushes. I let a quick smile escape; Eveline is so beautiful. "I didn't want to be rude."

"I just got embarrassed," she comments, tucking some strands behind her ear. "I'm shy, you know? But you make me feel this way."

"Feel how?"

"So hot like hell," she confesses, and I'm surprised. I didn't expect her to be so honest. "It feels like all the teachings I received at the orphanage vanished from my mind. They didn't really talk about sex but rather how I should behave and not have impure thoughts. But the conversation I had with Ellen was so enlightening and important for me."

"You spent the afternoon talking about this?"

"We talked about many things," her gaze shines in my direction, "but as I said before, it's women's talk."

"You..." I begin, but as soon as she looks at me, I shake my head. "Never mind."

"What? Don't start and then stop like that." She's smiling, but I notice her embarrassment. "I...?"

I shift uncomfortably in my seat; I really am a masochist. Bringing up a topic that caused my jealousy.

"You really haven't been kissed by them?"

Eveline smiles, and I know she's calling me jealous in her mind.

"You were my first kiss, Skull," I realize she's being sincere, and that makes me relax. I feel like an idiot for caring about that. "By the way, when they were kissing, I wondered what your kiss would be like."

I stare intensely at her.

"And how is it?"

I watch her sigh with a small smile as she gazes at my lips.

"I felt like I was floating when we finished," she states, then bites her lip. "You kiss well, Skull."

"You do too, Eveline. You surprised me and made me jealous." I decide to be honest as well. "And you're right; I can't stand the thought of someone else touching you."

She smiles shyly.

"I think I'm also jealous of you with someone else."

"You think so?" I smile, making her blush more. "I'm sure of it."

Her head shakes in denial, and she stops smiling.

"Layla said I'm not your type," as she speaks, I feel confused. "That you prefer mature women who can offer you something and drive you crazy in bed."

I frown.

"Eveline..."

"Did I drive you crazy in bed?" she interrupts. I turn my face toward her; she looks tense. How can she ask me this? "I wanted to continue, but you got tired. And I know it's normal for men to get tired; Tracy said some can't handle two in a row. I didn't understand this 'two in a row,' but I think it has something to do with sex."

"I can handle two in a row!" I respond nervously; she just smiles. "We didn't continue yesterday because it was late, and..."

"And you got tired," she finishes. I look at her seriously. "It's okay, Skull. I'm not judging you; I just commented."

"You're playing with fire, Eveline," I murmur, my tone coming out slightly like a threat. "Be aware."

I refocus on the road, hoping to reach Oklahoma before lunch. The next stop would only be in Albuquerque. Out of the corner of my eye, I notice Eveline smiling. Is she teasing me? I smile back, knowing that later she won't escape me.

As planned, we arrive in Oklahoma before lunch. We eat quickly, and I wait for Eveline to use the bathroom before we continue our journey.

We arrive in Albuquerque, New Mexico, at night. As we drive along the deserted road, the shadows of the mountains rise on the horizon, creating dark and imposing shapes against the starry sky. Beside me, Eveline rests peacefully, wrapped in the jacket I bought at a convenience store a few miles back. Her serene face is bathed in the soft light of the moon, creating an aura of tranquility around her. Her blonde hair sways gently in the night breeze coming through the partially open car window as she snuggles comfortably in her seat.

As we drive down the deserted road, I get lost in thought. After settling things with the President... what would I do next? Would I go back to see her? What would I say? Would she wait for me? Or would she forget me quickly?

With a bitter taste in my mouth, I take a deep breath. I couldn't bear to see her with another man or see her kissing lips that weren't mine. I run my hand over my beard, then let my fingers touch her cheek. I caress her softness, and she lets out a low purr. I want her for myself, but I know I can't.

I have enemies, many who want me dead and wouldn't hesitate to take someone from me again. Would I be so selfish as to put her at risk? My choices don't allow me to have someone. So I would settle for a little house in the middle of nowhere, with a small farm for chickens and ducks. I smile. Would she accept that life? To live simply with me?

She stirs, and I pull my hand away.

"Skull?" she calls sleepily. "Are we there yet?"

"Yes," I reply, pointing to the car's GPS. "We're going to stop at a hotel, and tomorrow we'll head to the location."

She looks at me and smiles, and to my surprise, she unbuckles her seatbelt and leans in to kiss me on the cheek.

"Thank you," she says and returns to the window. My chest tightens; I should have kept the barrier between us and continued treating her with the rudeness intended for anyone close to me. Because now, looking at her as just a mission is so difficult for me.

"Wow! This city is as beautiful as it is cold."

She quickly wraps herself more snugly in the jacket.

"In Afghanistan, we dealt with unbearable cold peaks," I comment, looking at her curiously. "And during the day, the heat was relentless. We wore our combat gear, which is already heavy due to protection against the cold and other threats, along with bulletproof vests."

"Miller told me you served together."

"That's right."

"And that you stabbed him and shot your friend."

I smile to the side and glance briefly at her. Eveline smiles, waiting for my response.

"Miller is no saint; he tried to kill me. Did he say that?"

"He mentioned something," she replies, then looks at me after a few seconds. "Why did you quit serving?"

Uncomfortable with that question, I just shake my head.

"In 22 minutes, we'll arrive at the hotel."

"Are you going to stop answering my questions again?" she asks, crossing her arms. "I want to get to know you, Skull. What you like to eat, if you have family or..."

"I don't want to talk about that, Eveline!"

I take a deep breath and look out the window. She doesn't ask me anything else, and I know I was rude, and I hate myself for it. Finally, I park in front of the hotel and get out of the car, followed closely. I grab our backpacks, and Eveline is silent beside me. We enter the lobby, which is quite small compared to the motel, and go to the reception.

At the desk, I request a room, preferably one with windows facing the road. I briefly sign a form, pay with the card Miller gave me, and wait for the key to be handed over.

As soon as I have it in hand, a staff member approaches to take the backpacks, but I just shake my head. Then, he, in a helpful manner, indicates the way, leading the way. I subtly glance at Eveline, and she has a sad expression. I look away, feeling guilty. We go up a flight of stairs, and when the staff member stops in front of the door, I step forward to open it.

"Have a good night!"

I nod and wait for Eveline to enter first. She passes by me quietly; I follow her and close the door. When I realize she's about to pull away, I hold her hand. Her gaze meets mine, and I see her as so fragile. I feel even more guilty.

"I don't like talking about my past," I warn, and she nods. "I have nothing good to say."

"That's okay," she says softly, and I step closer to her. "I'm just too curious; I'm sorry."

"No." I shake my head and kiss her gently. Just that contact makes my body vibrate. "I need to learn to be kinder to you. Forgive me."

Then she smiles, and I feel my chest warm. I kiss her again, and easily lift her into my arms. I make her legs wrap around me and walk until I feel the bed right in front of me. I lay her on the mattress and position myself above her, our tongues rubbing together erotically. My hand slides down her body, and I quickly squeeze her breast. She interrupts the kiss and moans sensually.

"How I wish I could see you in that dress again."

She looks at me, surprised, and gasps when I squeeze the other breast.

"So you really liked it?"

I kiss her once more, demanding her lips with hunger.

"It would be so much easier to make you mine with him," I reply, and she looks at me confused. "If I were using it right now, I would have you on all fours, wide open for me, lifting your dress, pulling your panties to the side, and burying my cock deep inside you."

Eveline bites her lip, and I notice her eyes sparkling. Does she desire this?

"A-All of it?" she asks nervously. I nod, and she shakes her head. "It wouldn't fit, Skull."

"It will fit," I assert, and I slide my fingers down to her pussy, protected by her pants. I rub it, feeling the heat, and the desire to taste her. "With a little care, it will go in completely, and I'll fuck you in every possible position."

I kiss her neck, and each time she sighs, I increase the caresses.

"Skull?" she calls when I think about putting a breast in my mouth; she grabs my hair. "C-Can I take a shower?"

I smile at the question and place both hands beside her head. Eveline looks embarrassed; anyone could tell.

"That's fine, but don't take too long."

I allow her to slide out from under me, and she rushes with the backpack to the bathroom. I sit on the mattress and observe my erection through my jeans. I squeeze it and let out a sigh; it's been a while since my last time. I get up and go to the window; everything is calm. The car is parked right in front, and I hope it won't let us down.

I lie back down on the bed, waiting for Eveline.

I grab the phone Miller gave me and decide to send a message to Pablo. I left the money with Miller, intending for a third plan. If I can't come back, the money I received for saving her will stay with her. Pablo will take care of the necessary fake documents, and Eveline can live a comfortable life for a while. I still haven't told her, but it will depend on how things turn out.

Before I can type, the bathroom door opens.

Eveline is wearing the white dress she wore on her birthday, smiling shyly as she stops in front of the bed. I stand up, ready to throw her on all fours and bury myself deep inside her warmth, but before I can do that, she stops me with her hand.

"Aren't you hungry?"

"For you? Yes, very hungry."

I try to embrace her once more, and she stops me.

"Can we eat first?"

I frown; her gaze is anxious. Then she kisses me, just a touch of lips.

"Are you nervous because you don't want to, or because you do?"

She smiles and holds onto the hem of my shirt.

"Don't think I'm silly," she asks, and I shake my head. I would never think that. "I'm afraid it won't fit or it will hurt a lot. Tracy was right when she said you're well-endowed."

My gaze is surprised, and because she's embarrassed, I don't question it. Finally, I kiss her again and give her a quick smile.

"If you don't want to do anything, I'll respect your decision," I murmur, and she sighs. "I'll take a shower, and you can call the reception. Order something to eat."

I kiss her one more time and head to the bathroom.

As soon as I enter, I leave the door ajar, place the gun on the sink, and start taking off my clothes. With a hard cock, I head to the shower and turn it on; the water is warm. I take a deep breath and switch it to cold. Maybe wanting Eveline to give herself to me today is too much, and I understand her concern. I've never been with a virgin; all the women I've been with had experience with casual relationships. I imagine that a woman's first time can be scary, so it's up to me to make that moment special for her.

I take a quick shower, and despite the cold water, my cock remains hard. Damn! Am I that needy? I frown, and the answer comes immediately. No. It was the effect of Eveline. I scrub my face with the towel and, before stepping out, cover my nudity. I grab the gun and exit the bathroom, surprised to not see the food cart. Eveline is sitting on her legs on the bed, and upon seeing me, her focus is entirely on my cock.

"Didn't you order food?" I ask, placing the gun at the edge of the mattress. Eveline doesn't respond, but when I go to the backpack to grab a clean pair of underwear, I feel something hit me in the back of the neck. I reach back and grab a piece of fabric. It was a pair of panties. On the bed, Eveline is on her knees. "You...?"

"I brought condoms," she interrupts, showing me the silver packets, "but be careful, okay?" she asks as she slowly gets on all fours.

Still in disbelief at her initiative, I approach and rub my fingers along her intimacy, confirming she's soaked and ready for me. Gently, I penetrate her with one finger, and she moans, tightening around me. I continue to caress her, but soon I lean in her direction. I need to taste her with my tongue, to feel her unique flavor, or I'm going to go crazy. I hold her by the backside, and with my thumbs, I part her little lips. Then I let my tongue gather all her pleasure; she moans louder and tries to shift out of position.

I slap her backside hard, and she looks at me from the side.

"If you try to move away, you'll get another slap!" When I receive no answer, I slap the other side. "Did you hear me?"

"Y-Yes!"

Satisfied, I give her two more slaps on each side, watching the marks become evident. I go back to sucking her, delighting in her clit, which I make sure to suck with hunger. Eveline moans and begins to grind against my face. I slide my tongue from her pleasure point to her tight opening.

"S-Skull...? Your beard..."

"Is it hurting?" I want to know, concerned, but she shakes her head and rubs against my face and tongue even more.

"It feels good..."

I smile and continue licking her. She's trembling, and as her moans grow louder, I realize she's about to reach orgasm. I alternate between sucking, licking, and nibbling on her flesh. After a few seconds, she moans softly and collapses her body onto the mattress. I remove the towel and toss it aside, grab one of the condoms, and open it with my teeth.

I put it on quickly and watch Eveline. Her body is still twitching, and she smiles. Her blonde hair is sprawled to the side, scattered around. I climb onto the bed and help her lie back on the mattress. Her gaze travels over me and stops at my cock. I kneel between her legs. I hold her wide open, and she looks at me nervously.

"Ready?" I say, and she nods, bringing her fingers to her lips. "I won't say it won't hurt, but I'll be gentle, okay?"

"Okay!"

I hold my cock and rub it against her intimacy. Then, I position it at her opening and push until the glans enters. Eveline places one hand on my arm and digs her short nails into me.

"Oh my God!" she moans, closing her eyes. "It burns! Skull!"

I control the instinct to thrust hard and gradually push deeper. I feel the barrier of her virginity and push a little more. I see the tears on her face and lean in to place soft kisses along her neck.

"Calm down, we're almost there!" I wipe her tears and decide to end her suffering. With a thrust, I penetrate her completely. Eveline screams as more tears fall.

I stay still, waiting for her to adjust. After a few seconds, I try to move when she stops crying, but her hand holds my arm.

"That's it, right?" she asks, and I nod. "I feel full inside."

I give a quick smile and support my arms beside her head. My lips demand hers intensely, hungrily, desperate for the sweet and hypnotic touch of Eveline, who is now entirely mine. Her delicate hands grasp my face as her lips try to keep up with my movements.

I snuggle closer to her, making her break the kiss to moan.

"Can I move?"

"Yes!"

Then I pull out completely before penetrating again. We moan in unison, and I repeat until her expression of pain changes to desire. It doesn't take long; the smile she gives me is contained but says a lot. I start thrusting slowly, gradually increasing speed as our moans rise. I can't contain the shivers coursing through my body, exploding in my neck. I have to maintain control to not cum right now.

I moan more hoarsely this time as I feel my cock sliding—now with ease—inside her, grazing her tight, warm walls. I lick two fingers and rub them in long circles on her engorged clit. Eveline moans louder and tries to close her legs, but I don't allow it.

The dress is bunched around her slim waist, so I have her take it off and quickly place one breast in my mouth. I nibble on the nipple and then give the same attention to the other. I sit up, and with both hands, I grip her waist firmly, pulling her toward me.

My cock is practically being milked by Eveline.

After a few minutes, the room feels strangely small, and the temperature oscillates—first like a Hawaiian volcano erupting, then a plunge into the South Pole coast. I moan hoarsely as she moans plaintively, grunting with pleasure. Our bodies tremble, and I hold her while continuing to move. Eveline grips me tightly and sighs before collapsing onto the bed, and I cum hard inside her.

Feeling the spasms, I pull her in for a kiss, tasting her tongue and exploring her mouth. Eveline is still clenching around me when I withdraw from her warmth.

It was the pinnacle; the highest peak of pleasure.

Realizing I've let my body fall on top of her, I roll to the side. I'm exhausted and breathing irregularly. I look at Eveline, and she's in the same state. Her breasts rise and fall, tired and panting. With open arms, I welcome her sweaty body as it snuggles against mine. There are no words to describe that moment.

"Is it normal..." Eveline takes a breath and looks at me. "Not to feel my body?"

I smile and keep my attention on her flushed and sweaty face. Her lips are swollen and red from my kisses, and her gaze is sleepy.

"I'll be right back."

I warn and get out of bed. As I walk to the bathroom, I remove the condom and tie a knot at the end. I clean up quickly and soon return to bed. Eveline is asleep, and I lie down beside her; she quickly searches for me. I relax my body and spend a few minutes watching her. What am I doing? Ruining her chances of getting involved and falling for someone else? That should embarrass me, but the effect is the opposite.

For the first time in years, I feel like my heart is in the right place.

And for the first time in a long time, I find myself afraid of my decisions.

CHAPTER FOURTEEN

Eveline

I slowly open my eyes, still wrapped in the post-sleep drowsiness. The soft morning light peeks through the slightly open curtains; I see our backpacks near the bed, but there's no sign of Skull. For a moment, I remain immersed in the comforting feeling of being nestled in soft, warm sheets.

Then, the memories of the previous night start to seep into my mind, and I can't help but smile, embarrassed. I gave myself to Skull and somehow— I don't know how— welcomed him inside me. I bring my fingers to my lips and close my eyes. I can remember the heat interspersed with suffocating waves of cold every time that huge cock hit me deep inside and pulled back with force to repeat the movements.

Always with more vigor and aggression.

I try to turn in bed, and a moan of pain escapes me. I pull the sheet off my body and observe my naked form; on my waist, there are some marks from yesterday's squeezes. On the sheet, I see dried blood, and that makes me feel ashamed. Did I sleep like this? I remember taking a few slaps, so I turn my body. My backside is red; my genuine reaction is to smile.

It was all so perfect for me.

I had never thought about this moment, but it couldn't have been better. As I sit up, I let out a brief moan; I'm sensitive down there.

The bedroom door opens slowly, and startled, I pull the sheet to cover my nudity. Skull enters the room, and when he sees me awake, he approaches the bed. He sits very close to me and pulls me in for a soft kiss.

"Are you okay?"

"Yes," I reply, unable to wipe the smile off my face. Skull gives me a brief smile. "Where did you go?"

His fingers touch my face, then tuck a strand of my hair behind my ear. Skull kisses me once more and pulls away. It feels like there are a thousand butterflies in my stomach, and my chest fills with a pleasant sensation. What was that?

"I went to the reception; the phone is silent. I asked them to bring you breakfast."

I nod, my gaze not leaving him. His blue eyes watch me closely, and I get lost in thought. If others looked at me so intensely, I would soon feel uncomfortable, but not with Skull. It's warm, comfortable; I feel nervous, yes, but it's not a bad feeling.

"Thank you for yesterday," I murmur, embarrassed, and he touches my chin. "Did you like it?"

"You don't have to thank me," he shakes his head and lets his gaze drift down my body. "It was one of the best nights I've ever had."

Hearing his words makes my heart leap in my chest, mingling with a wave of relief and joy. Skull enjoyed the night we spent together. His confession is like music to my ears, dissipating any trace of doubt or insecurity that might have crept into my mind.

But like a passing shadow, insecurity resurfaces, enveloping me in its invisible arms. One of the best nights he's ever had. Was I really able to satisfy him completely? Surely, Skull has had many more experienced women, and last night, I didn't do anything to please him. Tracy gave me tips, but I was so ecstatic that I didn't reciprocate at all. Just the kisses. A whirlwind of thoughts and worries begins to swirl in my mind, robbing me of the momentary peace his words brought.

Skull smiles and stands up.

"Aren't you going to take a shower?" he asks, and I quickly nod. "As soon as you eat and are ready, we'll leave."

I wrap the sheet around my body and, even though I'm sore, manage to get up and head to the bathroom. In front of the large mirror, I see my naked body. I turn to the side and observe more clearly the red marks on my backside, exact marks from the slaps on both sides. I enjoyed being spanked, but I would never say that out loud. I hold my breasts and feel them sensitive. Remembering the pleasure it brought when Skull practically sucked on them makes me thrum with a need for more.

Hearing a different voice in the room snaps me out of my daydream. I don't want to delay; I'm going to meet my mother and maybe my sisters. I smile in anticipation and open the drawer of the sink, grabbing a toothbrush and toothpaste. Would my mother recognize me? How would I introduce myself?

"Hi, my name is Eveline Novikov, and I'm your daughter!" I say to the mirror, but then I shake my head. "That's terrible." I accuse myself and take a deep breath. "Hi, Mom! I'm your daughter, the one who was in the orphanage."

I let out a sigh and place my hands on the sink. I really have no idea how to introduce myself. Not wanting to waste more time, I start brushing my teeth before taking a shower. My hair isn't dirty, so I decide not to wash it. After finishing my shower, I realize I didn't take the backpack, and even though I'm embarrassed and wrapped in a towel, I head back to the room.

Skull is sipping a cup of coffee when he sees me.

His hungry gaze travels over my body, and when I make a move to drop the towel, he slowly places the cup on the cart and approaches. His hands touch my arms, and anxiously, I wait for the kiss that comes swiftly. His lips take mine with intensity, and amidst the haze of desire, I taste coffee on his tongue. Being kissed by Skull is always so heated and electrifying. His lips explore mine with an overwhelming hunger, leaving me breathless and longing for more. The sensation of his strong hands around me sends shivers across my skin as our bodies draw close in a fervent embrace.

With the towel falling to the floor, I feel completely exposed before him, but also incredibly alive and excited. Wrapping my arms around his neck is like finding a safe harbor in the midst of a storm, and surrendering to him is all I desire at that moment.

With the intention of making that happen, I reach for his hand as we kiss and guide it between my legs. He quickly rubs his big finger over my intimacy, and then penetrates me with it. I pause the kiss and moan against his lips.

"Do you want to be mine once again?" he asks, and my first answer would be forever, but I just nod. "Aren't you tired?"

"Are you?" I retort with a sideways smile, but I'm startled when he looks at me seriously. "I..."

"You're very brave, Eveline," he warns softly, sending chills down my spine. "You have no idea how I held myself back this morning; if you knew, you wouldn't provoke me like that."

When I think about saying something, I'm thrown onto the bed. I bite my lip as I watch him take off his jacket, black t-shirt, and lower his hands to his jeans. I almost ask if we're going to be late, but I keep quiet. Being with Skull makes me forget the worries and fears I have. His gaze is fixed on me, and taking advantage of that, I run my fingers down my body, stopping in the middle of my legs. I rub my fingers there and let out a whiny moan. I'm sore but eager to feel him once again.

"I'll give you a chance," he begins, and I look at him anxiously. "To choose the position you want to be fucked in."

I gasp, not knowing what to say, then I watch him go to my backpack. I sit on the mattress; I don't know any positions. Just the one we did yesterday and the one on all fours, which I initially thought would take my virginity. He returns to me, and I'm impressed when he skillfully unwraps the condom along his length.

"I-I don't know positions," I reply. "What's your favorite?"

He quickly removes his shoes and climbs onto the bed, making it creak under his weight.

"I don't think you're ready for the position I have in mind, Eveline."

"I am!" I exclaim, kneeling. "I didn't give you pleasure yesterday, and that wasn't fair."

Skull frowns but smiles slightly.

"You think I didn't feel pleasure?" he asks, and I'm confused. "Eveline, Eveline... You took me from heaven to hell by surrendering to me. You drive me crazy!"

I smile and pull him in for a kiss.

"Then do as you said yesterday," I ask, gathering the courage to grab him by his cock. "I want it from behind, but... be careful."

I position myself, but his hand on my back makes me lean until my breasts and face are on the mattress. His tongue licks my entrance before penetrating me with it. Feeling his tongue inside my warmth is an intoxicating sensation. I grip the sheet tightly, and before I expect it, he gives me a hard slap. With one last lick, I open up even more for him.

"Do you like being spanked?"

"Y-Yes!"

He slaps me again, then pulls me by the waist until part of my feet is at the edge of the mattress. I then feel the glans rubbing against me and forcing its way in. Automatically, I push back for him, and perhaps taking that as an encouragement, he enters all at once.

I scream and lift my torso in shock, but soon I return to the same position.

My hair is grabbed forcefully, and I'm pulled back until my back is pressed against Skull. His lips travel along my neck, then he bites my nape.

"You will always be mine!" His rough voice, close to my ear, makes my body vibrate. "No matter what happens! Your body will always belong to me; did you hear me?"

"Yes!" I affirm, but I feel confused. His tone, though possessive, hints at a farewell.

Before I can question him, he throws me back onto the bed and forcefully pushes his hips against mine. My legs weaken, but I keep them firm. His hands grip my waist, pulling me as his hips return with force. Our bodies move in sync, at the same intensity, the heat igniting my body. I try to turn, but Skull quickly grabs my arm, pinning it behind my back.

I'm in pain, but I can't ask him to stop.

I try to pull my arm from his grip, and Skull allows it. Drunk with desire, I place my hands on the mattress and willingly begin to move against him. Then he stops and slaps me.

"Now roll your hips!"

I moan and look at him confused; realizing this, he holds my waist and shows me how to do it. I start rolling awkwardly, but soon get the hang of it. Each time I do this, I moan wantonly, unable to hold back. I let his cock slip out completely, then grip it and slowly bring it back in. I continue moving, being penetrated at my own pace, feeling multiple shivers running down my spine and bursting at my neck.

I knew what that was, and I smiled uncontrollably.

Perhaps noticing, Skull takes control again. He grabs my hair and penetrates me forcefully. I feel an absurd heat coursing through my body, tension building in my belly, and spasms taking over, making my moans louder. I continue trembling when I look back and see Skull removing the condom to cum on my backside. His muscles are tense, his breathing erratic, but soon he looks at me and rubs his glans against me.

He's sweating, just like I am.

Before pulling away, he gives me another slap on the ass. I would be more red than I already was. Skull goes to the cart and takes a large gulp of juice straight from the pitcher. I lie back, sleepy on the bed; my body is extremely tired. However, I know we need to leave.

"I don't know if I can go take a shower by myself," I say, and he sets the pitcher down in the same spot. I watch him approach, and when he's close enough, he lifts me into his arms as if I'm lightweight. My sensitive breasts press against his sweaty chest. "Want more?" I ask, surprised.

Then he smiles at me and walks with me to the bathroom.

"Are you already tired?" His tone is teasing. In response, I raise an eyebrow. "We're going to shower, then you'll eat, and we'll head out."

I smile. Would I always feel this way in his arms? Like we belonged to each other? I bring our lips closer and kiss him. Something more delicate, and surprisingly, he reciprocates. We kiss a little longer, and even though I don't want to, I take the initiative to start the shower. He sets me down, and under his gaze, I step under the showerhead.

Inevitably, I get my hair wet, but I don't care about that; I just want to have this time with Skull. And deep down, I wish every day could be like this.

CHAPTER FIFTEEN

Eveline

As soon as the car stops in front of a tree, I unbuckle my seatbelt. My gaze sweeps the neighborhood, and I'm enchanted by the beautiful houses, all in the same lovely style. I look at Skull, and he keeps his attention on the house in front of us. Then, I see a well-dressed man exit the house, followed by two girls—one almost my size and the other smaller. They get into the car and leave within seconds.

"Shall we?"

"Wait!" I ask nervously. "Do you think I look pretty in this outfit?"

I had picked out black jeans, a long-sleeved shirt, and boots. My hair is dry, straight as always, nothing too special.

"You're beautiful, Eveline. It doesn't matter what you wear."

I smile, feeling grateful, and follow him as he gets out of the car. We walk along the sidewalk, and my eyes scan the houses; everything is so quiet. We stop in front of a large residence, and Skull presses the doorbell. I adjust my hair, pulling it to the side, but quickly tuck it behind my ears. The door opens, and a woman in uniform smiles at us. She looks suspiciously at Skull but maintains a polite smile.

"Can I help you?"

"We'd like to speak with Professor Candice Adkins," Skull says when I don't respond. "Is she home?"

"Oh, yes. Mrs. Adkins is upstairs," she informs us, opening the door wider. "Please, come in. Who shall I announce?"

I enter and look around, impressed. The interior of the house is fully furnished, filled with photographs. I ignore the conversation between the two and move closer to the photos. I pick one up and see the blonde woman dressed as a bride, embraced by a man. I put the photo back and search for another. It's the girls we saw leave a few minutes ago; they're beautiful and resemble the woman. I approach another photo with the whole family and suppress a bad feeling.

Why am I not in that picture?

I hear a feminine voice just behind me, and I turn to see the homeowner descending the stairs. Her gaze lands on me, and she looks visibly startled. I approach in surprise; she seems so young, with shoulder-length blonde hair, and what catches my attention are her eyes—they're just like mine.

"Hi!" I smile and glance at Skull, who remains silent. "I don't even know how to introduce myself," I admit, somewhat nervously, and she swallows hard. "My name is..."

"I know who you are," she cuts me off in a rude tone that surprises me. "What are you doing here?"

This time, I'm the one who swallows hard.

"I-I wanted to meet you," I reply, and she shakes her head. "I..."

"You had no right to!" She interrupts me again. "Get out of my house, now!"

"Mrs. Adkins, I advise you to tone down your voice," Skull says, moving closer to sit in an armchair. My gaze returns to Candice. "You don't want to make a scene here."

"Make a scene?" she repeats, but then gestures with a cynical smile. "I want you to leave, and don't ever come back! It didn't occur to you—" she speaks to me this time, "—that if I wanted you, I would have you? Being in an orphanage in the middle of nowhere wasn't a hint?"

My eyes fill with tears.

"I just wanted to meet you," I murmur with a weak voice, my face burning with humiliation. "To understand why I was left."

"There's nothing to understand, Eveline. You should have accepted your fate, and that's it."

Skull stands up and pulls an orange envelope from his jacket. He hands it to Candice, who diverts her gaze to him.

"Accept which fate? The one that wants to kill her? We know your father worked at the government facility and was killed. You also went through there; now explain to me, Halina—" as soon as her real name is mentioned, she looks at him, startled. "What did your father discover? And please, don't waste my time."

She looks at me but soon returns her attention to the envelope. She opens it and begins reading silently. Minutes pass, and she shakes her head.

"You have no idea who you're messing with," she states and hands the envelope back to Skull. "You should have stayed in the orphanage! Why did you leave? The sisters were taking care of you!"

I'm confused.

"I was kidnapped from there," I confess, and she looks at me without understanding. "Skull rescued me."

"What do you mean? Kidnapped by whom?"

Skull stands beside me, arms crossed, his gaze meticulously analyzing the woman in front of us.

"The Diplomat hired me to rescue her," Candice looks at him, surprised. "He was afraid that if she fell into the wrong hands, their little secret would be discovered. However, he had other plans, like killing her."

I see her take a deep breath and glance at me quickly.

"How did you find me?" she asks, looking nervous. "Was it him?"

"No, but don't worry; the Diplomat might come after you. If you tell me what you know, I can stop him before that happens."

Candice sits on the sofa, her gaze troubled. She stays silent for a moment but then shakes her head.

"My father discovered that they were using some prisoners in biological experiments. Some substance found in a cave on the Asian continent; I don't remember exactly. He tried to gather evidence of what was happening because the things he saw were inhumane. Then he was killed, and I wanted to finish what he started."

"What did you do?" Skull asks.

"I put an end to it all," she murmurs; I see Skull's mouth open in surprise. "At the time, I got involved with that jerk; he swore eternal love to me, said he loved me. Until he found out who my father was and who I was. Months of relationship, and he ended it without even looking me in the eyes. I had the evidence; I could ruin his life and everyone around him. The Carter family would be destroyed politically for being complicit in all those atrocities. His guard dog found out I had the evidence and threatened me. But having that in my hands was my lifeline. I have money, and that made it easy for me to hide from his watchful eyes." She sighs and stands up again. "I wanted to start over, Eveline. I found out I was pregnant and didn't want you." As she utters those hurtful words, she begins to cry. "That's why I asked for you to be taken far away."

"If you didn't want me," I dry my tears and bring my hand to my back pocket. "Why did you leave this for me?"

I throw the picture onto the table in front of us; she picks it up.

"He's part of the past, just like you. Now get out! Don't go looking for trouble."

"Too late for that," Skull says, touching my arm. "Let's go." I nod and wipe my tears. "If you remember anything relevant, you can call this number."

Skull throws the card onto the table and gestures for me to leave. I walk past him, and when we're outside, we walk to the car. As soon as we get in, I allow myself to cry. My heart aches; I never imagined I would have such a reaction. Remembering her words hurts, especially in my chest. I glance to the side and see Skull watching me silently.

"Can we go, please?"

He nods and quickly starts the engine.

I try to stop crying the whole way, but it's in vain. If I had known it would be like this, I wouldn't have dared to show up at her house. I don't even know why I imagined her reaction would be positive. I'm such a fool. When we finally arrive at the hotel, I try to get out, but the door is locked.

"Skull...?"

He looks in the rearview mirror, then we hear a gunshot that shatters the back and front windows.

"Get down!"

I obey as he reverses, hitting something. The sound is loud and scares me. As he maneuvers the car to the other side, two vans stop in front of us. Skull curses, then, to my surprise, he accelerates, crashing into both cars. I turn in my seat and see a motorcycle following us.

"Skull!"

With a calmness that frightens me, he grabs his phone and types something. After a few minutes, he puts the phone away and reaches for his gun. We're taking an unknown route, with few people around, and I fear someone might get hurt. Skull rolls down the window and suddenly makes a sharp maneuver with the car. Without wasting time, with the gun cocked, he gets out and aims at the motorcyclist, firing three shots.

The motorcyclist falls abruptly onto the pavement, unconscious. Skull approaches. My anxious gaze sweeps the area, and then I see another motorcycle—just like the first—appear. Skull shoots at it, but this time it returns fire. I duck in fear of getting hit when I hear Skull curse.

With tears in my eyes, I see the black t-shirt he's wearing torn and blood oozing from the side of his body.

"Skull?!"

"It's okay! It was just a graze!" he reassures me as he sits down with difficulty. Then he touches my face. "I'll be fine; we need to get to the highway. I called a friend in the early morning; he's coming to pick us up. You'll be safe with him."

"What?" I ask, my heart racing. He drives at high speed, his gaze focused on the road. I can't take my eyes off his injury. "I'm not leaving you, Skull! You promised!"

"Eveline!"

"No! Let's go to a hospital; you're bleeding!" He shakes his head, and I take a deep breath. "Why are you so stubborn?!"

"My friend's name is Pablo."

"Let's go to the hospital!" I demand, and he ignores me. "I won't listen to you until you listen to me!"

Then he falls silent and presses on the wound.

In disbelief at such stubbornness, I close my eyes and shake my head. We're now on a highway with a desert landscape. There isn't a tree in sight, just some bushes and distant mountains on the horizon. Then, to my despair, Skull passes out, causing us to veer off the road. The car only stops when it falls into some sort of ditch. Desperate, I unbuckle my seatbelt and lean over him. I lift his shirt and see the gunshot wound. I grab my phone and dial the last number saved there; it barely rings before someone answers.

"I'm almost there, oh carajo!"

"H-He's been hit!" I cry, not caring anymore. "He passed out!"

"Where are you now?"

"I don't know!" I say, looking around; there's nothing. "We just left the city."

"I think I see you; if you hear the helicopter noise, get out of the car."

I frown, then hear a loud noise. I exit from the passenger side and look up. Shielding my eyes with my hand, I end the call and put the phone in my pocket. Two men jump out of a huge helicopter that blocks both highways and run towards us. I quickly turn back to Skull and grab his gun, aiming it at the newcomers.

"Hey, calm down niña, lower the gun," one commands. His gaze is cautious as he approaches. "I'm Pablo! You said he was hit?"

"Yes!" I lower the gun, and Pablo quickly takes it from me. He checks it, then stashes it behind his pants and runs to the driver. "Will he be okay?"

"Yes, he will," he asserts, and with the help of the other man, he supports Skull. "Grab what you need, and let's go."

I nod and grab our backpacks, opening the glove compartment to retrieve another phone. With everything in hand, I run after Pablo. He helps me get inside and closes the door. My gaze falls on Skull, who is asleep; I touch his face, praying he'll be okay.

"You don't need to worry," Pablo repeats as he assesses the wound. Then his fingers trace around Skull's injury and he smiles, showing me his fingers. "Exit wound; he'll be fine."

Incredulous, I watch him grab a first-aid kit. Didn't Skull have normal friends? Pablo pushes Skull's heavy body until he's on his side, and I quickly hold him against me. Then he takes a small bottle from the kit and takes a quick swig. After that, he pours some onto a crooked needle he has there and the rest on Skull's wound.

Immediately, he wakes up roaring in pain. His gaze finds mine, and he exhales deeply. Without holding back, I cry and lean our foreheads together.

"Are you okay?"

"Y-Yes!" I reply, a mix of fear and relief in my voice. "I thought you wouldn't wake up again."

He kisses my lips, not caring that his friend is watching us. Skull looks at him and nods.

"Thanks for coming."

"Don't make me cry," he says, focused on the thread and needle. When he finally gets it through the hole, he smiles. "This might hurt a little. How did you get shot?"

"We were going to wait for you at the hotel," Skull answers, his gaze on the wound, "but they were already there."

"Do you think you were followed?" Pablo asks as he begins to stitch up Skull's wound.

I divert my eyes, unable to handle the scene.

"I was careful," Skull says in a rough tone. "I need a plan to..."

"How about you rest a little?" Pablo interrupts, concerned. "You just got shot and you want to go for another one? She'll be even more scared."

Skull raises his gaze to me, and with a gentle gesture, wipes my tears. I feel a mix of relief and vulnerability in the face of his concern. His thumb continues to caress my face, and he only stops when he looks at his friend.

"Where are we going?"

"Home. You need to rest before you think about risking yourself again."

"Home?" Skull repeats and grimaces briefly as Pablo pulls the thread. "Yours?"

"We're going to Lanham; it will be kept safe until you recover. In two weeks, there will be a press conference with the candidates. Our darling, the favorite to win the election, will be there."

"Bastard!"

"Done!" As he says this, I check Pablo's work. The bullet wound is closed, but there's a lot of blood. He cleans it quickly and covers it from both sides. "Better than this, there isn't. In a few minutes, we'll land at a disused hangar; our ride is waiting for us there. Or did you think we'd come by car?"

"And still, yes, it took a while."

"For nothing!"

After retorting, he heads toward the seat next to the pilot. I stay there holding onto Skull. I want to ask him to forget about that Diplomat or President business, but I avoid speaking in front of others. My heart gradually calms, but every time I close my eyes, I can visualize the scene of him shot and passing out at the wheel.

If the bullet had been in another place, he wouldn't be here, and I wouldn't forgive myself. If there was any possibility of stopping this, I wouldn't think twice.

I feel a caress on my chin and look at him. I take his hand and place a kiss on it; we don't say anything, but his gaze is expressive. We fly for a few hours, but soon Pablo informs us that we have arrived. In the meantime, Skull has fallen asleep, and with help, we move him outside. As soon as I get out of the helicopter, I see a medium-sized plane right in front of us. I'm curious, but I don't say anything.

"When we get to the next hangar," Pablo says, watching two men carry Skull toward the plane, "we'll still have a 7-hour drive ahead. Quite the busy life, isn't it?"

I swallow hard and turn to face forward.

"Whose is all this?" I point, and he smiles.

"Mine," he informs and lets me go in first. "I won it in a bet; it's my favorite without a doubt."

Inside the plane, I observe everything with fascination. There are large seats that look very comfortable; I've never seen anything like this. At the end of the short aisle, I see Skull being placed on a bed. I walk up to him and sit close. Pablo thanks the two men and sits across from me.

"Want to tell me where you were before everything happened?"

I shake my head; I don't want to talk about my mother and her cruel words. I sigh as I look at Skull asleep, touching his scar and running my fingers down his beard. He looks so vulnerable there.

"It seems your relationship is quite advanced." I swallow hard but don't affirm or deny. "I'm not judging; I'm just surprised."

"I'm just a mission," I retort, this time looking at him. "Have you been friends for a long time?"

"Quite a while," he confirms, his gaze analyzing me attentively. "And I can assure you he cares about you."

I divert my gaze to Skull. I know he cares; his heart is good, but that's all it is. Deluding myself into thinking there's something more will only make me suffer. I adjust my hair to the side and look out the window. Pablo tells me to put on my seatbelt because we're about to take off. I comply, and when we're in the air, he tells me I can take it off. I lean my head back and close my eyes; I just want to live in peace. Maybe a family, children... I sigh; perhaps that dream will take a while.

I take one last look at Skull and decide to doze off. After all, we're safe here with Pablo.

CHAPTER SIXTEEN

Skull

I wake up in pain, and as soon as I open my eyes, I search for Eveline. I find her wrapped in a blanket, sleeping peacefully. I lean my body forward and, despite the pain, sit up. I scan the interior of the jet and then look out the window to get my bearings. It's night, and all I can see are the city lights.

"The sleeping beauty is awake." Pablo approaches, holding a mug. "You know it's been a long time since I saw your face?"

He offers me the drink and sits in the armchair.

I glance at Eveline, who is still asleep.

"Has she eaten?"

"Yes," he affirms as he watches me sip the coffee. "She only ate because I insisted; she wanted to wait for you."

I take another sip and look at him.

"Where are we?"

"We'll land in Virginia and then drive to the cabin."

I nod and lift my shirt, still wearing it; my wound is covered. I look at Eveline once more, allowing my thoughts to wander. It wasn't in my plans to get shot, not now that I'm so close to confronting the Diplomat.

"I need to know the exact location where they'll be," I say, and he sighs. "I can't let this opportunity slip away. If I let it go," I begin reluctantly, "the same thing will happen as five years ago."

Pablo doesn't move a muscle; he observes me in silence. Just when I think he's going to say something, Eveline stretches and opens her eyes. Upon seeing me awake, she throws off the blanket and hugs me. She squeezes me a little, causing me to groan in pain.

"I'm sorry!" she apologizes, but then smiles. "You slept the whole trip; I was worried, but Pablo said it was normal."

"I'm fine," I assure her, unable to hold back my smile. Then I remember that Pablo is watching us, and indeed, his gaze is surprised in our direction, so I look back at Eveline. "Did you manage to rest?"

"A little," she replies, her hand touching my face in a caress. "Does it hurt a lot?"

"Not really," my gaze shifts to Pablo, who stands up and leaves. Once he's gone, I look at Eveline. "Actually, maybe a little."

She quickly looks at me, concerned, and her hand goes down to my shirt, then lifts it. Up close, I can see the few freckles on her face; I hadn't noticed that before. Her left eye is green, and the other is blue. Both are so expressive, watching me as if they want to read my soul.

"Lie down a bit," she requests, and I obey. "I'll see if I can get something for the pain."

Seeing her about to leave makes me grab her hand. It's completely soft, her gaze still worried.

"I just need you to stay by my side."

Eveline pauses with a surprised look, but soon smiles and sits next to me. We stay there until Pablo announces the landing and gives the usual recommendations. The landing is successful, and from the corridor, I see my friend exiting the cockpit. He walks towards us, stopping with his hands on the backs of the chairs.

"Ready to go?"

He helps me stand, and we exit the jet. The cold night wind hits me; I quickly look back and see Eveline with our backpacks, looking around curiously. Then, as I look forward, I see my old jeep parked.

I analyze it quickly, and it seems to be just as I left it. Pablo, still helping me walk, chuckles.

"I took care of it lovingly," he mocks as we walk up to it.

With some difficulty, I sit in the back and wait for Eveline, who soon joins me. The backpacks are placed on the rack behind, and within minutes we're off. I watch Eveline, who looks extremely curious out the window, a smile escaping her lips, and I can't help but smile back. I divert my gaze forward and notice Pablo's look in the rearview mirror.

I adjust myself in the seat, which catches Eveline's attention.

"I can't imagine the pain you must be feeling."

"Skull in pain?" Pablo mocks, and I give him a serious look. "Don't worry, Eveline. He's used to it."

"That doesn't mean he doesn't feel pain."

Pablo smiles and goes silent. My instinct is to hug Eveline and tell her everything will be fine, that she doesn't need to be afraid anymore because I'll be with her, but I can't. I swallow hard and lean back comfortably. I close my eyes and allow myself a brief nap; my body is tired, as if all the accumulated stress has decided to overflow.

When I open my eyes again, I recognize the path we're following. Finally, we stop and get out. This is one of Pablo's cabins; I watch him as he quietly talks to Eveline. Not liking this, I move closer to them, positioning myself between them.

"Do you like it, Eveline?" he asks with his arms crossed. "This is a family heirloom; I renovated it some time ago."

"It's really beautiful," she comments, standing beside me. "You seem pretty rich."

"Yeah, I have a bit of money."

She nods, and we enter the cabin. Inside the very spacious living room, I see the huge L-shaped sofa, the fireplace being lit by one of the guards, the glass walls where the windows should be, and near a hallway, there's a staircase that likely leads to the upstairs bedrooms.

"Do you live in a house like this, Pablo?"

"Actually, no. Mine is smaller; I prefer to live in an isolated place. It's not like I can just appear in open spaces."

"What do you mean?" Eveline looks confused, which inevitably makes her beautiful.

"I have enemies, Eveline. I can't have a normal life. Like, a house in the city center, a wife and kids... I'll never be able to."

That hits me like a hint. I automatically look at Eveline; she watches us intently. She stays silent for a few seconds but soon nods.

"Apparently, I won't be able to either," she replies and sits on the sofa. "I have nothing, and maybe I never will."

"We could make a beautiful duo, couldn't we?"

I take a deep breath, catching the attention of both. My gaze is on Pablo, who smiles without concern.

"Well, I'm going to head out. Upstairs, there are clothes I brought just for her; I didn't expect to be shot. But I believe there's something of mine that will fit you, Skull. I bought supplies; they're in the kitchen." I nod, and he approaches me, extending his hand to the side, and one of the guards hands me my gun. "Upstairs, in the closet, there are some weapons and a first-aid kit. With what's up there, you'll be able to do other dressings."

"Thank you."

When he's at the door, he stops and turns to us.

"Oh! Eveline, he needs maximum rest. So, no sex for now; if he opens the stitches, he could die from bleeding."

I make a move to go to him, but the bastard quickly leaves the house. I return to Eveline, who is all red.

"Ignore him," I say, and she nods. "Are you hungry?"

I watch her stand up, and in a way I can't understand, she ties her hair back with her own hair.

"You stay here, and I'll see if I can find something for us to eat," she warns and hands me the remote for the big TV. "Try to distract yourself."

As soon as she disappears into the hallway, I let out a sigh and look once more at the bandage. I turn on the TV and start flipping through the channels. There's nothing that captures my attention; the only one on my mind is in the kitchen. My gaze goes to the hallway, and I decide to go after Eveline. I get up and feel a twinge in the wound, but I don't care. Slowly but surely, I make my way to the kitchen.

She is standing in front of the cooktop, her gaze is confused. She holds a pot of water.

"I don't understand," she murmurs without looking at me. "How do you turn this on?"

I approach her and stop by her side.

"It will only turn on if you place the pot on top."

Then she does so and smiles when the light on the screen turns on. I show her the functions, and she smiles at me.

"It wasn't like this in the orphanage," she warns, and I nod. "In the kitchen, there were three stoves, but they were different."

I nod to show I've heard, but my gaze doesn't leave her smooth movements. On the counter, there are two potatoes and two carrots. I notice the other ingredients are seasonings used in a soup.

"Since you're injured and it's cold," she starts looking at me. "I thought I'd make a vegetable soup."

"That sounds good."

"Tomorrow I'll take my time to see everything we have here," she promises, and I just nod. She smiles at me, and I feel like a fool responding the same way. It's so strange what I'm feeling. "Did Pablo serve with you?"

"No," I deny, and she looks at me, expecting more. When she realizes I'm not going to say anything else, she nods and goes back to cutting the potato. "I've known him for a long time, but it's for a different reason."

"That's fine," she smiles, but it doesn't reach her eyes. "Sometimes I forget that you don't talk much about your life."

I sit on the stool and grunt when I feel a twinge in the wound. She looks at me quickly but soon goes back to what she's doing. Her expression shows discomfort; noticing this, I let out a sigh. Maybe if I talk a bit, she won't feel so uneasy.

"We were once part of the same family," I reply, and she looks at me, surprised. "And after everything, we kept in touch; we have common interests."

"Enemies?" she asks, and reluctantly, I nod. "Does Miller know Pablo?"

"Yeah, they are the only people I trust and keep close."

After cutting the potatoes, she goes on to do the same with the carrots.

"Has Pablo ever been married?" she asks, and I shake my head, confused by that question. "So you were married to his sister?"

I'm completely taken aback; maybe my expression gave me away because she continues.

"It's just that if he wasn't married, and you didn't say anything about being raised together, that leaves only that answer. You were married, and what happened? Did she leave you? Did she die?"

"That's none of your business!" I shout, fearing what she might say next. "I won't allow you to meddle in my affairs!"

In anger, I get off the stool and walk to the bedroom. How could she have figured it out like that? Is it that obvious what happened? I take off my clothes in the room and head to the bathroom. Before stepping into the shower, I sit on the toilet with the lid down and let my mind wander. Gradually, I was forgetting some things about her, and it wasn't on purpose, but it's been a while since I've caught myself trying to remember her voice.

Sapphire.

Pablo's older sister, who worked in the police department, fascinated me when I first met her. Maybe it was her imposing aura, but at the same time, she was so attentive. Back then, I thought we could work out; we had chemistry. However, today I understand it was impulsive of me to propose. I smile remembering that she accepted without thinking twice. We married and lived five long years together—with ups and downs—but overall, everything was good.

I take a deep breath and go take my shower. I remove the bandage and toss it in the trash. Then my thoughts drift to Eveline; having her nearby is different from anything I've ever felt. With Sapphire, I had complicity and respect; we talked about everything. She told me about work and how she wanted to punch each of the clowns she worked with. The connection we had was unique, but nothing sexual, although the sex was good. We were two people with the same thoughts and conversations.

I frown at that realization.

With Eveline, it's different.

I've lost count of how many times my heart seemed ready to leap out of my mouth when she smiled at me or even when we kissed. That tingling in the pit of my stomach, wanting to protect her from everything and everyone, finally feeling at home, sheltered, safe? I shake my head.

"I can't be selfish again," I say aloud. "She deserves more. Safety, comfort, care, affection, love... Everything you can't offer."

I close my eyes and stand there for a few good minutes. I know the stitches might open, but my head is in a jumble. Finally, when I finish, my fingers are wrinkled. As I open the door, I see that Eveline has been there. The tray with the soup bowl is on the dresser. I approach and smell the delicious aroma coming from the food. With a spoon, I take some and savor it. I hold the bowl and head to the bed. When it's time to collect, I would apologize and make sure that this wouldn't happen again.

CHAPTER SEVENTEEN

Eveline

As soon as I leave Skull's dinner in his room, I head to the other one across the hall. I'm holding back my tears, but the moment I step into the room, I cry. I go to the bed and lie down with my weary body. Why didn't I just stay quiet and accept what Skull had to say for now? Discovering that he was once married surprised me, and by the way he reacted, maybe he still feels something for her.

I'm a complete fool because for a moment, when he was so affectionate with me, I imagined that a feeling might be arising. But now I realize it was just in my head. I recall our conversations from hours ago, and then I sit up when I remember something Pablo mentioned. He said he had clothes for me? Confused, I go to the dresser and open it; there are some women's clothes still with the tags on.

So if Skull hadn't been shot, would I be here alone?

I return to the bed and remain lying down.

Was it that easy to ignore my existence? Realizing that it is, I allow myself to cry more and curl up in the middle of the bed. I have no one, I am no one, and the fear of not knowing what to do consumes me.

I lie there and lose track of time, and when I think about getting up to take a shower, I hear the door open. Skull appears without a shirt, just in pants. My gaze sweeps over his scarred body and stops at his wound; there's a new bandage on it.

It's my fault that Skull was shot and nearly died.

"Please, leave me alone," I ask, and he stops by the door. "I'm sorry if I was rude; I don't want to interfere in your life in any way."

"Eveline..."

"Just let me be alone." My tears spill over, and I sit up. "You once told me I confuse you, but what about me? Everything about you is a confusion, Skull." As I accuse him, he watches me in silence. "During our first time, you treated me so well, you seem worried about me, and you're so affectionate, but a question of mine regarding you can start a war. Sometimes you make me forget that I'm just a mission for you."

"That's you saying that."

"No! That's what I can see," I retort, wiping my tears. "Actually, it's what you show me."

I lie back down, ignoring him.

When I think he's gone, I hear him speak in a low tone.

"What Pablo said is true," I look at him curiously. "Because of our way of life, we can't have a family, or kids, nothing. I thought I could, and it was the same as putting a target on Safira's head. Pablo's sister."

I see the internal struggle in his eyes, then I sigh.

"You don't have to tell me, Skull. It's not my business."

"The reason I said that in the kitchen," he continues, "was because I feared what you might say. The fact is I failed one person, and she died because of me."

"But it wasn't your fault," I murmur, and he shakes his head. "Skull..."

"That's why I told you I'm not a man for you," his voice is serious. "That's why I need to kill whoever it is, so you don't have to carry that fear."

"And then? Will you pretend you don't know me?" He looks at me surprised, then swallows hard. "Skull, we could run away together," I propose, kneeling on the mattress. "I don't care where, but if we're together..."

"My wife died, Eveline. She died because she was my weak point. There's no room for you in my life."

As soon as he finishes speaking, I feel a pain in my chest. A crushing pain that seems to tear my heart apart. I have no reaction; I just watch him leave the room. The moment the door closes, I lie back down and allow myself to cry.

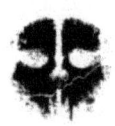

When dawn finally breaks, I remain in the room. A mix of sadness, shame, and heartbreak envelops me, along with a headache. I never thought I would go through this, and I wouldn't wish it on my worst enemy. With great effort, I get out of bed and head to the dresser. I open a drawer and grab a pair of black lace panties. They are so tiny that I find it impossible for them to cover anything. Since my backpack is still in the living room and I don't want to go downstairs right now, I take these. In the next drawer, I see some dresses, thicker fabric pants, and many blouses. I grab a flowery dress, the panties, and head to the bathroom.

After I'm ready and hungry, I go to the kitchen. To my surprise, Skull is sitting at the counter. He isn't wearing a shirt but has on the same pants as yesterday. I want to ask about the bandage and whether the wound bothered him last night, but remembering his words hurts me, so I ignore him. His gaze slowly sweeps over my body, almost like a caress. In front of him is a plate with scrambled eggs, bacon, and juice. There's another plate prepared, and I walk past it, heading to the fridge. I grab the pudding I saw the day before and look for a spoon in the drawer.

"I made our breakfast."

I remain silent, having no desire to respond. I take a spoonful of pudding and moan in satisfaction; I've never eaten anything as delicious as this. I start to walk out.
"Are you going to ignore me now?"
I glance at him and leave the room.
What does he expect me to do? To pretend nothing happened? Or that his words didn't hurt me? I know there was never a promise for us to be together as man and woman, but I still feel betrayed, hurt, upset.
I sit on the sofa and watch the daylight flood through the huge glass windows. It's warm, unlike last night, which was freezing. I try to focus my mind on something else, but it always betrays me and brings back yesterday's words. I spend a few minutes staring at the pudding, considering the possibility of going back to Chicago with Ellen. She invited me, and maybe I could help in the kitchen, cooking or cleaning. I don't necessarily have to sleep with anyone.
Minutes pass, and I hear Skull's footsteps approaching.
Without saying anything, he sits beside me and turns on the TV. I pull my legs up on the sofa—against my chest—and while I eat, I watch the cartoon on the screen. Out of the corner of my eye, I notice Skull is looking at me. If he thinks I'm going to speak, he's very mistaken. My pudding is almost gone, and in an attempt to savor it, I start to coat the spoon and slowly lick it.
"Your soup was really good."
I glance at him, then lick the coated spoon. His eyes follow my movement, and I see him take a deep breath as he adjusts himself on the sofa. Is he in pain? I lower my gaze to his bandage, and it seems fine. I return my attention to the TV. Why is Skull suddenly more talkative than usual? As soon as I finish, I stand up and head to the kitchen. After washing and putting away the spoon, I return to the living room. Skull has a serious expression, arms crossed.
I sit at the edge of the sofa and let out a sigh.

"Are you going to stay silent with me forever?"

"Will it make any difference to you?" I retort without taking my eyes off the TV. "Ignoring my existence isn't hard."

"I'm worried about your safety."

"That's fine! I don't care about that, Skull."

He turns off the TV, and I face him.

"I know I hurt you last night, but I'm thinking of your well-being," he says, and I watch his lips. "All of this is for you; if I didn't care, I would leave."

"I know," I nod, taking a deep breath to avoid crying. "I appreciate you putting yourself at risk for me, and don't worry about me when it's all over; I already know what I'm going to do." As I speak, he watches me intently. "Ellen invited me to stay with her and the girls. Maybe I'll help in the kitchen; I don't know. I don't think I could sleep with other men."

His gaze is incredulous.

"Are you serious?"

"Yes, she invited me. And since I can't go back to the orphanage or stay with my mother, that's all I have left."

"You can go to several other places."

"I'm not going to venture into other cities I don't know. I'm not that brave, Skull. So if Ellen accepts me, I'm going."

I notice he wants to argue, but he seems to hold back. However, his gaze doesn't leave me.

"You're not going there!"

I frown and cross my arms.

"I am going! Maybe there I'll even meet a nice guy who really wants me and not just to warm his bed."

I stand up and walk past him. However, my arm is grabbed, and Skull stands in front of me.

"Do you think I think that of you?" he asks aggressively. "That you were just another one in my bed?"

"Let go of my arm!" I command, and he pulls me closer. "I don't think anything, Skull! But you know what I've realized?" I question, allowing myself to cry. "That our last time together was a goodbye! Because even promising me you wouldn't leave, you planned to put me here and go. Doesn't it cross your mind that I have feelings? That after losing my mother, losing you would hurt me too? What do you think I am?" After my numerous questions, he remains silent. "How do you think I feel knowing that to you, I'm disposable?"

I free myself from his grip and turn my back to him.

"What do you think they will do, Eveline?" he asks, and I turn to him. "When they find out you're my weakness?" I look at him in surprise, waiting for him to step closer until he's right in front of me. "I won't be able to handle it if something happens to you. There's no space for you in my life because I'm afraid of losing you. I can't ask you to stay with me. I would be sentencing you to death."

His fingers touch my cheek, and I feel his thumb dry a tear of mine.

"You can't decide that for me, Skull," I murmur, holding his hand. "You need to give me the chance to choose."

"Please, Eveline."

"I want to be with you!" I declare, and he smiles, but then shakes his head. "When we kiss, or even when you just look at me, it feels like I have a thousand butterflies in my stomach. These are feelings I've never experienced before."

"A thousand butterflies?" he repeats, and I smile and nod. "You deserve more, Eveline. I don't have a home; I move from city to city."

"I don't care," I respond firmly. "I would live with you isolated from everyone. In fact, I would love to live in a smaller house than this one. Maybe with a few animals and a big garden."

Skull seems surprised, remaining silent for a few minutes before nodding.

"I would too, Eveline. I still think you're making a big mistake wanting to be with me, but the thought of you with someone else or far from me drives me crazy just imagining it."

I smile, resting my hands on his chest.

"So what do we do? You're not going to leave me again, are you? I choose to be with you."

I see him swallow hard but agree.

"I just need to finish what I promised before we can be together," he murmurs, and I nod with a sigh. "Is that okay?"

"That's fine," I agree and kiss his lips. I try to pull away, but he pulls me back. "What's wrong?"

"Don't ignore me anymore."

"You deserve it," I warn, and he hugs me. "You made me cry all night."

"Forgive me," he pleads and kisses my lips. "I have to be careful with your vengeful side; I was surprised."

He sits down and makes me stay by his side.

"What do you mean?"

"You ignored me, didn't eat the breakfast I made for you as an apology, and licked that spoon in front of me. Leaving my cock hard and jealous."

Embarrassed, I look away; so he enjoyed watching?

"You also like to ignore some of my questions," I comment, crossing my arms. "So you know how I feel."

"I won't do that anymore."

I stretch towards him and take his lips in a kiss. Skull holds my face and tilts it, deepening our contact. His tongue rubs against mine, and with a sudden movement, he tries to pull me onto his lap. However, I stop him.

"What?" he questions, close to my lips.

"No." I shake my head, and he looks at me surprised. "You're injured; remember? No sex."

"But we can."

"Not like this." I smile and stand up. "Want to see something?"

"What?" he asks, rubbing his hand across his beard. Skull really is impatient.

As I stop in front of him, I lift my dress, showing my tiny black lace panties. He brings his hand to his cock and squeezes it over his pants. Still looking at him, I turn my body to show my ass, and I'm surprised when I feel a strong smack. He turns me back to face him, rubs two fingers against my intimacy, and when they invade inside my panties, I let out a sigh but quickly push him away.

"There are many more in my drawer," I smile while fixing my dress.

I feel my intimacy craving, but I won't put his life at risk. The look in his eyes, a mix of anger and contained desire, makes me laugh more.

"Evil, Evil," he calls me, and I'm surprised by the nickname. "What do I need to do for you to sit that sweet pussy on my tongue?"

I feel a shiver run through my entire body and swallow hard. My gaze goes to the bandage, and I'm afraid of worsening his condition. Before I can say anything, Skull pulls down his pants, exposing his erect member. The sight of him looking at me, his hand moving up and down with a suffocating slowness on his cock, makes me burn with desire.

"It seems you're not taking what Pablo said seriously," I say, but my eyes are on his thick length. It's so pleasurable to see his hand working around it. "You could die from bleeding if the stitches open."

"He's being dramatic," he replies, lowering his body a bit more while keeping his legs spread. "Now take off those panties, and don't make me tell you again."

CHAPTER EIGHTEEN

Skull

I continue to masturbate without averting our gazes. Then Eveline bites her lip, looks at the large window beside us, but soon obeys. My eyes trace the path of her panties until they're gone. I stretch out my hand in a silent request, and she hands me the piece. I bring the lace to my nose and inhale; Eveline looks shy in front of me.

"Come here."

"Skull, you're hurt," she retorts without moving. "Why are you so stubborn?"

"Don't worry, *Evil*ine," as soon as I say this, she crosses her arms. "I won't exert myself, but you will."

"Don't call me Evil," she requests as she approaches. "I'm not bad."

I lower my body, practically lying on the sofa, feeling a sharp pain in my wound, but I show no sign of pain.

"When you want to be naughty," I murmur, placing my cock against my stomach. "You do it with excellence." She shakes her head, but her gaze is on my erection. "Now be nice, and take care of it."

"What do you want me to do?"

I make a motion with my finger, and she turns her back to me. Without penetrating her, I make her sit on my cock. Her wet pussy is on top of my erection, and with both hands on her waist, I show her what she should do.

"You're going to rub yourself nicely on my cock," I warn, gathering her dress at her waist. "And if you stop before the time, you'll get a spanking."

She looks back at me over her shoulder and nods obediently. I turn my attention back down and swallow hard as Eveline slowly begins to move, rocking back and forth. I let out a brief groan and place both hands on her waist, squeezing and pulling her closer to me. She's so wet that I feel her desire slicking my cock, making me imagine being inside her at that very moment.

As soon as I hear a moan escape her lips, I grab her blonde hair and pull it aggressively. Eveline moans louder but doesn't complain; on the contrary, I see her push her body toward me and quicken her movements. I release her hair for a moment, then she stops and looks at me. I quickly give her two strong slaps on her ass, and she smiles at me.

"Did you do that on purpose?"

"No," she denies, still looking at me, and resumes her movements, "but I like it when you pull my hair."

I smile at that and, with just one hand, gather her blonde hair into a ponytail. She lets out a whiny moan as I make her arch more and rub her slick intimacy against me. I can see the pre-cum oozing from my cock, and I feel chills running through my body. My groan comes out huskier, she moans loudly, and even while trembling in my lap, she doesn't stop moving.

Her moans in my lap drive me crazy for more.

With a few more movements, I finally come on my stomach. I hug her around the waist, and we moan together. Eveline still writhes on top of me, and I watch. Seconds later, I hold my cock by the base and rub it all over her intimacy. It glides easily between her little lips, and I hold myself back from penetrating her forcefully.

"You drive me completely crazy, Eveline."

"You make me feel the same way," she replies weakly, but soon stands up. "Now you're going to clean yourself and rest."

"But we're not done yet," I say, pointing to my hard cock. "I need you, Eveline."

"I need to prepare our food, you know?" she asks, adjusting her dress. "And you were shot; why is it so hard to understand that?"

"Eveline, a bullet is nothing to me," I warn, looking into her eyes. "I've taken worse than this, and I'm still here. Firm and strong, healthy..."

"But I'm saying you're going to rest and recover first," she states, arms crossed. "Or I'll make a point of sleeping only in my tiny panties next to you, and you won't have the right to touch me."

I'm surprised, even more so when she smiles challengingly. Am I creating a monster?

"You wouldn't dare," I murmur confidently, and then Eveline smiles openly.

"Just know that Ellen taught me many things," she comments in a teasing tone. "And I haven't used all of those lessons with you yet."

I take a deep breath and watch her pick up the panties to put them on.

"And when do you plan to do that?"

She smiles, leaning her body until her hands rest on my thighs.

Her lovely scent makes me close my eyes, but soon I look back at her. Her red lips, so inviting to me, are mere inches from mine.

"If you behave, who knows?" she kisses me quickly and pulls away. "I just want you to get better soon. I'm afraid it will worsen; we can't even go to the hospital, and we're in the middle of nowhere. I don't know how to drive, and what if we need to run? Or I don't know. So be nice, okay?"

I notice her worried expression and decide to comply with her wishes, but she won't escape tonight.

"All right."

She smiles and kisses my cheek.

I sigh and watch her disappear down the hallway. I shift my gaze to my slick stomach and stand up, but before leaving the room, I grab both backpacks. Upon reaching the bedroom, I go to the bathroom and clean myself up. I'm still in front of the mirror when I hear a phone ringing. I go to it, which is in my backpack, and answer on the fourth ring. It's Miller.

"Yes?"

"Pablo told me you got shot?"

"I didn't know you guys were gossipers," I say as I walk to the bedroom window, "but I'm glad you called. I need help; I need you to find a young woman named Abby."

"Abby from Abigail? Abela? Abriele?"

I furrow my brow.

"She's Eveline's friend," I reply, heading toward the exit. "She lived at the orphanage. On the day of the raid, she had gone into town. She's blonde, younger than Eveline, with blue eyes."

"Pretty uncommon, huh?" Miller mocks, and I remain silent as I go down the stairs. "But fine, I'm used to working with you. I'll see what I can find out. If you need anything, just let me know."

"Thank you."

I end the call and tuck the phone into my sweatpants pocket. I head to the kitchen and stop at the doorframe. Eveline already has some things cooking, and I stand there quietly watching her. It doesn't take long for her to notice me and smile. I return the smile, but I can't fully shake off my concerns. I opened up to her in a way I'm not used to; I shared my fears and had already resigned myself to the fact that we wouldn't be together. However, I received a declaration and her certainty that she wants to be with me.

We're both crazy, for sure.

Her gestures are so gentle that I become hypnotized by the scene. I must look like a lovesick fool. Realizing this, I stop smiling, totally surprised. Am I really in love with Eveline this quickly?

"What's wrong?" she asks, alarmed, as she approaches. "Is your wound hurting?"

She examines the bandage, but upon seeing that it's fine, she looks at me. I haven't felt all these emotions in a long time, and analyzing them, I'm sure they don't compare to what I thought I felt before. Having Safira was something different, but now? The feeling of being at home, my heart racing, a flutter in my stomach, or rather... a thousand butterflies in my stomach. I smile uncontrollably. All these feelings are, in a way, new to me.

"You know what happens if you ignore me, right?"

Eveline smiles provocatively, and I nod.

"I'm aware of that," I affirm, and she returns to what she was doing before. "What are we having for dinner?"

"Since I don't know what you like," she shrugs without looking at me, "I'm making meatloaf and steamed asparagus. I saw we have some berries, so I thought dessert could be a pie."

I nod a bit surprised by the menu. I remain silent for a few seconds before letting out a sigh.

"I like berry pie," as soon as I say this, she looks at me with a smile. "I like meatloaf and macaroni and cheese."

Eveline tries to suppress her smile, but it's in vain. I want her to know me, but I'm still hesitant to talk about everything I've done.

"And asparagus, do you like it?"

"Not much."

"But you're going to eat it," she murmurs, and I nod obediently. "When I finish here, I'll start on the pie. I hope you like it."

"Do you need help?"

I watch her grab a dish towel and dry her hands.

"I need you to go rest," she says, and I sigh while nodding. "When everything's ready, I'll let you know. You being hurt isn't going to help here."

She comes closer and gestures for me to leave, but before I go, I steal a kiss. Eveline watches me with a smile, and my heart warms in that moment.

I head to the living room and settle onto the sofa. Would it be strange for me to start making plans for us? Maybe buy a house on a farm? Somewhere warmer and isolated from dangers. I turn on the TV and then see him. The bastard is talking about the president's upcoming trips and how excited they are about the campaign. I curse myself for allowing myself to be hit because by now, I would have dealt with both of them. My thoughts drift to Candice, Eveline's mother, and how strong her words were. The fact that she knows about her daughter and hasn't kept her close makes me curious. I didn't mention anything to Eveline because I know it's a sensitive topic, but I'd like to understand her reasons.

From what I could gather, her words didn't come from hatred but rather concern. Fear.

If Eveline's whereabouts were a secret, how did the Diplomat find out? Did someone contact him? If so, who? Candice isn't on the list of suspects, but someone who lived with Eveline might be. Someone with an interest in gaining something from that information? Someone higher up in the orphanage's hierarchy?

I grab my phone and check the news from the month. Nothing has been reported about the orphanage, as if the case had been buried, and I only know one person who has the power to do that.

The president.

I let out a sigh and gather more information in an attempt to better understand what I have available.

From what Candice implied, the only ones who knew about Eveline were her and the sisters. Then I remember something about

Eveline's file being open on the director's desk. Could it have been her? She would have her reasons; after all, maintaining an orphanage isn't cheap, and without government help, things get worse. The fact that they had to choose between staying to work or leaving says a lot about the financial situation of the place.

I spend a few more minutes thinking when Eveline approaches with a glass of juice and smiles at me.

"Lunch is going to take a little while."

I take what's offered and take a sip. Her smile is so beautiful; how can anyone think of doing her harm? It's inevitable; I'm completely in love with Eveline. Realizing that I am, in fact, in love, makes me tense.

I thank her and watch her go.

Her walk is graceful, the dress is short, and I remember her indecent panties. How can she show them to me and not let me taste them? To feel her flavor on my tongue, her warmth around my cock, to hear her whiny moans... I try to change the direction of my thoughts, but gradually I feel my cock harden.

I look down and squeeze it, stifling a groan.

After a few hours, Eveline calls me to eat, and as soon as I arrive in the kitchen, I see the plates already set on the counter. I approach and sit down to start the meal. I taste it hungrily and am surprised by how delicious it is. Eveline mentions that the pie is in the oven, which delayed the preparation, but I quickly assure her that it's okay. She didn't need to put in so much effort, but in return, I receive an answer that leaves me speechless.

"I want to take care of you, Skull. While you're here, I'll do everything I can to make you feel comfortable."

Just being with her makes me feel comfortable. Having her in my arms, receiving her smiles and trust. I realize I need to open up more.

We talk about how huge the cabin is and how the night before she wanted to see the other rooms. Every moment she spoke, I found myself analyzing her so thoroughly. Listening to her voice and watching her while she talks brings me peace; it makes me focus solely on her. Her beautiful, well-shaped lips, her white teeth, her sharp nose, and her rosy cheeks.

Her blonde hair is dull, but it doesn't detract from her beauty.

When she notices she's being stared at, she stops talking, and I frown.

"You can continue."

"No," she denies, taking a sip of water. "You must be thinking about something important while I'm rambling on."

"You can talk, Eveline; hearing your voice calms me."

She smiles at me, and I can't help but notice her face turning a shade of red. Is she embarrassed? I smile and reach for the glass of water. We finish eating, and while the dishwasher works, I head to the living room with Eveline. I sit down and patiently wait for her to sit beside me. With the remote in hand, she searches for a movie on the TV, and when she finds one, she snuggles up to me. I wrap my arm around her shoulders and sigh.

That's what I want.

Peace, Eveline, and a life together.

"In the orphanage, we didn't watch movies," she says, and I watch her. "We had other chores, and even the computers were old. The internet didn't work properly."

"I don't like those movies," I warn, and she looks at me. "They exaggerate some events, especially action ones. There's no way a guy can jump from the sixth floor and still run. Either he breaks something or dies."

She nods, and I see several questions in her eyes.

"What was it like in Afghanistan?" she asks, and I notice her curious gaze. "What exactly did you go there for?"

I swallow hard but decide to respond. She needs to know me, after all.

"A few operations, mostly to combat terrorism," I reply, and she turns her body toward me, paying attention to what I say. "To promote stability in the region; there are good people there who don't deserve to pay for the actions of terrorist groups."

I notice her breathing change; she remains silent, but it doesn't last long.

"Those men in the cabin..." she murmurs, then swallows hard. "Were they terrorists?"

"Mercenaries," I correct her and inevitably recall my actions. "Forgive me for that."

"It's okay, I..."

"No," I gently interrupt her. "If they had done something to you, I wouldn't be able to forgive myself. When they passed me that call, it was the diplomat himself who warned me that he was arriving and that I didn't need to worry about you, that nothing would happen to you. I went, but I couldn't really go."

She cries, perhaps remembering.

"You came back and saved me," she says, and I caress her cheek. "I don't want to remember that, Skull."

"Okay." I affirm, my eyes not leaving her lips. "I just need you to know that you'll never be hurt again, okay?" I receive a nod and a kiss. She tries to pull away, but I hold one side of her face to deepen the kiss.

Feeling her lips, the way she kisses me, keeps me ignited and alive like never before. Taking advantage of her being lost in the kiss, I pull her to sit on my lap. She tries to protest, but I won't allow it and demand the passionate kiss that burns me everywhere. I move my hands down to her waist, hips, stopping at her ass, where I squeeze firmly. Our tongues intertwine erotically, and I pull her closer.

Eveline interrupts the kiss and looks at me.

"You're not going to rest, are you?" She smiles, but to my surprise, she lowers the neckline of her dress. Her medium-sized, firm breasts, with pink nipples pointing in my direction, make me curse softly, and before she can do anything, I take one breast into my mouth.

I suck and nibble on the nipple, savoring it with hunger and desire. I do the same with the other, receiving a whiny moan, and just when I think of continuing, she stops me. I watch her trembling hands move to my pants and open them. My cock is already hard, and I eagerly await her reaction.

She gives me a kiss and gets off my lap. I'm about to complain, but I stop when I see her pull my underwear with my pants and then take off her own panties. I hold my cock upright, eager to feel her slowly descend onto it. However, she snuggles back onto my lap like we did earlier, but this time she looks me in the eye.

"I liked the sex we had this morning," she warns, and in slow movements, she starts rubbing against my cock. "Did you like it too?" Her voice comes out as a whisper.

I grab her face and kiss her passionately. My hot body is in search of relief.

"I wanted to bury myself in you," I say, and with a swift motion, I stand up, holding her firmly. "I can't wait any longer."

Eveline kisses my face, neck, and finally my lips.

As soon as we reach the bedroom, I lay her down on the mattress and position myself on top of her. I rub my erection against her slick folds, and I see her squirming beneath me while letting out whiny moans. I grip my cock at the base and press against her opening, then remember the condom. I curse and, reluctantly, get out of bed to go to Eveline's backpack in search of the leftover condoms.

On the bed, she takes off her dress and kneels, waiting for me.

Now wearing the condom, I watch her smile and beckon me with her finger. I try to get on top again, but this time she makes me sit down and climbs onto my lap.

CHAPTER NINETEEN

Eveline

I'm completely trembling, but I know exactly what I need. Skull lies down and adjusts the pillows behind him. His fingers penetrate me, and involuntarily, I close my eyes. Then, I see his wound, just below the ribcage, slightly stained with blood. In that moment, I become worried, perhaps sensing this, Skull watches me.

"Don't worry about it," he pleads, stroking my thighs. "If you stop there, yes, I might die with the purple balls."

Amid my concern, I smile and shake my head. I push away his hand that grips his shaft and carefully guide it to my folds. I rub the robust head all over my intimacy, forcing it into my tight entrance and moaning softly. I feel the glans invade me and stop right there. He hasn't even fully entered, but I know it won't be easy to move in that position.

"Take me all the way, Eveline."

I look at him scared and shake my head. I place my hands on his chest and slowly move back. I feel him go in a bit more, and I automatically bite my lower lip. With both hands on my waist, he forces me down and then gives me a smack.

Before I can say anything, I hear a muffled rumble in the background. I stop startled and look toward the window.

"Was that thunder?"

"Are you scared?" he asks, and when I meet his gaze, he realizes that I am. "Come here."

I lean over his body and stifle a moan as my breasts press against Skull. His hands travel down my back; I feel him sink into the mattress and penetrate me forcefully. I arch my back on top of him and then take his lips for myself. Our bodies are on fire, and his hand leaves a hot trail as it glides over my body. Skull starts to move with me on top, and each time he enters, I feel like I'm going to heaven. I toss my hair to the side and kiss Skull's lips, loving how his beard grazes my face.

The sound of our hips colliding forcefully and our moans echo throughout the room. I can barely think straight, and the only thing I can do is beg for more.

"Skull!" I moan, my hips adopting the rhythm he sets. "More..."

I sit up straight and squeeze my breasts as my body vibrates. Then, wanting to intensify the sensations, I start bouncing, calling for Skull. I feel him slide inside me so fast and intensely. I'm completely soaked down there, but he doesn't seem to care. He quickly sits up and pulls me close. Gripped around my waist, he stands up with a swift motion. His strong, tattooed arms hold me easily; I hardly feel heavy.

His blue eyes lock onto mine, and holding onto him, I kiss him, feeling him penetrate me again in that position. It's incredible because I can perfectly feel him invading me deeply and then pulling back slowly to thrust powerfully. Choked with so many delicious sensations, I break the kiss and struggle to catch my breath. Skull breathes the same way, but his gaze never leaves me.

I want this.

I want to surrender to Skull every day, confide what's going on in my head, sleep in the same bed, share my life with him. My chest warms just imagining having him every day, receiving his rare smiles, his protective way... I want it all!

I kiss his scar and trail kisses down his beard and neck.

Sensations begin in my lower abdomen, and when I realize it, I'm trembling in Skull's arms. I contract tightly and let out a loud moan. He keeps moving, lasting a few minutes, but finally, he moans in my ear and grips me under my thighs. I can't feel my legs, which feel like jelly. He holds me against him for a good while, but soon lays me back on the bed, and I watch him take off the condom filled with a white liquid.

Skull ties the end and heads toward the bathroom.

In the room, I smile as I stretch out on the mattress. Once again, I had sex with Skull, and it was even better than the first time. A cold breeze sweeps in through the window, and I notice the rain. I pull the sheet to cover my body and gesture to close the window. However, Skull comes out of the bathroom and gestures with his hand. He goes to the window and closes it, then returns to the bed.

"Looks like it's going to rain all night," he says as he lies down, and I quickly snuggle up to him. "I like the rain."

"I don't," I warn, lying on his chest. "And your wound? Does it hurt? Let me see?"

"It doesn't hurt; you don't need to worry, Eveline. I have iron health; it'll heal."

"You're stubborn, that's for sure."

He smiles at me, and once again, the thousand and three butterflies are there in my stomach.

"So you don't like the rain?" His voice sounds lazy.

I trace a scar on his chest.

"No, at the orphanage, there were lots of leaks, and one annoying one right above my head in the dormitory," I remember with a small smile. "When it rained like this, I slept with my clothes on, but then my feet would get wet. I even slept in the same bed as Abby, but director Aaron scolded me."

"Really?"

"Yes," I affirm and sit up to look at him better. "During the last rain, the wall collapsed. I had two uniforms and four pairs of underwear. None for cold. We didn't have many things there."

"I can imagine," he comments, his fingers touching my face. "They weren't tiny panties, were they?"

I smile, shaking my head.

"They were more modest, but these new ones are interesting. I looked pretty good in them... Ellen told me that men find them sexy, but I thought I looked sexy."

Skull crosses his arms, his gaze narrowing.

"I would really like to know what else Ellen has been teaching you."

I let a cheeky smile slip out, then shrug as if I don't care about what I'm about to say.

"A few things about sex, like how I could drive my future boyfriend crazy with excitement. Things like that."

"Your future boyfriend?" His gaze narrows toward me.

"Yeah," I try to hold back my smile, but I can't. "Some guy I might happen to meet."

"I thought the lessons were meant to be used on me."

I swallow the urge to laugh and continue.

"You were too busy thinking about Layla," I say, and automatically feel a pang of jealousy. "I can't believe you let her kiss you."

"It was on the neck."

"Doesn't matter," I retort, and he pulls me into an embrace. "That guy, Liam, you didn't let him get close to me."

"You know very well why I didn't."

His tone is serious; Skull seems to be jealous.

"He wanted to take me to my room."

In a swift move that startles me, he positions himself above me.

"You are mine!" His voice is intense, sending shivers down my spine. "Your body, your smiles, everything Eveline is mine. And if any man tries to touch you, you can be sure I'll take care of him."

"And are you mine?" I question boldly, my voice unwavering. "I'll only be completely yours if you're mine, Skull."

To my surprise, he takes my hand and places it on his chest, over his heart.

"As long as I live, I...," I see him swallow hard, "Ryder Marshall, will be yours. There will be no one else, only you." Then he smiles at me, but quickly becomes serious. "I don't know what you've done to me, Eveline, but I only think about you."

Ryder Marshall? He only thinks of me? I'm completely taken aback. My smile is so genuine that it is soon returned.

"I don't know what I've done to you either, Ryder Marshall," I say, and then he kisses my lips. "But lately, I only think about you."

"It will be our promise," he whispers against my lips. "Okay?"

"Okay," I smile and pull him in for a kiss. Amid our fog of desire, thunder cracks in the sky, making a loud noise. "I really don't like thunder."

His fingers trail down my back, and I gradually begin to calm down. I rest my head on his chest and listen to his serene breathing.

"When I was younger, I was also afraid of thunder," he murmurs, and I look at him. I can see his well-defined jaw and the huge scar that crosses his face. "I got over it when I was a teenager. In fact, when I started my military career."

"Did you meet the Diplomat there?"

"No, after I was discharged from military service," his voice lowers. I stay silent, waiting for him to finish. "For inappropriate conduct," he murmurs, seeming cautious. "I started doing some freelance work."

"What do you mean?"

Skull takes a deep breath, and even while waiting, I'm attentive.

"I've worked as a debt collector, a hitman..." He pauses, and I can feel his tension. I gently touch his chest, making soft movements over his scarred skin. "I killed those responsible for Safira's death. One by one. When I was hired to save you, I had just killed a group from a cartel."

"They were also responsible for her death?"

"No, that was another matter." He comments, then looks at me. His brow is furrowed. "When I said I made many enemies, I wasn't joking, Eveline."

"I want to be with you, Skull."

His smile calms me, and I bury my face in his chest again.

"I think you're crazy."

"Maybe I am," I retort, my fingers touch a scar near his neck. "What happened there?"

"Glass shrapnel," he replies, then holds my hand and kisses my fingers. "I like it when you touch me. It's gentle; it brings me peace."

"I like it when you talk like this," I smile and touch his scar on his face. "And when you're affectionate."

I hope he continues to open up, but he falls silent. Out of respect for him, I simply accept it. Then he starts to speak again.

"In Colombia, I was kidnapped by enemies and subjected to interrogations. This scar on my face was a gift from them."

I sit up startled and pull the sheet to cover my breasts.

"Kidnapped? Why?"

"We had taken their support base, and two rebels died. I was going to open fire on a group, but I couldn't."

"Why not?"

Skull looks at me uncertainly, diverting his attention as if he's thinking about it, but soon he stares back at me.

"They used children as shields." As he responds, I swallow hard. "Then I was kidnapped and kept in one of their buildings. But I managed to escape; I was missing some nails, my face was torn, but I got out."

"D-Did you think about continuing with that?" I ask, frightened. "I mean..."

"No," he interrupts me, and I feel calm. "Saving you would be my last job."

I nod and suppress some tears. For a moment, the possibility of something like that happening to him knocked the wind out of me. A tightness in my chest, a bad feeling.

"I didn't change your plans too much, did I?" I murmur, hoping to change the subject. "Or disrupt things too much?"

"No, you didn't disrupt anything," he replies, and I smile. "You mentioned something about a smaller cabin than this one?" I nod my head. "I share that idea."

I stroke his beard, which is getting longer, and smile.

"Do you already know where?"

He pulls me into his arms, and I go willingly.

"A warm place; I want you in nothing but a tiny thong."

I can't contain my surprised laughter.

"Don't you think you're asking for too much?"

"Maybe naked and ready for me?"

I shake my head, my face burning with embarrassment just imagining it.

"Are you going to be naked too?"

"I'll do whatever you want, Eveline."

His expression becomes more serious; I feel his words are sincere, and it warms my heart. Slowly, I bring our lips together in a gentle kiss. As I pull away, I caress his face.

"So your name is Ryder Marshall?"

"But it's a secret," he whispers softly, his thumb brushes against my cheek. "You can't tell anyone."

"I promise," I reply while touching my fingers to my lips. "Your parents...?"

"They are alive," he interrupts me, but soon makes a confused expression. "I think... It's been many years since I looked for them. From a distance." Skull lets out a sigh. "My last conversation with my father wasn't good. He didn't accept my discharge from military service. After all, he was one. It's a family thing. To keep them safe, I had to die to everyone I knew."

"You faked your death to them?"

His expression shifts, and he shakes his head as he gets out of bed. I watch his naked body move close to the window.

"'You made me feel like I failed as a father'" his voice is weak, and worried, I get out of bed and go to him. "That's what he said to me when minutes later he sent me away."

"Skull..." I hug him from behind. His anguished voice tears me apart inside. "Maybe he was just upset; he said it in the heat of the moment. Everything happened, and you couldn't talk again."

"You don't know him, Eveline. He meant everything he said."

Still holding the sheet around my body, I make him turn to face me. His gaze is a mix of sadness and anger.

"Have you ever thought that when he received the news that you died," I start, and he watches me. "Everything he said, even his anger, is gone? I bet if he had the chance to talk to you, he would hug you? I never had a father or a mother, but you were loved by them, cared for... A heated argument can't be greater than their love for you."

I wait for him to retort, but then he sighs and lowers his head. He embraces me protectively, comforting me as his enormous arms wrap around my body. We stay there for a while, but soon we return to bed, and this time I am his mattress. I give a small smile and close my eyes, allowing myself to give the affection that Skull needs. Nothing sexual, just us two in that bed, him thinking about his parents and me knowing for sure that the feeling I have for Ryder Marshall is love.

CHAPTER TWENTY

Skull

Two days after our conversation in the room, my mind kept returning to Eveline's words about my father and our fight. The way she managed to understand me and speak with such certainty brought doubts I never had before. The subject of family had died for me; I was used to loneliness. The only people I cared about were Pablo and Miller, but now? I'm completely confused, not knowing what to do.

Could her words have truth about my father? After all, he had always been a very strict man regarding values and principles. Discovering that I was discharged for insubordination felt like disrespecting him. He didn't even let me explain what had happened because nothing would justify me advancing against my superior, even if he had almost killed a fellow soldier in my platoon.

I snap out of my thoughts and see Eveline approaching with a bowl of popcorn. She smiles at me, and I return the gesture. It's late afternoon, but it hardly feels like it. The day has been filled with constant rain, and if the house weren't heated, we would probably be cold.

"What are we going to watch now?"

Her dress comes just above her thighs, looking more like a sensual nightgown. I lose myself in her body; Eveline enchants me effortlessly.

"I have no idea," I respond, glancing at the TV, then remembering I've seen that actor before. "A man who flies and shoots laser beams from his eyes."

"Oh, he's quite handsome," she says innocently, looking at me with a furrowed brow. "Why does he fly? Isn't he human?"

"I don't know," I mutter reluctantly, "but I know there's a pretty redhead in this movie."

Okay. I might be sounding quite childish, and I probably said something foolish judging by the way she looks at me.

"So you think redheads are pretty," her voice is low, as if analyzing. "Remember who else is a redhead? Layla." When I think of saying something, she continues. "That's the third time you've mentioned her."

"Actually, that was you. I didn't even think of her."

"But she was the first name that came to your mind that day."

I fall silent to analyze my mistake better. I could have simply stayed quiet, but I let my jealousy speak louder, and this is what happens. I glance out of the corner of my eye and notice her eating with a serious expression. I get an idea and slowly stretch, deliberately leaving my arm on the backrest behind her head. Eveline doesn't move but continues eating.

Time passes, and as the movie nears its end, Eveline leans over to the coffee table to set the empty bowl down. She then crosses her arms and remains silent.

"The movie wasn't half bad."

"Uh-huh."

Receiving the monosyllabic response, I swallow hard.

"Did you like it?"

"No." She shakes her head, leaving me surprised. "But you must have liked it; the pretty redhead appeared a lot."

"Eveline..."

"No, it's fine," she shrugs. "I thought Superman was handsome; you think redheads are pretty. There's no problem with that."

I accept what she says and return to watching TV.

Miller still hasn't contacted me about Eveline's friend, and this would be a great time to give her some good news. I let out a sigh and look at her; her expression is angry. I think for a few minutes. I didn't mention Layla, so why is Eveline apparently upset? I cited the redhead who's the girlfriend of that strange ET, but it's not my fault she remembers that Layla.

"Are you upset with me?"

"Why would I be?" she replies with a question. I take a deep breath; I've never liked being answered with a question. "Actually, I'm thinking about which panties I'm going to wear to bed tonight. It's a tough task."

I swallow hard, hoping she continues, but she smiles.

"I can help if you want."

She looks at me, and when she's about to respond, she pauses for a few seconds. Her gaze travels across my face, then she nods.

"Of course, that would help me a lot."

I'm genuinely surprised because I expected a refusal. Eveline returns to watching with a sideways smile, and even though I want to relax, I can't. It seemed too easy. What is she planning? Another movie starts in sequence, and this time it's a cheesy romance. It's not something I enjoy, but I stay there to keep her company. As the movie unfolds, I subtly glance at Eveline, who is drying a few tears.

I let a smile escape, feeling extremely relaxed. For a moment, I even forgot why we were there; the seriousness of the situation demanded a firmer stance from me. However, how can I be indifferent to Eveline? How can I not do everything to make those days normal for her?

I slide my hand under the gray T-shirt and touch the bandage.

"What's wrong?" she asks, quickly lifting the fabric. "Does it hurt? I told you to rest. Lying down, to be more exact. Let me see?"

I allow her to examine the bandage; it's dry. Her face is so perfect—lips, nose, everything about her enchants me. How is it possible?

"You're so beautiful, Eveline," I say, and she gives me an awkward smile. "Really very beautiful."

"You're not trying to sweet-talk me, are you?" she questions, arms crossed. "Because that compliment won't save you from punishment later."

I smile instantly; I knew it.

"Punish me? I didn't do anything; you're the one who kept calling another man handsome in front of me."

She kneels on the couch, then sits on my legs.

"But unlike Superman, he didn't keep kissing me on the neck and wanting something from me like Layla did to you."

I grab her by the waist and pull her to sit on my lap. Her blonde hair spills over her beautiful face and shoulders. Eveline smiles and snuggles closer to me.

"I'm yours, Eveline."

Her hand glides up my chest, stopping on my face.

"You won't let her get close to you, will you?"

"No, and if it happens, I'll let you know that I'm yours. Jealous."

Eveline shakes her head.

"And you, aren't you?"

"A little, maybe."

"Just a little?" she repeats. I nod and start kissing her neck. Her scent drives me crazy. "I'm almost sure you're not being sincere."

I pull her in for a kiss and grab her hair in a messy ponytail. My lips work on hers with hunger and desire, always seeking more. Our tongues rub against each other, and I feel Eveline pulling off my T-shirt. In that brief moment, she lowers the top of her dress, exposing her breasts to me. Not one to hesitate, I have a nipple between my lips within seconds.

As I start sucking and nibbling, Eveline moans loudly and grips my hair. I give the same attention to her other breast while she writhes restlessly over my erection. My hands slide down to her behind, where I give a smack followed by a squeeze.

"Do you want to do it again?" she asks in a low voice, kissing me quickly. Her lips are red, and her taste is unique, addictive, urging me to have more. "I feel guilty because I should be the first to stop you."

"Stop me?" I repeat, confused, and after holding her firmly, I stand up. "You don't want to?"

She smiles shyly, warming my heart. That smile can completely disarm me. I press my lips against her neck and kiss my way up to near her ear.

"It's just that you're hurt," she whines as I start walking toward the stairs. "I don't want you to get worse."

"Eveline," I begin smiling. "Don't worry about anything; I want you, and you can't deny me that."

Once inside the room, we tumble onto the bed, and I snuggle on top of her body. My hand explores the mattress, and as soon as I reach under the pillow, I grab a condom.

"W-Wait!" she pleads, pushing me until I lie down. "I'll do this."

I smile and let her take the silver packet from my hands. To help her, I slide down my pants along with my underwear. Eveline kneels between my legs and, with a look of desire, begins to masturbate me. I close my eyes quickly but soon return my focus to her. Her tongue sensually glides over her slightly parted lips, making my cock throb. I'm completely hard, desperate for Eveline. Then, slowly, she descends and envelops my glans between her lips. One hand grips me at the base while the other supports herself on the mattress.

I feel the rhythmic sucking, and it's paradise for me. Without me asking, Eveline opens her lips wider, allowing me to enter further.

Totally surprised that she can accommodate a few inches of my erection, I caress her cheek. Her face turns red, and she pulls away quickly, saliva and remnants of my pleasure glistening on her red lips. Unable to contain myself, I pull her in for a kiss, sucking her lips and tongue, and I can't wait any longer to be in her warmth.

I'm completely naked and watch her smile as she opens the condom. Gently, she rolls it down my shaft, and once suited up, I pull her onto my lap. Her tiny thong remains, and I rip it off aggressively.

Eveline closes her eyes as I invade her slowly, but I hear a noise coming from outside. She moans in my arms; however, my attention is on the rustling sounds and footsteps I hear in the distance. I'm about to speak to her when I see a man appear at the bedroom door, gun in hand. In a swift motion, I grab Eveline and throw us off the bed, avoiding bullets hitting her. I make her hide under the bed and hear the intruder rushing toward us.

In instinctive combat mode, I manage to stand up skillfully and grab the gun, forcing it down. A shot hits the floor, and with a savage twist, I hear a crack and the howl of pain. I elbow him in the nose, causing it to bleed instantly, and there we begin to fight, him always trying to aim the gun at me. I hear more footsteps in the hallway, and two more men appear, advancing toward us. Both are armed. I move my body to the side and kick the second one who entered, making him drop his weapon.

The third aims at me, but I use the arm I just broke as a shield. I dodge another blow and kick the third in the chest, making one fall. In the meantime, I manage to take the weapon and shoot under the jaw of the one I have hold of, and to finish, I shoot the other two. My breath is quickening, and I feel the adrenaline burning through my veins.

"Eveline, let's go!"

When I don't hear her respond, I run to where I left her, finding her crying and trembling. She comes into my arms and grips me tightly. I know I can't push her away, but it's only a matter of time before more reinforcements arrive.

"It's all right! I'm here," I murmur, kissing her forehead, "but we need to go, okay? I need you to be strong with me, all right?"

"Y-Yes!" she responds, and I take a deep breath. Her gaze goes to the dead men, but I quickly touch her face, making her look at me. "Skull..."

"Hey, you don't need to be afraid," I say in a calm voice, but inside I'm furious. I almost lost her, and that only increases my determination to kill those two bastards. "We need to go now!"

I pull her up to stand, noticing she seems disoriented, and I grow worried. I quickly put my clothes back on and go to the closet, finding some weapons that Pablo mentioned. I glance at Eveline as she packs clothes into the backpack. With everything ready and a gun in hand, we head outside. Inside the backpack, I grab my phone and send a message to Pablo. My Jeep is parked just ahead. I walk over to it with Eveline by my side and settle into the driver's seat, watching Eveline sit in the passenger seat. She wipes away some tears but doesn't say anything.

"We're going to Washington D.C.," I announce, and she nods. "Are you hurt?"

She shakes her head, and I take a deep breath as I start the engine and drive away quickly.

AS SOON AS WE ARRIVE at a roadside motel, it's already night. I make the payment and take a key. Quickly, I enter the room, followed by Eveline. She throws her backpack on the floor and lies down on the bed with her arms outstretched.

"How were we discovered?" Her voice is low, and when she looks at me, I see the sadness. "I didn't even hear when they came in."

"I don't know," I reply to her first question and sit down close. "By now, Pablo has probably sent someone to clean up the mess."

She nods and, after a sigh, sits up.

"I was so scared you would get hurt," she warns. I stretch my arm toward her, and she comes without complaint. I hug her around the waist, feeling her arms wrap around my neck. "Skull, can we leave?"

Eveline pulls away, and somewhat confused, I watch her sit on my lap.

"You know I can't until this is over."

"I'm scared, Skull."

I let out a sigh, then my phone starts ringing. Eveline sits beside me as I answer the call.

— *Are you both okay?*

"Yes," I confirm to Pablo. "We're safe."

I hear his sigh, and I stand up, walking to the door.

— *I'm here at the cabin; everything is turned upside down. It looks like they were looking for some clue about where you are. We need to talk tomorrow.*

"Okay."

I end the call and turn back to Eveline, who remains seated on my legs. I walk over to her and kiss her, stroking her cheek and feeling how soft she is to my touch.

"Have I told you that you're beautiful?"

She smiles and places her hands on me. Her smile can completely disarm me.

"I think you've said it twice; I don't even remember," she murmurs, standing in front of me. "Even scared under the bed, I was surprised you fought naked. Weren't you afraid of something happening... with him?"

I smile, but it doesn't last long.

"Not with him, but if something had happened to you, I wouldn't forgive myself, Eveline. For you, I would take a bullet, a knife... whatever. Keeping you safe is my life's goal from now on."

I receive her tight hug and spend a good few seconds feeling at home. Her scent calms me; I love how I feel about her. Realizing this, I freeze in the embrace. Do I love Eveline?

"Skull," she pulls away and looks at me, her beautiful smile still there. "I'm going to take a shower," she comments, and I nod. "I need to change my panties; I'm still wearing the torn ones."

I lick my lips and lower my gaze down her body. Slowly, I bring my hand to the middle of her legs and caress her, feeling her desire moistening my fingers.

"Need help taking them off?"

Her hand grabs my shirt as she opens her legs for me.

"Aren't you tired?"

She smiles, and I quickly lift her into my arms. I kiss her lips, and when I feel her tongue touch mine, my body vibrates. I pull my face back just enough to meet her beautiful eyes and smile, sure of what I'm feeling. I kiss her again, and blindly make my way to the suite of the room.

CHAPTER TWENTY-ONE

Eveline

As soon as we wake up the next day, we prepare to meet Pablo. I'm sitting on the bed, watching Skull put on his clothes with a serious expression. Earlier, Miller called, and whatever he said left Skull worried. While we were at the cabin, even though it was just a few days, I fantasized about a world that was just ours. There, I forgot everything else, and it was just the two of us.

My heart was constantly sending me signals about Skull. About what we were doing, the new feelings I had for him, and that made me anxious. I wanted to talk about how I felt, but something held me back. Perhaps the fear of potential rejection? He said he wanted me too, but what if opening up pushed him away?

Or was my presence in his thoughts, as he claimed, a sign that I could, indeed, speak up?

"Worried?"

I quickly shake my head and let a smile escape.

"Just thinking."

He approaches me without a shirt and sits down very close. I touch his face, letting out a sigh of satisfaction. I look at his lips and remember how they kissed me intimately. Whenever he could, Skull would spread my legs and make me come with his tongue and lips. It's something he truly enjoys doing, and I equally love returning the favor.

"Can I know what you're thinking about?"

"No." I shake my head, and he smiles.

He kisses my lips, and just as he thinks of deepening it, someone knocks on the door.

Skull gestures for me to stay quiet, and with his gun in hand, he goes to the window covered by the curtain. Upon seeing who is behind the door through the crack, he puts the gun away in his waistband and opens the door. Pablo enters and waves to me, while Skull grabs a shirt and puts it on, his gaze scrutinizing Pablo.

"Yesterday was pretty hectic," he says, and Skull nods.

Pablo's phone rings, and he looks at the screen for a few seconds before quickly showing it to Skull. Their gazes meet mine, and I'm left confused. Just as I'm about to ask what's happening, we hear another knock at the door, but this time I recognize Miller's voice. As the door opens, I see him, and to my surprise, Ellen is with him.

I get up from where I am and go to her to hug her. She embraces me, and I can't help but let the tears fall.

"Oh, my dear," she murmurs while still holding me. "I was so worried about you."

"I'm fine," I reply, stepping back with a smile. "And the girls?"

"They stayed, but Tracy sent you a kiss."

I smile and look at Skull, who has his arms crossed. He watches us silently while Miller and Pablo whisper something to each other.

"So? What did you decide to do about her friend?"

In an instant, Pablo and Skull glare at Miller, who looks confused. I furrow my brow, a bit puzzled.

"My friend? What about her? Did you find her?"

Miller looks at me without understanding, but when his gaze lands on Skull, he gets it.

"I thought you all talked about it," he shrugs. "I found your friend, Eveline. She was taken to the Diplomat."

I freeze at that.

I search for Skull with my eyes, and he doesn't look surprised.

"You knew and didn't tell me?"

"I found out this morning," he murmurs, approaching me, his hands touching my arms. "You weren't supposed to know; I don't want you to worry. We'll figure it out."

I shake my head, looking at everyone present, finally resting on Ellen. She remains serious, her gaze not reflecting surprise but apprehension.

"Why did you come?"

Ellen swallows hard but then smiles at me.

"I came to bring you back with me," she warns, looking at Skull. "Let them handle this, and you'll be safe with me."

I divert my gaze to the guys standing side by side.

"And what's the plan?"

"Well..."

"We're still working on that," Skull interrupts Miller deliberately, and the two of them glare at each other. "But we already know where she is."

"So, are you going to act today?"

"We need a plan to get in, Eveline," Pablo says, arms crossed. "It's risky, and we don't want to compromise your friend's safety."

"Can I do something?"

"No, Eveline!" Skull says, his face contorted. "You're going with Ellen!"

"If I can do something to save my friend, I will, Skull!" I retort, and he takes a deep breath. "Is there anything I can do?"

"Actually, yes," Miller replies, looking at Skull with concern. "My plan is to infiltrate you into their hideout, to be our eyes until we can invade and..."

"Alright, I'm in."

"No! *Damn it! No!*" Skull roars, practically furious. "You're not putting yourself at risk like this, Eveline!"

"She's my friend!"

"You're not going!" He shouts and steps closer to me, standing in front of me. His expression is desperate, and I realize something. Is Skull scared? "I'm not going to let you put yourself at risk like this! You're prohibited!"

I touch his face, disregarding the audience, and kiss him.

"You can't forbid me and send me away when my friend is there because of me." I make it clear, and when he opens his mouth to speak, I continue: "I'm not leaving; I'm staying and helping save Abby."

"*Eveline, please...*" he whispers, touching my cheek. "I can't let you go," his gaze is almost pleading. "I can't lose you, please..."

"I'll be fine," I interrupt him. Skull closes his eyes, remaining like that for a few minutes, but then he stares at me. "I just need you to support me. It will work out."

He shakes his head, then rubs his hand over his beard.

"Why are you so stubborn?" he asks, and I give him a smile.

"I learned from you."

He kisses me again, and I feel his lips trembling; I've never seen Skull like that. When I pull away, I notice everyone is looking at us. Ellen smiles, Miller looks confused, and Pablo has a satisfied expression.

"Did I miss something?" Miller asks Pablo, who keeps smiling. "Are you two together?"

"I noticed the moment I laid eyes on you two," he replies to his friend. "As someone who loves a love story, I support it."

"I suspected it, okay?" Miller retorts. "I was almost sure when Skull wanted to kill one of my clients just because the poor guy wanted a chance with her."

Surprised, I look at Skull.

"Why can he call you Skull?" Pablo questions while pulling out a chair to sit. "I thought I was your best friend."

I smile, but Skull remains silent. His gaze is distant; the concern is evident. I touch his face, making him look at me, and I kiss him once more.

"Don't worry."

I receive a nod, and when he takes a deep breath, he turns back to his friends.

"Let's focus," he asks, and soon he has their attention. "I'm going undercover with Eveline; that's not up for discussion."

"Are we following my plan?" Miller asks, and Skull nods.

"God help us," Pablo adds, then looks at me. "We've learned about the things they've plotted, but since we don't have proof, it would be good if you could record them admitting what they did."

"And how do I do that?"

"We'll put a wire on you," he responds, looking at me. "They won't notice, but you need to act natural about it. We'll transmit it to the press, the police, and send the content of the flash drive Skull showed me. They'll be leaving there in handcuffs."

I confirm and see his gaze shift to Skull. The two share a look without saying anything; after a few seconds, Pablo looks away. I step away from them as they start talking about a basilica and walk over to Ellen, hugging her.

"So you sorted things out with the handsome guy?"

Embarrassed, I notice Skull listening and glancing at us quickly. I look at Ellen, and she smiles softly.

"We talked and came to an agreement to be together when this is all over."

Ellen touches my hair. Her gaze is so affectionate, so comforting.

"I'm happy for you two," she smiles, but soon stops and pulls me into a hug. "Are you sure you don't want to come back with me?"

"Abby is my best friend," I respond in her embrace. "If I can help, then I will."

"You're brave, Eveline. I feel proud but worried too."

We pull away, and I watch Skull with his arms crossed, listening to what the others are saying. He looks serious, and I automatically remember when I first met him. We were both strangers to each other, but now it's different. I can't see myself away from him; I worry about his safety and his reactions from moments ago. He feels the same way too.

I want to ask Ellen what it's like to love someone, but they're too close, and I don't want them to hear. However, something inside me screams that this feeling is love. I feel a hand on my arm and look at Ellen. Her gaze goes from Skull to me, and then she smiles.

"You make a lovely couple," she compliments, and I smile shyly. "Are you two taking precautions?"

The question came in a whisper, which didn't draw attention to us.

"Yes," I affirm, feeling my face burn with embarrassment. "And we've done some things, but not everything."

"There will be time for that," she responds, and I nod.

I turn my gaze back to the guys who are talking among themselves, and I can barely hear what they're saying. Skull is the only one quiet, his angry and imposing expression would frighten anyone who didn't know him. The conversation doesn't last long, and when Miller and Pablo shake hands, I realize it's over. Skull takes a deep breath and rubs his hand through his hair.

"Well, let's go to my place," Pablo says, looking directly at me. "Tomorrow, we'll put the plan into action." He glances at Skull. "Are you sure, Eveline? Even if you don't go, we won't spare any effort to save your friend."

"I'm sure," I say, and he nods. "If there's a way I can help, then I want to."

I look at Skull, and he remains serious.

He might not agree with my decision, but it's what feels right for me. Abby is my best friend, and I don't want anything to happen to her. If I'm there, I can calm her down and make sure she'll be okay when everything goes down.

Pablo invites Miller and Ellen, who accept to spend the night at his house. Then, quickly, Skull grabs our backpacks, and I walk alongside him to the car. Miller, Ellen, and Pablo go in separate cars ahead while we follow behind.

I glance at Skull; he still hasn't spoken to me.

"Hey, it's going to be okay," I murmur, touching his thigh. "Just don't be upset with me. She's my friend."

"I'm not upset with you."

I nod and wait for him to continue, but he stays silent. Accepting that, I turn my attention back to Miller's car in front. The drive is long, and soon I notice we've exited the highway and are on a dirt road. Minutes pass, and just as I'm about to ask if it's taking long, I see a mansion partially hidden in the forest. The large gates open, and I'm enchanted when I notice the grand fountain with a large eagle sculpture.

Security guards approach around.

"Wow, it's huge."

Skull only looks at the yard, and something comes to my mind: Did he and Safira stay around here?

We get out, and I grab my backpack, but Skull quickly holds it. We walk to the entrance, and inside it's even bigger.

"Do you live alone in this place?"

"No, I like staying in my cabin," he replies, starting to climb the stairs, "but since I have guests, I prefer for them to be comfortable."

I follow him up the stairs, passing through a hallway until he stops in front of a door. Once it's opened, he encourages us to enter. The room is so luxurious; there's a huge bed against the wall, and the furniture is beautiful. There's a door on the other side that I imagine leads to the bathroom.

"It's all beautiful, Pablo."

"Rest for a bit," he says, giving Skull a pat on the shoulder. "Then come down to eat."

I nod at Ellen, and when everyone leaves, I sit on the bed. I'm barefoot, and my gaze follows Skull as he sits on a sofa against the opposite wall. His hands rub his face; he seems impatient, which makes me sad.

"If you're not upset with me," I call his attention. "Why are you ignoring me?"

"I'm just thinking, Eveline," he retorts, leaning back against the sofa, his body sliding down more. "This isn't how I imagined rescuing your friend."

I get off the bed, walk over to him, and sit on his lap.

My hand touches his chest and moves up to his neck. The other rests over his heart, feeling it beat rapidly.

"But you understand me, right?" I ask softly. "I don't want to do this to you like this."

"Going back with Ellen?" he asks once more, and I shake my head. "You're very stubborn, Eveline."

"Trust me," I plead, and without holding back, I kiss his lips. "Let's do this! When all this is over, I'm up for going anywhere you want. A warm country, a small house where I can stay in nothing but a tiny thong."

It takes a few seconds, but he soon smiles. I feel his hands pull me closer by the waist.

"No thong, right? An island, or a village."

"We can start over there," I finish, and he smiles, but then it fades. "What's wrong?"

"We'll have a good life, Eveline," he says as I feel him caress my face. "I mentioned a warm place, but we can go wherever you want. Have the life you desire."

"A life of husband and wife?" I question, and for a few seconds, he looks at me somewhat surprised. "I'm not asking for a proposal," I say quickly, nervous. "I just asked because you said we'd be together, but you didn't say what we'd be. Someone might ask, and..."

"A life of husband and wife," he confirms, taking my hand and kissing it right after. "If you want it, I'm okay with it."

I try to hold back my smile, but it's in vain.

"If you make a decent request, then we can talk."

"But you were the one who proposed," I retort with a challenging look. "So you should be the one to ask."

"It's chivalrous for you to ask, Skull."

I cross my arms, and he simply gives me a smile.

"That's old-fashioned," he shrugs. "I'll wait for you to ask me."

I smile as I shake my head. After a few seconds, he stops smiling and embraces me. I return the hug, and in that moment, my chest feels warmer, and my eyes fill with tears. I want to say, "I love you, Skull," but I can't. Something holds me back, and I don't know what it is anymore. Maybe it's because I don't think the moment is right, but would there ever be a right moment? His arms tighten around me, pulling me closer, but I don't complain; I relish the feeling of being completely safe in his warmth.

CHAPTER TWENTY-TWO

Eveline

Night quickly arrives, and we all have dinner in a very fancy room. Miller and Pablo chat animatedly, and Ellen occasionally laughs at Miller's comments. Skull, however, remains quiet, lost in thought. They don't talk about tomorrow, and even though I want to know, I appreciate this moment of relaxation. At the end of dinner, we retreat since we'll be getting up early. Before stepping away, Ellen hugs me, wishing me sweet dreams.

Inside the room with Skull, already ready for bed in one of his T-shirts, I lie on the mattress and wait for him to take the place beside me.

"Ellen really likes you," he says, moving closer. "Almost like a mother to you."

I look at him in surprise and nod my head. That's exactly it, like a mother. I never had one, but I feel it's something like that, more maternal. I smile at the realization and watch him lie down, wearing only thick pants. I turn toward him, but when he opens his arms in an invitation, I snuggle against him quickly.

"Skull?"

"Yes?"

"Thank you for supporting me," I murmur. "I know you don't want me to go, but it's important to me."

He remains silent, but soon speaks again.

"Alright, I understand, and I'll be there to make sure nothing happens to you."

I lean over his body and kiss him. I'm met with affection, and I subtly move my hand down to his waistband. I caress over the fabric, and he begins to harden, but I quickly remember we need to sleep. I separate our lips and smile.

"Good night, Skull."

"You're going to leave me hard and go to sleep, *Evil*ine?"

"Don't call me that," I ask once more, and I watch him pull his cock out. He's so robust, virile... There's just a little pubic hair, as if it's just starting to grow, and I find it extremely sexy. I raise my gaze to his face and touch his beard. "Evil is bad, and I'm not like that."

"No, you're my sin, Eveline," he replies, and I'm taken aback. "The feelings I have for you, I don't think I should feel."

My fingers trail down the numerous scars on his body, then I give him a smile. What feelings? Why isn't he more specific?

"Just because you're older?" I ask, and in a quick movement, he positions himself over me. His hard cock rubs against my tiny thong, and his expression is intense. "I don't care about that."

"You think I'm old?"

"No." I shake my head, but I can't hide my nervous laugh. "I don't think so."

Then I feel his fingers pull aside my thong, followed by his cock forcing its way in. I writhe on the mattress and let out a soft moan when he stops penetrating me. Skull keeps his eyes on me, and I watch, mesmerized, as he brings his fingers to his tongue before rubbing it on my intimacy. Automatically, I open my legs more for him and wrap my arms around his neck. His fingers exert a slow, rhythmic pressure that leaves me on the edge.

"Skull!"

"Ryder!" His voice is low but demanding, dangerously echoing in my ears. "I want to hear you moaning my name! And if you don't obey me..."

"Am I going to get spanked?" I ask with anticipation, and I smile when two fingers penetrate me, making a "come here" motion. "Oh! More!"

"More of what, Eveline?" he questions, and stops. I immediately complain, and he smiles. "When you say the words, who knows, maybe I'll continue?"

Under his gaze, I remove my thong and turn on the mattress, getting on all fours. I hug the pillow and push my hips up, completely needing him.

"Please, Ryder! I'm yours... Please."

First, I feel a finger rubbing against my wet intimacy.

"Don't make a sound," he commands, and I nod my head frantically. "Do you like to provoke me?"

Involuntarily, I roll my hips toward the fingers that slowly penetrate me. It's torture feeling him entering me with his fingers so patiently, as if he's punishing me?

"Ryder... don't torture me like this..."

I brace my hands on the mattress and twist until my lips touch his. A kiss begins, and I feel my body ignite. Between my legs, it's as if flames consume me rapidly. Licks of fire that only calm when Skull touches me, so experienced and precise. I grab his hair and moan against his lips.

Our breaths mix, heightening the erotic atmosphere. The movements increase, and when I can't hold back my contractions any longer, I moan loudly, but I'm quickly silenced by a kiss. His tongue caresses mine, and as I reciprocate, I feel the spasms fade away.

"We don't have any condoms," he warns, and I make a sad expression, but he continues, "but you can still suck me off."

I smile shyly but nod.

He promptly lies down and watches me.

I get on my knees between his muscular legs, and as I grab him with both hands, I lean down to lick his glans. I collect his pleasure with my tongue and swallow under his attentive gaze. I suck him while feeling my intimacy pulsate with desire. I move my lips up and down, and Skull moans; that sight is so sensual.

I hold him with just one hand and try to take him to the back of my throat, but I can't. My eyes close as I feel so sensitive, and I let out a soft moan. I release his cock and lovingly rub my entrance with my own fingers. Without waiting for an invitation, I approach him and sit on his lap.

"I want you so much, Ryder... It's even hurting."

"Horny!" he exclaims, grabbing my ass. "We can't do it now..."

"Please!" I practically whine. "Just a little, please!"

I bite my lip and stare at him; I know I could get pregnant, but we would be quick, and there wouldn't be a risk. I kiss his lips and, in the meantime, I grab his member from behind and guide it toward my folds.

"Stubborn as always," he accuses, stopping me; his tone isn't one of fighting but rather one of observation.

"Another guy in your place would take me right now," I provoke, and he glares at me angrily. "He wouldn't let me suffer like this... full of desire."

Skull turns our bodies, positioning himself on top of me, his face very close to mine.

"Another guy wouldn't even come close to you, Eveline," he whispers in a threatening tone, but I'm not afraid; desire speaks for me. "I'd kill him without thinking twice!"

"Then make me yours, here and now! What are you waiting for?"

He kisses me hard and then turns me on the bed. I'm propped up, and when I feel his fingers touching me intimately, I try to look back. However, Skull grabs my hair and forces me to look forward. I bite my lip as I feel him slowly penetrate me to the hilt. The sensation of fullness quickly washes over me, and I can't speak.

His hand pulls my hair dominantly, and almost simultaneously, Skull forces his hips against mine. I breathe heavily, unable to think, only feel.

"Is this how you wanted it?" he asks, and in response, I let out a moan. "My cock all the way inside this pussy?"

I try to move, but I can't. Then, in that position—where Skull's body exerts weight on mine—he starts to move vigorously. Each time he hits me, I feel him strike deep, and it's heaven for me. I open my legs wider, and Skull grips my waist fiercely. I moan louder and try to plant my knees on the mattress for support, but it's impossible. My feverish, limp body writhes with difficulty. Perhaps noticing this, he positions his hands beside my head and lifts the weight of his body off me.

The sound of our pelvises colliding fills the room, just like the heat that envelops us. Even with my breath uneven, I try to regulate my heartbeat, but it's in vain. With great effort, I manage to support my knees on the mattress, and, surprisingly, I feel Skull hitting new places inside me.

My skin tingles, sending pleasant sensations throughout my body. Then, I turn toward him and scratch his chest. Skull lets out a loud groan with his hoarse tone, and I find it so delicious to hear. I close my eyes when I feel a contraction starting in my lower belly and try to escape that position.

However, Skull notices and forces his hips deeper into mine.

"You're not going anywhere!" he says, and to my surprise, a finger penetrates between my cheeks. It's so strange, yet at the same time, so pleasurable to feel. "You're going to come on my cock, and then I'm going to fuck you right here."

I'm alarmed, but I don't say anything.

The movements intensify, and when I feel him deep inside, I cover my mouth with my hands to prevent my moans from escaping loudly. With a trembling body, I lie on the mattress and try to regain my senses. His cock slowly withdraws, and, as he warned, he positions the head at my other entrance.

"Skull!"

I turn with a trembling hand to stop him, but he's quicker and grabs it.

"Calm down," he asks, rubbing his head against my folds, sometimes pressing against my butt. "It's not going to be now, but when it's just us, I'm going to fuck this ass hard."

I bite my lip, embarrassed, and enjoy the caress I receive there. He hasn't come yet, but I think he's very close. Then, he makes me grab one side of my ass while he holds the other and continues rubbing the head. Sometimes he forces penetration, but when I flinch, he stops. Minutes pass, and I hear his guttural roar. Looking back, I realize he's coming. I feel his semen dripping between my cheeks, making my sensitive intimacy throb.

Skull throws himself beside me, and my gaze goes to his member, which is a bit flaccid. I raise my sight to his face, and he smiles contentedly. One of his rare smiles; he's so handsome. What will tomorrow be like? Will he go in with me anyway? But what if the Diplomat recognizes him? Would he be killed?

As if doused with a bucket of cold water, my body trembles with fear, and I understand how dangerous tomorrow will be. In that moment, I'm afraid I won't be able to be with him anymore. My earlier courage abandoned me without a second thought.

"Hey, why are you crying? Did I hurt you?"

I bring my fingers to my face, and yes, I am crying. Skull sits up, his concerned gaze sweeping over my body.

"No." I shake my head and sit up, then hug him. "I'm scared, Skull! I don't want you to get hurt tomorrow."

His arms wrap around me, and I feel his natural scent and sweat. I love that smell! I love being protected in his arms; I love when he's affectionate and even when he's rough. I love Skull completely! Realizing the obvious of what I'm feeling makes me smile between my tears.

I love Skull.

"You don't need to be afraid, Eveline. We'll put an end to this, and the only concern will be our next destination."

I pull away slightly from him, and he gently wipes away my tears. His gaze is completely affectionate and confident; how can I not love him? I touch his face, tracing his scar, and lean in to kiss his lips.

"Skull... I want to say something," I warn him, and then swallow hard. He just nods and watches me with his beautiful blue eyes. He seems anxious, expectant; his gaze doesn't leave mine. "I..."

"You...?" he encourages me when I hesitate, but I freeze. "Are you sure I didn't hurt you?"

I smile and run my fingers along his beard.

"You were perfect, Skull. It was exactly what I wanted."

He scans my face analytically and then smiles.

"Catholic orphanage, right?" His voice sounds mocking.

I dry the traces of my tears and give him a shy smile. Maybe confessing my feelings now isn't a good idea; he might feel obligated to say something to avoid hurting me, and that would be the end for me. Or perhaps occupying his mind with that would be dangerous? After all, we were going to war.

"I think the company led me down the wrong path," I joke, but deep down, I feel cowardly. "I wasn't like this; I barely thought about sex, I was just curious."

Skull snuggles between the pillows and opens his arms. I quickly nestle into his warmth and accept his affection as he runs his fingers through my hair.

"Sleep, Eveline. And don't worry about anything; I will protect you."

I close my eyes and, even with a bad feeling in my chest, I force myself to fall asleep, knowing that by morning, our future would be at stake.

CHAPTER TWENTY-THREE

Eveline

As soon as I stretch in bed, my body tilts to the side, and I open my eyes. Through the bedroom window, I can see the rays of sunlight escaping through the cracks. I sit up with the sheet covering my breasts and look around for Skull; he isn't there. I rub my eyes and get out of bed, heading to the bathroom with the intention of taking a shower before meeting Skull downstairs.

I don't spend much time in the shower; I'm anxious and, at the same time, have a bad feeling. Already ready to start the day and our plan, I leave the room. I put on a pair of jeans, boots, a soft fabric top, and my jacket. As I descend the stairs, I hear some whispers coming from the large living room. Ellen is the first one I see; she's sitting there, her expression worried. The moment she sees me, she stands up. The security guards in front of her quickly excuse themselves and leave.

"Good morning! Where are Skull and the guys?"

Ellen clears her throat and approaches me.

"Eveline..." she murmurs cautiously. "They went to rescue your friend."

Hearing that, I frown and shake my head.

"No! I said I was going, he agreed, and..."

"He just didn't want to leave on bad terms with you," Ellen interrupts me. "They left a few minutes ago."

Tears stream down my face, and I don't care if she sees me like this. My heart is shattered; how could he go without me? Was our last night together a goodbye again?

"No! How could they agree to this?!"

"Eveline..."

"No!" I cut her off rudely. "He can't have done this to me."

Ellen steps closer and touches my arm.

"He was really worried about you, Eveline," her voice is gentle. "He knows what he's doing, and he's not alone."

"He's hurt!" I retort, crying more. "The plan was..."

"They will come back."

I shake my head and dry my tears. I had two options: either keep crying or take action. So, even though something inside me screamed, I turned around and walked toward the exit.

"Where are you going, Eveline?"

"I'm not going to just stand here not knowing what's happening!"

I hear Ellen's footsteps behind me, but I don't stop.

"Eveline, please! Let's wait for them here."

I turn to her suddenly; her look is anxious, but I don't let it shake me.

"I love him, Ellen! I can't just stay here and wait without knowing what will happen. If I can help in any way, then I'm going to help."

I don't wait for a response and leave the mansion. As I step onto the large patio, I see some security guards scattered around. A few look at me suspiciously, but they don't approach. My stride is confident, yet I wonder what I will do and how I will get to where they are. I try to remember and recall hearing something about a Basilica. That would be where the President and the Diplomat would be. Near the iron gate, I look at two of the guards staring at me.

"What is it, miss?"

"I need to leave."

"We have orders not to let you leave," one warns, and I cross my arms. "So..."

"I'm a guest, not a prisoner," I interrupt him. "I demand that you open this gate, or I'll call the police."

They glance at each other, and for a moment, I swallow hard with fear. I see him about to respond, but he falls silent as he looks behind me. I mimic him and am surprised to see a car approaching; I notice Ellen is driving. As soon as she stops beside me, she looks at me.

"Since you're stubborn and not going to stay, at least let me take you there."

I suppress a smile and practically run to the passenger seat. She talks to the guard, and then we are allowed to leave.

With the car in motion, she looks at me.

"What do you plan to do?"

"I don't know," I reply. Her look is frightened. "I just know I won't stay here."

We spend a few hours on the road, the entire trip in silence. Each lost in her thoughts, and I have a slight suspicion that Pablo or Miller already knew we were going. When we reach civilization, I notice the streets are crowded with people and cars. There are several flags scattered throughout the area; I am enchanted by the beauty of the streets and everything in them, but I know that soon I would be face-to-face with those who want me dead.

Next to me, Ellen curses as the road is blocked by cars. My gaze scans the crowd outside, and right at the entrance of the Basilica, there's a platform with some people on it.

"Are you sure you want to go there? There's no turning back once you do."

I swallow hard and then nod.

I get out of the car and briefly close my eyes when the cold morning wind touches my skin. I fix my hair and start walking through the crowd. There are so many people here: young, adults, children, and the elderly. Everyone is holding small flags with the President's photo on one side and the country's flag on the other. I weave through a narrow path, and then I see him waving and smiling.

He's wearing a dark blue suit, his dark blonde hair slicked back, and his thick beard gives him a more serious look. I manage to get in front to see him better, hoping he notices me. Right behind him is the Diplomat, with a more closed-off expression. His attention is focused on his phone as he types quickly, but he soon looks around. He taps the President's shoulder and points to the entrance of the Basilica. A bit alarmed and impulsively, I make my decision.

"*Dad!*"

I shout as loud as I can, and when they both look directly at me, I swallow hard. The President quickly averts his gaze, but the Diplomat stares at me, shocked. I hold his gaze, and after a few seconds, he resumes walking. I'm confused, and some people around me look at me quizzically but don't ask anything. Something makes me look back, and I notice Miller, dressed in a suit and tie, walking toward me. I excuse myself to a few people and head in the opposite direction to shake him off. As I pass a group of people, I spot a staircase leading down to a door. I quickly descend, and to my surprise, the path is clear. The passage is a bit dark, but at the end of the long corridor, I can see light. I walk toward it, even though I'm completely terrified inside.

The closer I get, the more voices I can hear. In the lit corridor, I see a few people. They are all dressed alike; even the women are in suits. From the other corridor, the Diplomat emerges, accompanied by four security guards. He looks furious, his hands gesturing as if something has driven him mad. I hide in the darkness; when they move away and I don't hear any more conversations, I take a deep breath and follow the path he took out.

My steps are quick, and as I near the door, I push it open and am surprised to see a huge room. I enter cautiously, my gaze scanning several paintings on the walls. All are protected by glass; I stop in front of one and touch the plaque with different writing. Then I hear a noise coming from my left. I fix my gaze on the large wooden door and walk toward it. I test the doorknob, and it slowly opens.

I try to breathe more slowly, as if that could hide my position. As I step into the room, in the darkest corner, I see someone gagged.

"Abby!"

I run to my friend and hug her tightly. My tears escape my eyes; I can't hold back. I then remove the tape covering her lips.

"Evie, be careful!" she screams, looking behind me.

I turn quickly, only to see Ethan slap me, making me fall.

"Well, well, you were right," from the ground I see the President sitting by the door. He stands up and adjusts his suit. "She came for her friend. Very well, Eveline. Loyalty is a beautiful thing."

I sit up with difficulty; my face hurts a lot.

"You old bastard!" Abby roars. "You're lucky I'm tied up, because if I were free..."

"Shut your mouth, Abigail," Ethan places the tape back over her lips and turns to me. "It's been a while, Eveline."

With aggression, he grabs me by the hair and pushes me against the wall. He pulls my hands behind my back and holds them tightly. I feel his nose brush my neck, and I squirm in disgust.

"Finally met you," my father says. Ethan quickly turns me to face him. "I have to admit, discovering you are alive was an unpleasant surprise for me, and even more so because of the blackmail I received from your superior."

I frown, not comprehending.

"I-I don't know..."

"No," he interrupts me, and I swallow hard. "Of course, you didn't know. The only one to blame is your mother; after all, she told me she had put an end to you. You shouldn't have trusted her; I was a fool, you could say."

My mind is racing with all of this. My mother had saved my life? So she knew who I was and where I was? But why didn't she tell me when I visited her?

"What are we going to do with her, Sir?"

He gestures for silence, his gaze never leaving mine.

"Where have you been, Eveline? None of the men I hired to kill you were successful. Answer me; I'm genuinely curious."

I swallow hard again and observe everyone in the room. Then I remember what my mother said about him. I can't show fear, and I won't.

"You should worry about other things," I murmur, trying to keep my voice calm. He stares at me, surprised, crossing his arms in a relaxed manner. "Like the experiments with the prisoners, the trip to Afghanistan, the deaths of the scientists... Focus on that, Mr. President."

He remains silent for a few seconds, then smiles.

"As bold as your mother," he says, touching my cheek. "How can you be so much like her without having even known her?" he asks, and I turn my face away. "Or was it with her that you were?"

"Your problem is with me!" I exclaim, feeling my arm, still held by Ethan, tighten. "So why don't you let her go?"

His gaze shifts to Abby but soon returns to me.

"I don't leave loose ends, Eveline. How do you think I got here?"

"By lying and being a bad person?" I retort, and then I receive another slap.

His hand rises once more to hit me, but he stops as soon as his phone begins to ring. Even with his furious expression, he takes a deep breath and then reaches for the phone. His gaze lingers on the screen for a few seconds before he stares at me.

"Stay here with them," he says and heads for the exit without another word.

Left alone with Ethan, I look at Abby, who is squirming in her chair.

"You know something, Eveline?" Ethan's voice puts me on high alert. "I was glad to find out you're alive."

As soon as he finishes, his hand roams over my stomach. Then, catching him by surprise, I stomp on his foot with all my strength. I try to run, but he grabs me by the hair, throwing me to the ground.

"We're going to have a little chat, Evie."

After finishing his sentence, I see a gun in his hand.

Skull

I FINISH ADJUSTING the earpiece in my ear, my vest, and then check my gun. I let my gaze drift to Pablo, who is working on the computer installed in the van. We are two blocks away from where our targets are. On the attached monitors, we have clear live feeds of the events happening in front of the Basilica. I put my gun in the holster and grab my mask. Before I can put it on, my phone vibrates, leaving me confused. However, I answer it.

"*You're unbelievable!*"

I frown, not recognizing the voice. At the same time, Pablo's phone rings, and he answers.

"Who's speaking?"

"*You gave me your number when you were at my house,*" she warns, and I immediately remember: Eveline's mother. "*What do you think you're doing?*"

"Mrs. Adkins, I..."

"*I'll give you what I have against that bastard! But please, don't let her in.*" Her voice is urgent. "*I kept her away from all this to keep her safe, and you bring her here?*"

"What?" I'm confused; my gaze shifts to Pablo, and he looks startled. "What are you talking about?"

My phone beeps, and I notice the message in the notifications. It's a compressed file. Pablo curses, drawing my attention, and points something out on the screen. I move closer as Candice continues to speak on the call.

It's Miller's car parked in front of the Basilica.

I clench my jaw and quickly end the call.

"I'm going in now! Check the file I just received," I murmur as I hand over my phone, and I exit the van with my mask already on. "I can't believe Eveline is here."

"Try not to kill anyone."

I look at Pablo but soon make my way.

I walk through the dirty alley, carrying only ammunition, grenades, and a tactical knife. Spotting the large manhole cover, I head toward it; that's how I plan to infiltrate the Basilica. The tunnel layout I studied minutes ago remains fresh in my mind—an underground path with limited escape routes.

With force, I open the cover and see the rusty ladder. I glance around one last time and proceed. The damp, foul air envelops my body as I plunge into the depths of the duct. Darkness embraces me, but it doesn't intimidate me. Step by step, I move through the narrow tunnel, the sound of dripping water echoing around me.

My heart pounds in my chest, not because of what I'm about to do, but because I know Eveline is there. Alone, unprotected, and likely scared. I quicken my pace, and before I know it, I'm running.

After a few minutes of running, I finally see the exit that will lead me to my goal. I climb the stairs, and when I sense the silence outside, I push the cover open.

"I'm coming, my love!"

CHAPTER TWENTY-FOUR

Skull

I walk through the underground corridor with firm steps; few people know that beneath that Basilica are paths and private rooms. Wings dedicated to guarding valuable treasures, like sacred relics, historical artifacts, or precious offerings. The one I'm in right now is the Maintenance Access Wing. As I reach the end of the corridor, I see a door, retrieve my weapon and the silencer. After attaching it to the barrel, I grip the gun firmly and exit the corridor.

I hear muffled conversations coming my way, and I grip the weapon; then I remember Pablo's words. I curse under my breath and put the gun away.

Two security guards turn the corner, and upon seeing me, they try to draw their weapons. But I'm quick, and I swiftly advance, landing a kick on one and a punch on the other. I grab the first one's arm and twist it, turning to the second and knocking him out, making him fall to the ground unconscious. I soon do the same to the first guard, throwing him against the wall. I grab both by their collars and place them in a darker corner of the corridor. Before leaving, I tie them up and grab a *walkie-talkie*, hooking it to my vest.

"Did you manage to get in?" I hear Pablo ask in my ear.

"Yes, and what about Miller?"

"He's already inside."

I don't respond, and when I push through a door that's ajar, I see the room with the sacred relics. From where I am, I can hear noise from the outside area. I'm about to enter another corridor when I hear a scream coming from just ahead. The voices are agitated, but I recognize one: Eveline's.

"No, Ethan! Let me go!"

Ethan? I grab my gun, and right in front of the door, I kick it open in fury. Eveline is against the wall, and a man with a gun stands behind her. I tremble with rage as it takes hold of my body while I approach.

"Skull?" Her voice is weak; she looks at me as if she can't believe I'm here.

"You'd better stay there, man," he says, aiming the gun at Eveline. "Or I'll shoot her."

"You should point it at me," I retort, my gaze fixed on him. "I'm the one armed and aiming at your head."

"If you take another step..." His voice is trembling. "Look here, man, I'm not *playing*!"

I stop but continue aiming at his forehead. He laughs, and without taking his eyes off me, he smells Eveline's hair.

"Ethan, right?" I ask. In response, he looks at me confused. "The same one from the Orphanage?"

"How do you know?" He replies with a question, then smiles. "Been talking about me, Eveline? You know each other, don't you? Is he your boyfriend? I can't believe you slept with him... Did you tell him what happened in my room?"

The question makes me sick with more rage, and when my hand with the gun wavers for a moment, I fire. He screams and instinctively brings his hand to his bleeding arm, stepping back. He tries to shoot me, but I decide to end it, and my second shot is in his forehead. His body drops lifelessly, and without wasting time, I rush to Eveline.

"Skull, I... I'm sorry!" she murmurs nervously, handcuffed. I search the dead man's pockets for the keys. "I woke up and you weren't there! I got scared because you were hurt, and I was upset for being abandoned again. I didn't want to be there not knowing and..." Her voice trails off when she realizes I'm still silent. "Skull, will you forgive me?"

I release her and hold her delicate face. My heart is pounding in my chest; the fear of losing her consumes me.

"I'm the one who should apologize," I say, and she frowns. "I'd die if something happened to you, Eveline." I swallow hard; her eyes are locked on mine. Her hands touch me over the mask. "I love you more than anything in this world. I love you, Eveline!"

She's surprised but smiles at me and kisses me through the mask. "Skull, I do too..."

Two gunshots interrupt us, and I roar, leaning my body over her, which makes her scream in fright. My back aches, but I skillfully turn around and see the President holding a gun. Before he can shoot again, I hit him in the chest. He falls, clutching his wound, and almost immediately the Diplomat enters and sees the scene. He screams for help, and when he reaches for his gun, I fire nearby, preventing him from grabbing it.

He glares at me with fury.

"Bastard! You'll be arrested, and I'll do everything to make sure you die in prison!"

"Funny for you to say that," I murmur, standing up. "The press already knows about the crimes you two committed."

Albert smiles and adjusts his tie.

"With what evidence?" he questions arrogantly. "Your word? Do you really think they'll believe a deserter who kills for money?"

"Not mine," I smile, even though he can't see it, "but Halina Novikov's." He looks scared but tries to hide it. "She delivered the evidence of your crimes, and I'm sure that right at this moment, it's in all the newspapers around the world."

And, as if confirming, his phone starts ringing, just like the president's somewhere in his suit. He looks at the device, and I see his breathing change, then, without waiting, he starts to laugh.

"Man, how bizarre."

I glance quickly to the side and notice that it was Eveline's friend who spoke. The two are hugging, and I slowly indicate for them to stay behind me.

"Yeah." He shakes his head. "If we had searched deeper, we would have discovered that this bitch was alive, and with luck, we would have killed her and that whore Halina. This isn't going to amount to anything." He shrugs. "After all, I'm just following orders, and the one at the forefront of it all was the president, who's now dead."

From the corridor, I hear footsteps coming in our direction, and I'm ready for a fight.

"You have a part in this too, Mr. Diplomat. No need to be modest."

I finish speaking and keep my eyes on the door.

"When you're in jail, she'll be the next to die," he threatens, and I tighten my grip around the gun. "But don't worry; I'll make it look like an accident. Two deaths that no one will miss." As soon as the footsteps stop at the door, the Diplomat smiles. "This assassin killed the president! Kill him right now!"

As he finishes accusing me, the shot is low and muffled due to the silencer, and when the Diplomat drops with a bullet in his head, Miller approaches with a furrowed brow.

"What the hell! I just killed the most beloved diplomat in the country. God bless America."

"Why did you take so long?" I ask, turning to Eveline. She quickly comes into my embrace, but I pull her away. "We need to go." I look at the blonde girl beside her; there are few similarities between the two. "What I tell you to do is to obey without question, both of you in silence and..."

"How rude." I look at her, surprised. "Yeah, you're rude!"

"Abby," Eveline scolds and hugs her by the arm. "He's just a little."

Without retorting, I hold Eveline's hand, and we start walking with Miller guiding our way. I grab the *walkie-talkie* and tune in to the released radio frequency.

"Attention, the President has allowed civilians inside the Basilica. Only civilians, no press," I say as I walk toward the empty corridor. "Evacuate the car exit and wait until further notice."

"Understood!" a male voice responds after a few seconds.

I end the transmission of the *walkie-talkie*.

As soon as we reach the main path, Miller tucks the gun under his suit and watches the movement. I take the opportunity to turn to Eveline. Her face is stained, and I'm confused as to why I didn't see that before.

"What happened?"

"Nothing!"

"That old man and Ethan hit her," Abby responds, and Eveline looks at her alarmed. "I'm not lying."

I take a deep breath, and as if sensing my state, she touches my face.

"It's over, Skull," she murmurs and gets closer to me. "How are we going to get out?"

"You two will go with Miller to the main exit. No one will suspect you."

Eveline frowns.

"But what about you? Why aren't you coming with us?"

"I can't leave like this, Eveline," I respond, and when I see she's about to retort, I continue, "I'll meet up with you outside, I promise! Is that okay?"

I can't risk and let her come with me. If I get caught on the way to the exit, I don't want Eveline to be present.

"Let's go!" Miller calls as he adjusts his tie. "I hate this suit."

Eveline quickly hugs me; she's trembling.

"I love you, Skull!" Hearing that makes my chest warm and my breath weak. A thousand butterflies in my stomach? She pulls away and smiles at me. "That's what I wanted to say yesterday! That I love you, and that outside, I'm going to propose to you."

"It's all very beautiful, but let's go, everyone. They're going to look for the president."

I look at Miller, who has an anxious expression. I nod and watch the two go with him. They easily blend into the crowd. I quickly run down the path that led me to that room, pass through the dimly lit corridor, and automatically look for the two guards. I sigh in relief when I see them still unconscious, and I place the *walkie-talkie* near them. When I realize the corridor is clear, I run to the sewage passage at the end of the maintenance area wing.

Eveline

ABBY TIGHTLY GRIPS my hand, and when we're finally outside, I hear my friend whispering her thanks. My gaze meets hers, and we smile. I have so many questions to ask, but I still can't calm down. I look for Skull around us but don't find him. We quickly descend the steps, but Miller turns and gestures for us to remain calm. I see some police cars stop right in front of us, and I freeze in fear, but they pass us by as if we were invisible.

In the distance, I hear the sound of a car approaching, and it's Ellen. She stops beside us and fixes her gaze on Miller, who, even without speaking, I can tell is silently arguing.

"Get in."

"And what about Skull?" I ask as he opens the back door for me. "Aren't we waiting for him?"

"He'll come back with Pablo. Now, if you could just get in, I'd appreciate it."

I suppress a rude reply, and before settling into my seat, I glance around. Once inside the car, Abby quickly holds my hand, making me look at her.

"You really came for me."

I hug her tightly.

"You're my best friend, Abby," I say fondly. "I'd never leave you behind."

Abby pulls away and touches my hair, then analyzes Miller and Ellen.

"Who are they? And don't tell me you're with that rude masked guy?"

I lean my head back and allow myself a brief smile.

"He's not rude, Abby. Skull is a good man."

"And why is his name Skull?"

"It's a nickname we gave him," Miller replies, removing his tie. "In the past, Skull was more merciless; he had a deadly and remorseless approach. But now? He's a big coward."

"Sorry," Abby says, crossing her arms, "but are we talking about the same person? Because the man who saved us killed two people."

"If you were on our combat missions, you'd understand, little girl."

I see Abby frown at the nickname. She looks at me, and I silently wave my hand, asking her not to say anything. My head is pounding, and my heart is tight; I feel I'll only be okay when I can hug Skull tightly. I close my eyes, feeling the car in motion, and then I smile, feeling completely giddy.

Skull loves me and said it plainly: "I love you, Eveline." I want to scream, hug him, kiss him... My God! How I want him in my arms right now! I feel my hand being held, and I smile at Abby. Having my best friend safe and sound by my side lifts some of the weight off my shoulders. Finally, I know she's safe.

As soon as the car enters the large courtyard, I look at two vans parked near the flower bed. Ellen barely parks, and I practically leap out. Before I can slam the door, it's opened, and Pablo smiles at me. I pass by him, not caring if I sound rude. I quicken my steps, and the moment I stop at the entrance of the room, I see him. Skull still wears the mask, and upon seeing me, he moves towards me. With tears in my eyes, I run to him and jump into his arms. One arm holds me by the waist while his other hand caresses my back.

"I'm here!" he whispers softly, his voice muffled, then makes me look at him. "Are you okay?"

I nod my head, and still in his arms, I pull his mask down until his lips are exposed. Skull kisses me and pulls me against him, making my body respond with intense shivers. I tilt my head to deepen the kiss, allowing Skull to devour my lips. Then I remember the audience, and I force myself to end the kiss.

"I was so scared," I murmur, and Skull wipes my tears. "I never want to go through that again."

"No, never again."

He kisses me one last time, and I'm placed on the ground. Without separating from him, I look around. Abby is sitting on the couch, drinking a glass of water while Ellen is beside her. Miller soon flops down next to her, now without his suit.

"I have a lot of questions," Pablo walks past us and heads to the large TV. "At least now everything will be clarified."

On the screen, I can see several blurry images of injured men, and the caption in huge letters reads, "Scandal: President Authorizes Experiments on Prisoners to Turn Them into Biological Weapons."

"Evie?" I look at Abby, who has a confused expression. "Was he your father?"

I nod and walk over to her.

"What happened, Abby? Where were you? How did you end up with them?"

"When I returned from the city with the lawyer and Sister Trambley," she began. "Everything was destroyed; the entrance was all on fire, and the black-clad police said it was a gas incident."

"Black-clad police?" Miller asks.

"FBI," Skull replies, stepping closer and crossing his arms in front of us. He's still wearing the mask. "Did they take you? Did they ask anything?"

Abby mimics him by crossing her arms and looks at me.

"What's his name again?"

"Skull."

"So, Skull," she says, looking at him. "Why don't you take off the mask? I don't feel comfortable talking to someone who doesn't show their face."

Skull looks at me, his eyes fixed in my direction. I give a small smile, feeling grateful when he removes the mask and puts it away in his vest. I turn to Abby; she has her lips slightly parted, and when her attention focuses on me, I can almost imagine what she's thinking.

"They asked for my name, but I was worried about you and asked if you were in there. Ethan was there; he said we were friends, so we were taken. I was left alone in a huge apartment; Mr. Ritchson said you were okay, that he would find us. But two days later, Ethan was already working for them and told me you and I would be killed. I got scared and tried to escape, but I got caught."

"But what about your family?" I ask, concerned.

"I don't know," she shrugs. "They took my blood, and I don't know the result. I don't know what to do."

I hold her hand, and when I think about speaking, Skull takes the lead.

"Miller can find them."

We look at him, and he nods his head.

"Well, then let's rest," Ellen murmurs, standing up. "What a day this has been!"

"I'll take you to a room," Pablo says to Abby. "Follow me."

"Are you coming with me, Evie?"

"Of course!"

I glance at Skull, who slightly nods his head. Then I stand up, and before stepping away, I pause in front of him.

"You're not leaving here, right?" I ask, and he shakes his head. "I love you!" I whisper, and in response, he kisses me and then smiles.

I run after Abby; she's standing on the stairs, and her mischievous smile is so inevitable. Pablo shows her the room and quickly leaves. Barely has the door closed when Abby jumps on me.

"I can't believe you're dating!" Her tone isn't accusatory; it's more surprised. "And wow! What a man he is! Have you two had sex? You're not pregnant, are you? Did he ask you out? How did all of this happen?"

I can't stop smiling. I've missed all that craziness with my friend by my side.

"I'm not pregnant, but yes, we've had sex. He asked in his own way, but I was pretty difficult."

Abby looks at me with one eyebrow raised and pulls me to the bed.

"Tell me everything."

As soon as she finishes speaking, she lies back but doesn't break our gaze. I take off the jacket I'm still wearing and then lie down. I start recounting everything from the day I was kidnapped from the orphanage. Reliving those moments sends chills down my spine because if Skull hadn't shown up, I could be dead right now.

As I speak, I realize when everything changed between Skull and me. Him caring about little things to make me comfortable, the kiss, our first time together... The fact that he trusts me enough to open up about his real name and his family was a huge proof of love that I hadn't noticed before. When I finish telling my story, Abby has a small smile and hugs me. After a few minutes, she looks at me and grins.

"Now tell me what it's like to have sex," she asks, sitting up. "I can't believe you did it before I did. Come on, tell me! What's it like?"

I smile somewhat shyly, but I know that if I don't say anything, she won't let me off the hook. I roll my eyes; she claps her hands, and then I start to talk.

CHAPTER TWENTY-FIVE

Skull

The warm water embraces my body, calming every tense muscle and dissipating any remnants of worry that may have lingered. I'm immersed in the hot tub, the first time I've ever entered one. My half-closed eyes allow me to glimpse the soft light playing on the surface of the water, creating a spectacle of golden reflections dancing to the rhythm of the rising steam. Through the window, I observe the city in the background against the orange sky. I think of the chaos that is unfolding at this very moment, with so much dirt being uncovered, but deep down, I regret nothing.

To keep Eveline safe, I would kill as many men as necessary.

I release a sigh and sink deeper into the water, feeling the foam envelop my entire body.

"Skull?"

"Here," I reply, and soon I see the bathroom door open. Eveline looks at me from head to toe before biting her lip. I stretch my hand toward her, needing to feel her lips, her body against mine, to love Eveline as she deserves. "I was with Abby; she went down to eat with Ellen. Pablo told me you were here."

"Why don't you take off your clothes and stay here with me?"

Eveline smiles, and I automatically return the gesture. Under my gaze of pure desire, she removes her boots, her top, and then her pants. Unable to contain myself, I run my hand along her thigh, then rub my fingers against her panties.

"Should I take these off too?"

I nod and slide my fingers under the fabric, caressing her soft lips. She opens her legs, giving me more access to her warmth. My middle finger slips inside her opening, and Eveline moans, clutching my hand. I pull her tiny panties aside just as she removes her bra. I take her hand and help her step in. I receive her body over mine and relax.

I feel as if I'm floating in a sea of tranquility. There's no rush in my caresses on her skin, no worry, just the present moment, wrapped in the arms of the woman I love.

My muscles loosen under the gentle pressure of the water, releasing all accumulated tension. Our faces are very close, and amidst the mist of the moment, I kiss her softly. Our noses touch, and Eveline snuggles closer to me. Her fingers trace my face, a gentle touch that makes me close my eyes.

"You're so beautiful, Skull."

I smile and bring my fingers to her chin.

"Said the most beautiful woman in the world," I retort, and she kisses my scar.

Her lips are soft, and I kiss her with longing. My fingers tangle in her golden hair while Eveline surrenders to my kiss with fervor. Our tongues entwine, and when my erection becomes apparent, I feel Eveline's hand grasping it and leading it to her backside. I'm surprised, but I let her do whatever she wants with me. She pauses the kiss and rests our foreheads together; her expression is pure desire, intensifying my arousal even more.

"Quite greedy, aren't you?" Our breaths mix, but she doesn't stop. "And brave."

"As if you didn't want to as well," she comments softly.

The head pushes to enter and manages to get in, but soon it slips back out. Eveline frowns and tries to look back. Quickly, I rub my fingers on my tongue and bring them to her tight entrance. I coat it completely while putting one breast in my mouth. Eveline moans softly, and taking that as encouragement, I continue. I grip my shaft and, sucking on her breast hungrily, I penetrate Eveline again.

Her hands grab my hair, and she moans loudly. I feel her clench around me, and it feels so good. I pause, hoping she can relax, but to my surprise, she wriggles, making me enter completely. Eveline takes a deep breath, sighing with her eyes closed. I pay attention to her other breast, and this time she looks at me.

"Does it hurt?"

"A-little," she replies, biting her lip, "but it feels so good!"

I wrap my arms around her waist and begin to move slowly, never breaking our gazes. After a few seconds, I gradually increase the rhythm, not caring about the soapy water soaking the bathroom floor. She searches for my lips and devours them with desire while the sound of our bodies echoes around us. I grip her blonde hair tightly and pull, leaving her pale neck at my disposal. My tongue glides over her soft skin, then I suck on it.

"Ah!" she moans and smiles.

My shaft enters forcefully into her backside, reaching the hilt, always in short, precise movements. One hand rests on my chest while the other continues to grasp my short hair. I embrace her and this time quicken the pace, letting out brief, hoarse groans.

"Oh Skull!" Eveline moans, and I feel her tighten around me.

Trembling in my arms, she moans softly in my ear. The shivers travel down my skin, bursting at the back of my neck, and knowing what that sensation is, I thrust harder. I push Eveline's hips down while I cum deep inside her backside.

I observe her face and smile at seeing her exhausted but well-fucked expression.

"I have a surprise for you," I say, and she looks at me, her face completely red and sweaty. "First, you need a shower, so let's go down."

"What's the surprise?"

"A surprise," I reply, smiling as I caress her face. "If I tell you, it won't be a surprise."

She smiles and kisses me slowly.

"All sweet, how did I not realize that you love me?"

My chest warms as I gaze at her beautiful face.

"Maybe because you were too busy being jealous."

I feel a slap on my chest, which brings a laugh from me.

"Or because you were afraid to open up to me?" Her voice is challenging, and I smile but soon nod.

"Falling in love with you scared me," I murmur, and she looks at me intently, "but discovering that it's love left me completely afraid of losing you. That almost happened today, and I wouldn't forgive myself. Never. You brought me a purpose in life, Eveline. I want you, I want our own family, with kids... Maybe in a few years?"

Eveline lets some tears fall, but she nods and kisses me.

"Is that a marriage proposal?"

"I thought you were going to ask me," I reply. Eveline smiles, the most beautiful smile I've ever seen. "I don't have a ring with me, but I want you to be my wife. Will you accept?"

"Yes! A thousand times yes!"

I kiss her to seal the agreement, and then I feel her grinding in my lap, causing my erection to harden slowly. I smile amidst the kiss, knowing we wouldn't be going down anytime soon.

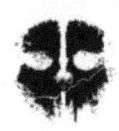

When we finally finished and went downstairs, it was already night. Eveline smiles, and I remain more serious, but inside I feel more alive than ever. We walk toward the familiar voices, and as soon as we stop at the entrance, I take in everyone present. Abby, Eveline's friend, stares at us and can't hide her smile.

"Finally!" Miller mocks without taking his eyes off the cards he's playing with Pablo. "Are you hungry? Oh, of course you are; what a silly question."

Eveline shoots me an embarrassed glance but says nothing.

"Any news?"

"Nothing to worry about," Pablo replies, looking at us. "What are you planning to do now? Do you know where you're going?"

"We need some documents," I murmur as I head to the drink cart while Eveline sits down next to her friend. "And we need them fast."

"We can get them without any problems." Miller says, focused. "Are you going to use what I made for her, or will they be new?"

I glance at Eveline, who looks confused but doesn't ask anything. Then, before the blabbermouth can say anything more, I continue.

"New ones, as if we were married."

This time, they stare at me.

"That's great, my friend," Pablo smiles, stands up, and puts the game on the table. "I'm very happy for you."

We hug, and I feel he is sincere, as he always has been. I look at Miller, who is peeking at someone else's game, and shake my head.

"Thank you, it means a lot to me."

Miller comes over to greet me, while Eveline is on the couch, being hugged by Ellen. In the midst of the congratulations, we hear the doorbell ring, and minutes later, the newcomer appears. I search for Eveline's gaze; she looks surprised.

"Good evening!" Halina, Eveline's mother, approaches cautiously. "I'm moving," she says, looking directly at Eveline, who remains seated. "Actually, I should be at the airport right now, but I needed to talk to you, Eveline."

"Do you want privacy?" I ask.

"No, I'll be brief," she says as she walks until she stops in front of Eveline. "I just wanted to know if you were okay, and I came to ask for your forgiveness for what I said that day."

Eveline stays silent for a few seconds, her gaze fixed on her mother, but she soon looks away.

"It's okay, I understand."

"No," Halina shakes her head and sits down, taking her daughter's hands. "I couldn't stay with you, Eveline. Leaving you in that orphanage was my way of ensuring that nothing bad would happen to you, because if they caught me, only I would die. You have no idea how I suffered without you, without being able to hold you in my arms, to protect you." As she spoke, tears fell from both her and Eveline's eyes. "For your safety, I had to do everything I did."

"Why did you tell me those lies?"

"I was surprised to see you there," I move closer to observe the scene better. "The last time I spoke with Director Aarons, she told me you were fine. Your birthday was coming up, so I sent a little extra money compared to what I usually did; I wanted them to do something special for you. Then, suddenly, you were in my office, and I was afraid he would find out and know you were here."

"It was brave of you, Halina."

She looks at me but soon shifts her attention back to Eveline.

"Only God knows how hard it was to stay away from you, daughter. I was standing in front of the Basilica, I needed to make sure I wouldn't see you there. Then, I saw you running, someone behind you. I was terrified, so I called him," she points at me, "and gave him everything I had. I thought that way those bastards would be caught, and you would be safe."

I cross my arms. I feel the truth in what Halina has just said, and I imagine how hard it must have been for them to be apart all this time.

"I-I don't even know what to think," Eveline responds to her mother. "I thought you hated me for being his daughter."

"No! I don't hate you, and I don't regret having you! You are my daughter, I love you. I know all about you, about your best friend Abigail, how you two used to get into trouble at the orphanage."

She laughs, followed by Eveline.

"Actually, it was Abby who caused trouble. I only accompanied her to knock some sense into her."

"But I never did anything!" This time, it's the friend who speaks up. "How ungrateful! I made your days better, you can say."

Halina smiles but soon focuses back on Eveline.

"Will you forgive me, daughter?"

Eveline takes a deep breath and nods.

"Of course, it's all right."

"Ah! How wonderful!" Halina hugs her, and the two stay that way for a few minutes. "Now that they're dead, you can come back with me." As she speaks, I freeze. "Your sisters don't know about you, but my husband does. He's a good man; he'll love meeting you. You'll get to know them slowly, and..."

"I'm not going," Eveline interrupts her, and Halina looks at her in shock. "We can talk, and maybe visit each other, but I can't go."

"And where will you go?"

"I don't know yet," she shrugs, then looks at me and stands by my side. "I'm going to marry Skull; we're going to start a family."

I keep my gaze on Halina, who stares at me without hiding her feelings.

"Are you sure, daughter?" she asks, but quickly continues, "It's nothing against you...?"

"Skull."

"Skull," she repeats. Then, after a few seconds of silence, she shakes her head. "So, can we keep talking? I don't want to lose you again."

"That's fine," Eveline responds and hugs her. "Thank you for coming to clear everything up. You said you're moving?"

"Yes, goodbye Albuquerque – New Mexico." She laughs but soon touches Eveline's face. "You are so beautiful, daughter. I'm so happy you've become such a lovely woman with such a good heart." The two smile at each other. "I'll be going then. Will you still have that same number?"

"Yes, you can always call that number." I respond and receive a nod.

"Take care of my daughter, Skull. I know you will, but I need to hear it from you."

"Don't worry; I'll protect her with my life if necessary."

"When he says that," Miller murmurs, coming to stand by my side, "you can believe he means it."

I step aside so Eveline can hug her mother once more, and then I watch her leave. For a moment, I feared she would go, but I would understand if she did.

"Was that my surprise?" My gaze meets hers, and I give her a smile. "Thank you, Skull. I love you!"

"When you say that," I murmur near her lips, not caring who sees us, "a thousand and three butterflies flutter in my stomach."

Eveline smiles and kisses me.

"I can't believe it," Miller exclaims, drawing our attention. "Skull the romantic?"

"Shall we eat?" Abby says, standing up. "I'm hungry."

Everyone agrees, and when Eveline tries to pull away, I stop her.

"What's wrong?"

"I love you! Thank you for staying."

Her arms wrap around my neck.

"I want a family with you, Skull."

I lift her up, and she gives me a cheeky smile.

"A warm place, tiny panties, and a lot of love?"

"I thought you were naked," I murmur innocently, causing her to swallow hard, "but tiny panties work too."

I lean in and take those delicious lips.

"Are you coming or not?"

Eveline kisses me softly, her lips touching mine tenderly as if they want to convey all the love she feels. I feel the warmth of her hand enveloping mine, and I allow myself to be guided by her.

In the kitchen, the atmosphere is filled with laughter and lively conversations. But even with our friends around us, my attention remains completely focused on Eveline. Her gestures, her words, every little detail enchants me and makes me feel grateful to have her by my side.

When our eyes meet, a smile lights up her face, and I can't hide my smile. At this moment, I realize that loving and protecting Eveline has become my noblest purpose, my reason for being. Every gesture, every word will be dedicated to her, for her smile is my greatest reward, and her love, my strongest fortress.

CHAPTER TWENTY-SIX

Eveline

As Skull drives silently beside me, I gaze, completely in love, at my new ring. We didn't have a huge wedding, just a small ceremony with only us: Miller, Ellen, Pablo, and Abby. That was six months ago, but it's so vivid in my memory. I didn't wear a wedding dress like in the movies; instead, I insisted on wearing the dress from my birthday. When Skull saw me in it, he was surprised.

I can't help but let a smile escape.

"Can I know what you're smiling about, Mrs. Morrison?"

"I was reminded of your reaction when you saw me walk in wearing that dress at our wedding."

He shakes his head.

"How did you want me to react? The justice of the peace couldn't focus on anything other than your cleavage," he murmurs, not taking his eyes off the road. "His luck was our wedding, because I was dying to grab my gun and..."

"Skull," I interrupt him with a smile. "You're such a hothead, so jealous."

I feel his gaze on me, and I can imagine exactly what he's thinking. That I'm jealous too, but he is more so. With his silence, I return to my daydream. As soon as I officially married Skull, now Simon Morrison, Miller and Ellen took charge of getting my friend to her grandmother. I was so happy when everything turned out well for her. I shift in my seat and glance one last time at my golden ring with a small diamond in the center.

I look ahead and see the sign announcing the city just a few kilometers away. I adjust my hair to the side and dare to look at Skull.

"Is everything okay?"

His answer takes a moment, but he soon agrees.

We were going to visit his parents, actually to announce that he's alive, and it wasn't an easy decision. It took months of thinking, sleepless nights, and at no point was I against it. I want Skull to be able to free himself from that burden and the uncertainty.

Minutes pass, and when we finally reach the city center, I feel anxious. Skull drives through some busy streets but soon takes another road, and this time everything is calm. I see some houses of different colors, many trees, and parked cars. Then, he stops in front of a light blue house. I remain silent, waiting for his decision; I know how difficult this is for him, and I will stand by him in any choice he makes.

Skull lets out a sigh and starts the car again.

From the door of the house, I see a lady with pale blonde hair and a floral outfit come out, holding a plant pot. Skull stops and watches her. I see him swallow hard, and I wonder if that's his mother. She notices us, the pot falls from her hand, and she starts walking toward us. Quickly, Skull gets out of the car and approaches her. I smile, get out of the car, and adjust my dress and the jacket I'm wearing.

The two embrace, and I feel emotional as she starts to cry, holding onto Skull. It isn't long before I see a man with white hair and a beard coming out of the house. He wears a checkered shirt, jeans, and closed shoes. His expression is one of confusion about what's happening.

"Look, Joseph!" she exclaims excitedly. "It's our Ryder! My God! My son!"

A bit tense, I watch the scene, but soon let my smile return when Skull's father approaches and hugs him. I take a deep breath and step closer, standing on the sidewalk.

"Dad, forgive me..."

"There's nothing to forgive!" he says, and I wipe my tears. They pull away, and I notice that just like him, the lady is now looking at me. "Who is this young lady?"

Skull comes to me and holds my hand. I smile to convey reassurance, and then I smile at the two of them in front of us.

"They are Joseph and Charlotte Marshall, my parents." As he finishes speaking, the woman smiles at me. "This is Hailey Morrison, my wife."

"Wife?" Charlotte repeats, and for a moment, I fear they won't like me. "Oh my God! It's a pleasure to meet you, Hailey."

She hugs me, and I return the embrace.

"Let's go inside," Joseph says, looking around. "Come in; we're alone."

I follow Charlotte, who smiles at me, and together we enter the house. Inside, I notice the living room is very cozy, and everything smells so good. Skull is hugging his mother, which brings a smile to my face.

"My God! I prayed so much for you, my son. I always knew you were alive! Why? Why, my son?"

"Forgive me, Mom," Skull swallows hard. "I did it to keep you safe."

"What?" Charlotte asks, genuinely confused. "What do you mean?"

"Lottie," Joseph shakes his head in a silent plea. She simply nods. "The important thing is that you're back. I'm happy to see you, son."

They embrace again, and I smile, extremely happy. After that, we sit down and chat. Both are curious to know how we met, what we were doing, and where we lived. Skull answered what he could, concealing much of what he had done all those years or how we met. Charlotte mentioned that she had never believed her son was dead, and deep down, something told her he was alive.

I felt touched by this; perhaps it was a mother's sixth sense, and it's something beautiful. I remember my own mother, who always calls me to ask how I am. In the meantime, I got to know my sisters. It was strange, but we didn't talk much. With Abby, though, we spoke almost every day.

"Where are you living?"

"We're in Hawaii," Skull replies, and the surprise on his parents' faces is evident. "It's really nice there."

"That's quite far, isn't it? But are you enjoying it?"

"It's a little far," I respond politely, "but it's so nice to live there. You're both invited to come visit."

Skull glances at me quickly and nods.

Charlotte smiles, but soon starts to cry. Skull goes to her and hugs her. I try to hold back my tears, but it's all so emotional.

"You look so handsome; you didn't have that scar on your face before."

"I know."

She gently touches his face.

"Thank you for coming back to us," she says as she hugs him. "Today is the best day of my life."

After more hugs and tears, we stay for dinner. Charlotte makes sure to update Skull on everyone in the family, even people he doesn't know. The rest of the evening goes the same way, and when it's time to leave, she starts crying again. We promise to come back soon, but before we go, Skull asks them not to talk about him. His parents agree, and we finally say our goodbyes.

Inside the car, as we drive back to the hotel, Skull can't hide his smile.

"It's so good to see you like this," I murmur, filled with love. "I liked them."

"I bet they liked you too."

I smile and lean over to kiss him on the cheek.

"Why are we staying at a hotel in another city?"

He glances at me quickly and thinks before responding.

"I thought you liked the hotel."

I look out the window and stay silent for a few minutes. Even though we are now "normal people," Skull is still very careful about our safety. Even in our house in Hawaii, he always checks to make sure everything is locked and that the alarm system is activated. I let out a brief sigh and watch the houses fade into the distance, giving way to bushes and trees.

"I liked it," I reply and look at him, "but it's so far, and you get so tempting when you're driving."

"What's that?" he asks with a sideways smile. "What are you going to give me this time?"

"Is that a complaint?"

"Never!" he replies promptly.

I bite my lip and place my hand on his thigh.

"We could pull over there," I point outside. "And let me make you happier."

"A quickie in the bushes?" he asks, half surprised and half laughing. "You don't want to use it as a bathroom; do you think you can fool me?"

"It's not the same thing," I say as I take off my boots. "I'm going to sit on you, not on the grass."

Skull looks at me and, after a few seconds, steers the car off the road. I smile, unbuckle my seatbelt, and wait to slide the seat back so I can snuggle onto his lap.

"Is that why you came in a dress?" he questions, and I smile shyly. "What a naughty woman; I just got married."

"As if you didn't like it," I retort and feel my panties being pushed aside. His long finger caresses me. "Skull... I want you deep inside me..."

I rub our noses together, then take his lips in a needy kiss. His scent, his hands, and kisses drive me crazy, always leaving me wanting more. While I suck on his tongue, I help him open his pants and pull his underwear down a bit. Skull pulls me in tightly, while I grasp him and guide him inside me.

I choke out a gasp and smile when a finger enters my other entrance.

"Can you roll for me nicely?" Skull whispers, and I obey immediately.

In that position, it feels so intense to feel that huge cock reaching deep inside. Around us, all we could hear were the crickets and the leaves rustling in the wind. Skull penetrates me with another finger, and I moan louder. I love surrendering my body and soul to him, for he always knows just where to touch me to leave me filled with desire. His tongue licks my neck and goes to my lips, where we start kissing.

Amid the lust, I try to open the buttons of his shirt, but I end up tearing them off.

"Sorry!"

"You deserve a spanking for that," Skull says with a smile. "Don't you think?"

I nod while continuing to move; I feel I'm very close to orgasm, and I bet Skull knows it too. His hips start to meet mine, and his heavy hand begins to slap my backside. My legs weaken as the orgasm overwhelms me, and I can only writhe on top of him. Then, in a sudden motion, Skull grabs my waist and thrusts into me hard. The pleasure intensifies, and totally fragile, I let out one last whiny moan and lean my body against Skull.

He releases inside me and groans close to my ear.

"Satisfied for now?"

I smile and nod. For now, yes, because when we get to the hotel, he won't get away from me. With some help, I get off him and sit beside him. I adjust my panties and watch him put his semi-hard cock back into his underwear. His gaze meets mine, and he smiles. With each passing day, I love him more, and it always feels like I'm going to explode from so much love. I close my eyes and rest my head against the window. I try to stay awake, but I end up falling asleep, knowing that I am safe and well-loved.

EPILOGUE

Skull

Eight years later

Furious, I pace back and forth in that empty hallway. I knew I shouldn't have gone to work! Being here at the hospital, alone and without news of Eveline, is a nightmare for me. Since we moved to this town, and I promised we would have a normal life, it took a few months for me to find a job. The same happened with Eveline, who studied and is now graduated in marine biology. Impatient, I head to where two nurses are talking.

"Do I have to break someone's face here to get noticed?" They immediately stop talking and look at me, startled. "My wife went into labor a few hours ago. They brought her here, and I've been waiting without any news about her or whether they even let me in to see her."

"Sir, first you need to..."

"Don't ask me to stay calm," I interrupt him, and he falls silent. "I'm not nervous; I'm pissed off! I want to know about my wife! Or should we find a doctor for you?" I threaten, making him take a step back. "That's right!"

"W-What is your wife's name?"

"Hailey Morrison."

Like a rocket, he rushes past me, and I head to the chairs. I sit in one, but quickly get back up. It's our first child, and I imagined I would be by her side to support her, but no. I rub my hand over my beard; if I had my gun, I would already be by the doctor's side. They say violence doesn't solve anything, but they are...

"Mr. Morrison?"

I turn to the doctor and approach him.

"My wife?"

"She's fine," he smiles and puts his hands in the pockets of his coat. "Your baby was born healthy; it's a beautiful girl. She weighed 2.5 kg and responded well to her initial exams. The two of them are resting in the room; I can take you there, but you cannot threaten the nurses."

"Where are they?"

"This way," he indicates the path, and I quickly follow him. We enter an elevator, and I keep my arms crossed. "The first child always brings these emotions," the doctor says, and I take a deep breath.

When the doors open, a wave of emotion washes over me. Eveline is there, lying down, holding our little bundle. Her blonde hair is spread over the pillow, and her smile is tired yet radiant, lighting up the room. My heart races as I approach her. It's just the two of us in the room.

"Love!" As I stop beside her, I see our baby sleeping peacefully. "This is our daughter."

I swallow hard, feeling a strange sensation in my chest; my eyes fill with tears, and like a fool, I let a few tears fall. I quickly dry them and lean down to see my daughter. Her fine blonde hair is sparse, giving the impression that she doesn't have any, but if you look closely, you can see.

"She's beautiful," I murmur, looking at Eveline. "I'm sorry for not being home; I didn't..."

"No, love! Don't think about that; it was her who hastened the delivery." Eveline smiles and touches our baby's cheek. "Heather Morrison?"

I look back at her and allow myself to smile.

"I like that name," I say, my eyes focused on Heather. "How are you? Was it very difficult?"

"Well, I pushed so hard that I thought I wouldn't make it," she comments while touching our daughter's fine hair, "but it was worth it."

I touch her face and place a kiss on her lips.

"I love you so much! Thank you for our family."

I kiss her again.

"I love you too," she says, and I smile widely. "Do you want to hold her?"

"What?" I ask, alarmed. "No, I-I don't know how to hold babies. I might drop her, or hold her too tightly."

I feel dizzy with the possibilities, but I try not to show it. Eveline's laughter catches my attention, and I'm left confused.

"You, the man who saved me from a group of terrorists and faced God knows what else, are afraid to hold our baby?"

"It's not fear," I retort, and she smiles more. "It's caution; I don't want to hurt her or..."

"Come here," she commands, and I obey, tense. "Hold her firmly around her body and at the base of her neck."

I rub my hands on my pants and, somewhat trembling, I take our daughter. She stirs and grumbles but doesn't open her eyes. She is light and, at the same time, limp, fragile, but so perfect. An involuntary smile forms on my lips as I realize that, despite my fears, holding her isn't as scary as I imagined. In fact, it's the opposite. I feel enveloped by a wave of love and protection that I had never experienced before.

"She's perfect," I murmur softly, then look at Eveline. "Thank you."

When the doctor returns, he explains to us about the care related to Eveline's feeding and informs us that we will spend the night here.

I don't hesitate to agree; after all, I want to ensure that my beloved and our little one are well taken care of. Throughout the night, I remained by their side, attentive to any needs that arose.

The next day, by late afternoon, we finally return home. I received two days off work to help Eveline during this crucial adjustment period. Our routine was always the same: I tidied the house, prepared our meals, and helped with our baby.

Every moment spent with them was precious and unique to me. I worked hard to learn everything I needed to know about caring for a newborn, from changing diapers to those special moments of breastfeeding. Watching Eveline recover well and our baby grow and develop each day was a feeling I couldn't describe.

Despite the exhaustion and sleepless nights, I felt fulfilled.

I turn in bed and search for Eveline's body; as soon as I find her, I pull her to me. She grumbles but continues to sleep. I place my arm around her waist, and soon I feel her hand on mine. Just as I'm about to drift off to sleep again, a soft cry starts in the background and quickly escalates into a wail.

"Heather is awake," Eveline murmurs sleepily, making a move to get up.

"I'll go," I say and kiss her on the neck. "Sleep."

"Thank you, love; I love you."

I smile and get out of bed wearing only my shorts. The pink room across from ours is all decorated by the two of us. As I push the door open, the crying intensifies, and I have to admit my daughter has good lungs.

How can someone so small scream so much?

"Daddy's here," I say, grabbing the floral diaper and placing it on my shoulder. Then, carefully, I pick up my baby. "Calm down; Mommy is sleeping; we don't want to wake her." I start rocking her while singing a lullaby.

I sit in the rocking chair there and continue to rock her. I stroke her chubby cheek, and I can't help but smile when she gives me a quick toothless grin. After a few minutes, she falls back asleep. I check her diaper, which was changed a few hours ago and is clean. I know I need to put her in the crib, but I linger a bit longer, rocking her.

"Love?" I look at the open door, and Eveline is standing there with her arms crossed. Her short nightgown gives me a view of her thick thighs, as well as her large breasts peeking from the lace neckline. "I miss you in bed."

"Two whiny girls in my life."

I joke, watching her smile and approach. She checks the crib and stands beside it. Carefully, I stand up and walk over to Eveline. I place Heather on the mattress and adjust her gently. Before leaving, Eveline kisses her on the forehead and pulls me by the hand. My gaze follows her backside, and unable to resist, I squeeze it tightly, hearing my wife's moan.

We enter the bedroom, and as I close the door behind me, Eveline wraps her arms around my neck.

"Do you know what we could do now?" she asks, and I raise an eyebrow. "Since she's asleep again, and since we're awake... we could do something?"

"Weren't you tired?"

"I was," she says, and with a burst of energy, I lift her into my arms, "but I dreamed of you. So I woke up to put it into practice."

I smile and lay us down on the bed, positioning myself over her warm body. Her legs open wider, and I smooth my hands over her skin, feeling its delicious softness.

"Tell me more about this dream."

My fingers slide under her nightgown and slip inside her panties. Eveline is completely slick with desire, so I slowly rub my fingers there and penetrate her.

"I dreamed that you tied me up," she murmurs with a moan. "And took me with fury and love."

"Tied up?" I repeat with a sideways smile. "Where are those handcuffs?"

"You're not going to handcuff me," she retorts, and I'm left confused. "In the dream, I wanted to touch you and couldn't."

"Then show me how you want to do it."

Quickly, she turns on the mattress and gets on all fours. Totally hard with desire, I remove her slick panties and trace my finger along her intimacy. I gather some of her slickness and rub it on her bottom. I slide one finger inside, then another. I feel the tightness around my fingers and imagine my cock in its place.

"Today I want to fuck here," I announce, and she spreads her legs wider. "Do you have something to say?"

"Why are you taking so long?"

I smile and slap her backside.

The grip leaves a mark of my hands on her pale skin. I lower my shorts and then spread her cheeks wide. Eveline wriggles anxiously and even grabs my cock, moving it up and down. Before penetrating her, I wet my fingers with my tongue and then rub them on her tight entrance. I force my cock in, and as it slowly enters, I allow it to go all the way. Eveline takes a deep breath and rolls her hips for me.

I start moving, listening to her soft sighs and moans.

In a swift motion, I lay on top of her and grab her by the hair. We are connected in such an intense way that I fear I might come first, as if it were my first time.

"S-Skull..." I smile; sometimes, she called me that. "M-More!"

I hold her affectionately, and we turn to the side. She smiles and turns her face toward me while I hold her leg to keep it open wider. Our lips touch, and there we begin a kiss.

"How I missed you!" I murmur, followed by a moan. "Your body, your scent..."

She smiles and licks my chin. The desire on her face is so palpable that it makes me harder. To increase the pleasure even more, I take my fingers to her pussy and penetrate her, moving them at the same time I thrust hard into her ass. I keep going until she digs her nails into my arm while writhing in my grasp. Our bodies collide forcefully, and I only stop when she tightens around me, trembling.

With a few more thrusts, I also come, pulling her closer to me.

We breathe heavily, and then I watch her turn to me and kiss my lips.

"Now I can sleep satisfied," Eveline jokes and closes her eyes. "I love you, love!"

Ready to hold her, Heather starts crying again. We look at each other and smile; soon Eveline gives me one last kiss and closes her eyes. I get out of bed, rejuvenated, adjusting my clothes. I walk back into the pink room and smile at my little one, who is crying at the top of her lungs. I carefully pick her up, and as I cradle Heather in my arms, I sing a lullaby, listening to her grumbles.

With a tender smile on my lips, I watch my daughter as she brings her little hand to her mouth, such a small gesture, but full of meaning for me. I kiss her forehead and mentally thank for the family I have. It never crossed my mind that a mission would become my world and that from this love we would create such a beautiful baby. Looking back, I'm sure that everything I did to get us here was worth it.

"I promise you, my baby. Daddy will always protect both of you."

Did you love *Unholy Passion*? Then you should read *Dangerous Affections* by Amara Holt!

Dangerous Affections

When you're the **consigliere** of the Italian mafia, love is the last thing on your mind.

Luigi, the **ruthless enforcer** of the Cosa Nostra, is feared for his **cold precision** and deadly methods. Trained in medicine to prolong his enemies' suffering, Luigi hides a **dark and traumatic past** beneath his controlled exterior. He thrives on order and lives by the rules—until Bella crashes into his world.

Bella is the opposite of Luigi in every way. She's **clumsy**, compassionate, and working three jobs just to survive. Behind her warm smile, however, she hides a **secret** that could shatter her life. When fate forces these two unlikely souls into a **fake relationship**, their worlds collide in an explosive mix of **danger**, passion, and **forbidden desire**.

As tension rises and sparks fly, Luigi and Bella must navigate a **perilous game of deception** where trust is fragile, and their hearts are on the line. Can love truly blossom in the shadow of vengeance, or will their **dangerous affections** lead to destruction?

Dangerous Affections is a gripping **enemies-to-lovers** mafia romance filled with **suspense**, steamy chemistry, and unforgettable characters. Perfect for readers who crave **high-stakes drama**, intense emotions, and a love story that defies the odds.

About the Author

Amara Holt is a storyteller whose novels immerse readers in a whirlwind of suspense, action, romance and adventure. With a keen eye for detail and a talent for crafting intricate plots, Amara captivates her audience with every twist and turn. Her compelling characters and atmospheric settings transport readers to thrilling worlds where danger lurks around every corner.

Milton Keynes UK
Ingram Content Group UK Ltd.
UKHW031348011224
451755UK00001B/56

9 798330 575749